Sweet Retribution

Taken – Mama, I want to come home.

A work of fiction by

Ernest John Swain

....The times I'd dreamt of revenge against this evil man, responsible for my daughter's abduction, were beyond count but now, here I was, in a moment of panic, trying to save him.

Readers please be aware that artistic license has slightly condensed the time-line of factual dates in this fictional story.

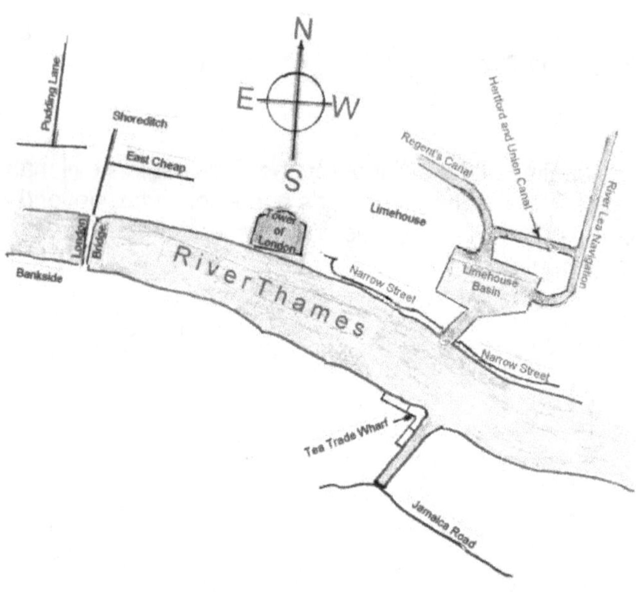

Summary of events so far:

Jack once more takes up the story of his and Pru's experiences in 'The Apprentice' ISBN 9798637147243.

Their little hideaway, remote in the Pennine moors had served as a safe haven away from Finkelstein, the wicked and violent under-world character and his partner, the despicable Lord Bouverie, shipping magnate, smuggler, and slave trader. Bouverie had unjustly blackened the name of Pru's husband Joe, causing his health to deteriorate and bringing him to an early grave.

Pru made Joe a promise as he died that she'd somehow take revenge upon Bouverie. She'd felt no pangs of conscience in taking Bouverie's assets from Finkelstein, and that's where I came into the plot. I was persuaded to use my skills to forge a legal document; convinced that we were morally justified. Pru's masquerade as Lady Bouverie was the final ploy that gained us the tainted treasures her husband had horded.

Sweet Retribution

Chapter 1

We'd intentionally disappeared into a life of obscurity in our remote little cottage, high on the Pennine moors away from the past. Our living would probably be considered quite basic, with an earth closet and all our water carried from the nearby stream, but we were living comfortably on what Pru had taken from the despicable Lord Bouverie's estate and from that slimy money-lender Finkelstein. Her confidence trick had been an act of revenge that had taken some nerve – but how sweet.

Two years had passed since Bouverie had died and we'd escaped the clutches of Finkelstein, but I couldn't throw off those memories, forever looking over my shoulder knowing of Finkelstein's reputation, always afraid that the past would catch up with us. I realise that you, the reader, might consider me spineless, but I'd been brought up as a God fearing, law abiding child, and I was clearly out of my element in a criminal enterprise and I knew just how dangerous Finkelstein was. He'd never give up until he'd had his revenge and recovered what we'd taken.

I was in my element once again with the freedom of the moors, the seasons and the wildlife that surrounded us, far away from all that troubled me, but I could sense Pru was restless. She was essentially a city girl and missed the busy life London offered. I, on the other hand, a country boy and orphan, raised by an uncle and placed in the apprenticeship with that Ancient Guild of Stationers in London, had found the city so far removed from my earlier environment, so impersonal and somewhat frightening.

Here, in this secluded moorland setting, life was so very different for Pru, not only lonely but with little to occupy her. She began to take occasional journeys back to London, alone which worried me but she was insistent. Initially I accepted they were necessary if only for her state of mind.

The love between us was as strong as ever which probably persuaded me to simply go along with the situation. However, curiosity grew and I eventually insisted that I should accompany her if only for her own safety. I was forever wondering what trouble she'd be getting herself into.

Now, with each of her visits to London, my apprehension was building again; why travel alone; who was she seeing; what was she up to? Always one to hold her cards close to her chest, reluctant to tell anyone what was on her mind; my questioning gradually began to annoy her. The memory of those early days and the seduction she employed to coerce me into the forgery, still remained a sexual thrill. I was still so infatuated, so in love with her that I'd allowed that laissez-faire attitude to flourish – until now. Now I was determined to return to London with her; discover what she was getting involved in.

Our journey down to the Blue Boar staging post entering the big city brought back all those memories I'd tried to suppress – of what had driven us away. However, the nearer to our destination we travelled, the more excited Pru became. It showed in her face and her chatter but still she kept the purpose of her journey to herself.

She'd still retained the cottage from which we fled and I thought we'd be heading there, but the hackney carriage took us from the Blue Boar to a wharf on the south side of the Thames. I didn't understand her purpose and despite my questioning Pru just smiled and coyishly said, "All will be revealed."

I was irritated having to follow along, not knowing where we were going or for what reason and my annoyance was showing through. Pru made straight for a majestic looking, three mast clipper, 'The Lady Ester', being gently rocked by the rising tide at its mooring alongside the Tea Wharf. Although the place was busy with loading and unloading of cargo on other boats, there was no visible activity aboard the Lady Ester. Never-the-less Pru made straight for the gang-plank. Surprisingly no-one appeared to question us or prevent us climbing aboard. To me, our being there aboard this vessel had no purpose and I felt we were trespassing and probably asking for trouble.

My annoyance was getting worse, and I was concerned that I was being led into something for which I wasn't prepared. I'd expected someone to at least challenge us, to insist we had no right to be there, but it appeared there was no-one aboard. Still Pru gave me no explanation of what we were doing there. She'd always shown confidence in everything she did and I suppose I shouldn't have been surprised that she was acting as though she had every right to be there. I was ready to turn about and leave but not Pru; confidently, she opened the door to what must have been the captain's cabin and stepped inside. I nervously looked about me to convince myself that no-one could see us and meekly followed her.

I was sure we were intruders but she opened a locker and brought out two glasses and a bottle, then brazenly poured two liberal drinks of rum. I confess it wasn't to my taste and it burned my throat. I felt distinctly uncomfortable – convinced we shouldn't be there and fearful of what mischief she was up to?

"With the rising tide Pru looked to the quay, seeming to anticipate the arrival of someone. I knew nothing of ship-board life but presumed the clipper would normally be leaving with the high tide and I began to wonder if she planned for us to embark on a journey. I was getting more anxious with every minute, and was about to insist that we left, but one by one, crew came aboard and still no-one paid us any attention which confused me even further. They set about the rigging, the moorings and hatches, obviously making ready to sail.

Sweet Retribution

"Finally, a rather large, muscular, bearded fellow with a rolling gait arrived with a bundle of papers under his arm. He beamed a huge smile and stretched his arms around Pru and kissed her on both cheeks; obviously someone very familiar to her, leaving me bewildered. Turning to me he said,

"You must be Jack? We've been expecting you," which confused me even more. Expecting me?
Pru smiled and said as though I'd finally understand,

"Jack this is Captain Blood. He's the master of my clipper the Lady Ester, and a good friend."

"Just a minute, **your** clipper? Did I really hear you say that – '**your**' clipper?" She smiled briefly but without answering she turned to Captain Blood, asking,

"Is she here, did you bring her along?"

"I've left her with Lottie. They're in the shipwright's shed..." he answered hesitating slightly, then continued, "...you must understand she's very frightened, this is a big step for her."

I didn't understand any of this, but was it any of my concern? I was so confused and beginning to feel as though I was in a fuzzy dream and would soon wake up to reality.

Captain Blood seemed a little agitated as he said,

"Look, we don't have much time we'll soon have to cast off if we're to catch the tide, so if you're going to meet her we'd better go now."

Pru rose from her seat and looked at me saying,

"Prepare yourself Jack. I didn't intend this should be sprung upon you quite so quickly but now I've no choice. Come on, we're going to introduce you to Chika."

"Chika, who or what is Chika?"

"You'll see. We've been working towards this for a long time. Prepare yourself, I really want you to be kind, Chika needs someone to take care of her."

I honestly had no idea what to expect. Was Chika a pet cat or something more exotic? In the event I followed Pru and Captain Blood down the gangplank onto the quay. As we entered the shipwright's work shed, there she stood, hiding her face in the folds of Mrs Blood's skirt; a waif, I guess about four years old, thin as a broom handle and dusky, obviously mixed blood, her head a mass of tight black curls. I looked at Pru hardly knowing what to say but she just beamed at me, her face a picture of delight.

"I must leave you..." said Captain Blood, "...or I'll miss the tide," and he turned, kissed his wife, patted Chika on the head, and hurried away with his parting words, "Look after her, Jack."

Pru lifted the child into her arms and looked anxiously at me. All that I could see was the wet shine on the girl's face where her tears ran.

Tears were also welling in Pru's eyes too as she said,

"She's coming home with us Jack."

What could I do? It wasn't a question of 'Do you mind?' or 'What do you think of the idea?" The decision had been made; there was nothing I could say. I think Lottie could see the shock in my face and she took my hand and gave a squeeze as she said,

"Let's all go back to my cottage, I've a pan of broth and fresh baked bread..." and looking again at me continued, "...I can see we need to have a good talk." Of that there was no doubt. We walked to Lottie's cottage just off the Jamaica Road, not far from the Tea Warf.

I'd realised for quite some time that Pru had wanted a child but despite our attempts we hadn't been successful. I'd blamed myself but although she'd never voiced her concerns, I believe she thought the problem was hers. Now, this was her answer, but why a child that so obviously wasn't white? Surely she could have taken her pick from an orphanage.

"Are you all hungry?" asked Lottie as we made ourselves comfortable. She produced four dishes and began to ladle broth into each. I'd not heard the child speak, and still she said nothing but eagerly spooned the broth into her mouth.

Sweet Retribution

"Jack, you look bewildered..." she said as she handed me my dish, "...help yourself to bread."

Bewildered was hardly the word, I was dumfounded; speechless. There were so many questions I wanted to ask but felt unable. Lottie sat down to eat but with every spoonful she paused to give me another snippet of the story.

"We've been friends a long time, Pru, me and my husband Tom. I remember the time when Joe – Pru's first husband – worked down here at the wharf for that scoundrel Bouverie. I know you shouldn't speak ill of the dead but he really was a scoundrel. I was cook in Bouverie's home until after he died." She paused to spoon some more broth.

"I don't know how much Pru has told you about him but apart from smuggling and defrauding the excise he was also involved in the slave trade, shipping them to the New World. To his high society friends he kept his activities secret but us below-stairs had a good idea of what he was up to. He kept two young black girls hidden from prying eyes – just for his personal entertainment, if you know what I mean?"

She paused again to see my reaction and watched me as she broke more bread that she dipped into the broth. She continued, speaking with her mouth full,

"Chika here was born to one of those girls, and they were only girls, not women yet."
She let the revelation hang in the air for a moment or two to let what she was telling me sink in.

"So, what happened to her mother?" I asked.

"When Chika was born, Polly – that was her mother's name – never really recovered. She named her baby Chika which apparently means 'God is greatest', and she managed to nurse her for a while, but gradually her milk dried as she became weaker and she finally died. Bouverie never gave her the proper medical care she needed – I suppose he didn't see her as a financial necessity. Chika would have died too but I took her and found her a wet nurse. When that arrangement ended she went to a widow woman who Pru and I paid."

Lottie put down her spoon and stared into her bowl, then shaking her head as though to show her disgust of the man, continued,

"I think Bouverie could see what was written in the stars; the Quakers and Wilberforce in parliament were gaining popular support; it was becoming obvious the slave trade would end, and ultimately, I think he was just pleased to be rid of Polly and what happened to Chika was of no concern to him. The other girl simply disappeared – we never did know what happened to her."

I could feel Pru's eyes burning into me, trying to judge my reaction. The truth was I found the story upsetting too. I looked at Chika and my heart sank, I couldn't imagine how someone could treat other human beings in such a callous way – especially a child. Lottie began again,

"The woman we paid to look after Chika sadly died and since then I've done my best for her but she needs more than I can give. Pru's been helping out and Chika's become more attached to her whenever she's been able to visit."

Pru had kept quiet throughout Lottie's explanation but now she said,

"Perhaps you can begin to understand what a despicable piece of filth Bouverie really was. Human beings, whatever their colour, should never be treated in such a way. Now, I feel justified in everything I've done and his filthy riches are being used to help put right those wrongs. Bouverie's gold and diamonds bought the Lady Ester and the tea warehouse and that in turn has provided the captain with a ship, a trade and Lottie with a home. Perhaps now you can understand my frequent journeys down here..." she looked at me with pleading eyes and continued, "...and understand how important your skill in forging that letter of administration was in all of this?" All that I could think to reply was,

"Why couldn't you have told me? I would have understood." Pru didn't reply but I realised that quite unknowingly I'd had a significant part to play. It was all a lot to take in but I suppose Pru at last had to lay her cards on the table if I was to accept Chika into our home.

Chapter 2

Pru was as excited as I'd ever seen her, fussing around the child, covering her with affection. Chika was much more relaxed in the familiar surroundings of Lottie's home. I took her upon my knee at every opportunity but I was completely out of my comfort area dealing with a child, and Chika was a little apprehensive of me, probably because all her contacts had previously been exclusively female. I understood to a degree as I too had been an orphan, raised by an uncle with no female input. However, Chika's initial shyness was soon forgotten and she soon began to accept me. I had a lot to learn about children.

As daylight faded Pru became agitated, pulling the curtains aside and looking outside, explaining that she would have to leave.

"There was business to attend to." she said,

"Well, I'm sure Mrs Blood – Lottie – will look after Chika whilst we're gone," I answered.

"Oh no, you must stay here with Chika. This is something I have to do on my own," Pru insisted.

"On your own? After dark?" I'd forgotten just how confident Pru was to be out after dark and how accepted she was amongst that disadvantaged community who lived on the edge of criminality. It was obvious her allegiances amongst the back-alleys and slums hadn't deserted her.

"Don't wait up, I'll probably be late," were her parting words. Not a word of where she was going or who she intended to see – so much for me being determined to find out what she was up to. It left me feeling quite inadequate and inconsequential. I was being sidelined yet again. What other surprises was she going to spring on me?

Lottie put Chika to bed in her usual cot and blew out the candle. The only light in the room was moonlight through the small window that looked out across the shimmering Thames. Whilst she waited for Chika to settle she stood and watched the unladen barges and lighters at the quay-side rocking to the movement of the water that lapped against their hulls. When the child had drifted off to sleep Lottie quietly returned downstairs.

I was feeling dispirited and lost in thought as she entered the room and I realised I'd allowed the fire to burn low. I rose to poke the fire into life and add a few more cobbles of coal. The thought crossed my mind that coal must be expensive and as if she read my mind she said,

"There's always a few cobbles to be had at the wharf where the lighters load," and it prompted me to say,

"That's most peculiar you seemed to know what I was thinking." And she replied,

"No wonder, I can almost read you like a book. Pru's told me so much about you."

We were obviously of a like mind and in tune with each other, and I could see we were going to get along. I asked about her husband's voyage and she replied,

"I guess that with the ebb tide he'll be beyond Margate," and catching my bewildered expression she continued, "Margate – the mouth of the Thames. He'll make for the Channel and then with a fair wind he'll no doubt be off the Scillies by mid-morning."

"Where's he sailing to?"

"India."

The thought of such a journey was filling me with wonder. I had no idea where these places were. I was like a child again at my uncle's knee, learning about the big wide world.

"India, is it a long way".

She smiled at my lack of knowledge and replied,

"A very long way, it'll take months to reach there, let me show you," and she invited me to kneel on the hearth with her as she began to draw a diagram on the ash dusty hearth-stone. She traced the bulge of Spain, and the entrance to the Mediterranean, then the huge expanse of Africa and its Cape of Good Hope, Madagascar and finally India. I was totally absorbed in her knowledge of the world. I began to realise that my education was quite basic. Uncle Charles had done his best but this was like a story teller, weaving her magic.

"He'll set his course for Madeira – and she pointed out the island off Portugal – and then south, praying for full sails through the Doldrums, then it's the rough seas of the Cape and onwards to West Bengal where he'll pick up his cargo of Darjeeling tea."

"Surely, there must be a quicker and easier route than right around the southern tip of Africa to get to India?"

"Not at the moment but there are plans to build a canal through Egypt that will allow ships to pass from the Mediterranean to the Red Sea. If it ever gets built it will halve the journey."

She sat down beside me on the sofa and looked at me with a smile on her face.

"I've heard quite a lot about you Jack. I always wondered what Pru saw in you to make her pursue you up north."

"You obviously know all about me. Pru must have told you?"

"She did, but I already knew all about your... *er...* fall from grace with the parlour maid when you were dismissed from your apprenticeship. Yes, I had the full story, you see, Pru and I were very close and I helped her to set up the trick to get Bouverie's assets from Finkelstein. I've done alright out of it. But Pru thought she'd lost you and she'd grown fond of you. She spent a lot of time trying to find you."

I replied, "Yes, I know – that is, I know she struggled to find me when I fled in panic – but I didn't know you had anything to do with the deception on Finkelstein."

"I'm not surprised. Pru always works on the assumption that the less people know, the less they can divulge. D'you understand?"

"Yes, I do. Even now she often tells me that."

Just then we heard small footsteps on the stairs and Chika emerged into the room rubbing her tired eyes.

"What's the matter Chika darling," asked Lottie.

"I want a drink."

Only a mere sip from a glass of water proved that the real reason she'd risen was the comfort of Lottie's arms. Climbing upon her knee she snuggled close and buried her face in Lottie's bosom.

The hour was now getting late and there was as yet no sign of Pru. Once again my thoughts returned to that night of waiting whilst she had gone to Finkelstein with my forged letter of administration – and the morning when men came hammering at the door. Surely I wasn't to go through all that again?

The clock on the mantelpiece struck twelve, then one, and I was getting really anxious when the latch lifted, the door opened, and in stepped Pru. I went to greet her but her mood was foul and it showed in her face.

It was natural enough I thought, for me to ask the reason, but with a shake of her head she waved the palms of her hands in front of me in a gesture that said, "Don't ask." It was quite usual when things had gone wrong that she wouldn't talk and I knew she'd only tell me in her own good time. Lottie never said a word, I think she understood too.

The following morning the atmosphere at breakfast was surprisingly pleasant. I was given the responsibility of looking after Chika, so I walked out with her down to the river. Pru and Lottie were engaged in whispered conversation when I left and were still so occupied when I returned. Their faces were a mask of concern as though confronted with some enormous problem.

I knew there was no point in asking Pru what her problem was and so I waited until I caught Lottie on her own, but when that moment arrived she shook her head saying,

"Sorry Jack, I'm sworn to secrecy. You'll have to wait until Pru is ready to tell you. All I'll say is that it's nothing for you to worry your head about," but how could I help but be worried? Not knowing was possibly worse than being aware because my imagination ran riot.

Sweet Retribution

Chika had been quite a surprise to me. I hadn't
anticipated that adoption of a child was on the agenda
and had to admit to myself that her being a coloured
child had thrown me completely. I tried hard to examine
my feelings; after all I'd never had any contact with
someone of colour. It wasn't a matter of prejudice,
there'd been French Huguenots, Ashkenazi and
Sephardic Jews, Irish, Chinese and other ethnicities
about the city whilst I was an apprentice, and
immigration was growing, especially around the docks,
so I wasn't quite sure what troubled me. Was it just the
thought of being a parent or was it the colour issue?

It's true I'd seen coloured men working in the docks
and in other jobs but they were usually labourers with
whom I'd had little contact, and I'd always associated
them with the slave market. I'd kept my distance and
when I began to examine my feelings I began to realise
the reason was fear. Probably because of the pictures
I'd seen of natives with a bone through their nose, and
usually toting a spear. They were usually big strong men
who I presumed spoke a different language and were
probably head hunters. How silly, now here I was with a
beautiful child who spoke as white children of Jamaica
Road speak and with the same Christian upbringing.

Chapter 3

That evening, as dusk approached, Pru prepared to go about her strange secretive business, and again I hadn't the slightest idea of what she was up to. However, this time, I was determined I'd follow. She may not have wanted my presence but I was not going to let anything happen to her. I was sure that whatever she was engaged in spelled danger. I knew Lottie would try to dissuade me but I'd leave her no choice. It was time I made an effort to exert myself.

As Pru left the house, Lottie took Chika to bed and I crept out without anyone's knowledge, intending to shadow Pru. She hadn't got more than five minutes start, and I ran to catch up with her. Jake the ferryman wouldn't be operating at that late hour so I knew she'd have to use the bridge. I followed the path she'd have to take, along the river, over the bridge and towards the slums I remembered. Surely I'd soon catch up with her.

Alas, she was nowhere to be found. I searched the gin palaces and the beer houses but she'd given me the slip. After an hour or more wandering the streets, I realised my mission was fruitless, and dejectedly I headed back to Lottie's home. Now I'd have to face the music.

"Whatever were you thinking? Pru's going to be so annoyed when she gets back."

"You don't have to tell her."

"Don't you think she'll know already? Nothing escapes the eyes and ears of that crowd. They'll know you were in and out of their drinking dens, searching."

"She'll understand. I'm concerned for her safety."

"Safety? You should know, she's told you before, she's safe amongst that crowd – they're her own people

"Well, if only she'd tell me what she was about it would probably ease my mind."

"I'd be breaking my promise if I told you. She'll tell you when she's good and ready."

Sweet Retribution

We settled down to wait, and wait. My stomach was churning with anxiety and although Lottie tried hard to take my mind off my worries, it was in vain. Again the hours ticked by and Lottie fell asleep in her chair. When the church clock struck two there was still no sign of Pru's return. I began to pace the floor and several times went outside into the street, hoping to see her approaching, but to no avail.

By the first rays of morning light I was outside again straining my eyes into the morning mist that hung about the river on those autumn days. There was a real chill and a feel of dampness to the air which added to the despair I felt.

Breakfast came and went but I never felt less like food. Lottie tried hard to keep an air of calm about her but was it a charade for my sake, because I was beginning to sense that she was now becoming concerned too? I could wait no longer and said,

"Lottie, the time's come to do something. Wherever she is, she's in trouble – I'm sure of it. You have to tell me what's going on.

Pru lay under the old rotting sail cloth of the derelict lighter that lay half submerged at the water's edge. Lying on her side on what remained of the sloping deck, she could just peep out to see the beginning of the wall of the quay. It had been a leap of faith from the quay to land on this old wreck in the dark and she dare not move whilst they were searching for her – so close. The mist hanging over the river had been a blessing. The hue and cry had lasted since well before daybreak and now there was so much activity on the quay and on the river; but were they longshoremen, stevedores or were they the searchers? A Hue and Cry meant that everyone had a responsibility to search for and pursue a criminal so how could she know when it was safe to leave her hiding place with so much activity about her? She clung to the book and held it safe; it had been worth all the drama.

Meanwhile, I was imploring Lottie to tell what she knew.

"There's not a lot I can tell you. You know how Pru works – *'the least you know, the less you can tell'*. If she's not back by the time the church clock strikes twelve. I'll tell you everything I know," she said. Another hour or more dragged by, time for the anxiety to turn my insides into a raging fire of torment.

"Oh, for God's sake, Lottie, tell me where she's gone. I can't wait that long."

"Alright, but don't go and spoil everything for her. She's put a lot of time and trouble into this. All I can tell you is it's to do with Finkelstein. He's been trying to frighten her with blackmail and if he was to succeed she could lose everything, the Lady Ester, the tea warehouse, your home – everything. Now do you understand why she didn't tell you?"

"Well, where's she gone?"

"Everything centres on Bread Street in East Cheap, which is over the new Westminster bridge, that's where Finkelstein operates, near the markets. I beg you, don't go there looking for her; you'll just end up in trouble yourself. Remember, Finkelstein knows Pru so she wouldn't approach him directly. There must have been some other angle she was working on."

"I'm going to search for her. Help me Lottie; tell me who I can talk to? Who will know what was happening – she must have involved someone if she couldn't approach Finkelstein herself?"

"Jack, why don't you stay here and look after Chika and let me go. I could give you names but you'd never find them, and if you did, it's doubtful they'd tell you anything."

It's difficult to think rationally in such circumstances but I knew in my heart Lottie was right. None of the villains and rogues of Pru's acquaintance was likely to give me the time of day, much less divulge what she was up to. Lottie, on the other hand, was in the know and was accepted amongst them in the same way as Pru.

Sweet Retribution

There was another consideration too – I might unwittingly talk to the wrong person and blow the whole thing – and so, but still with some misgivings, I agreed that Lottie should go.

I stayed behind with Chika, on tenterhooks, tormented by thoughts of what could have happened to Pru, whilst Lottie delved into that under-world of skulduggery and intrigue that Pru just couldn't leave behind. I couldn't control my emotions when Pru walked in the house, covered in dried mud and with scratches and bruises to her arms and legs. I honestly thought she'd been in the river.

I threw my arms around her and hugged her tight. The tears welled in my eyes, and I gulped,

"Pru, where the devil have you been? Look at the state of you. What's happened?"

"Oh, I had a little mishap. I had to hide from someone but it's all over now. Where's Lottie?"

"She's out looking for you. We were both worried out of our skin, convinced you'd come to some harm."

"Look, I keep telling you, there's no need for you to worry, I'm quite capable of looking after myself."

"Pru you're getting yourself into danger; don't deny it. I had to prise it all out of Lottie – what you were up to regarding Finkelstein – and you know you're playing with fire. He won't stop at blackmail. Why don't you leave well alone? You've done well enough out of what you got from him originally."

"Let me get cleaned up and a bite to eat and I'll explain it all to you," she said taking the book from her bodice.

"What have you got there?"

"Oh it's my insurance – our insurance," let me get cleaned up.

Lottie returned in a fluster as Pru scrubbed the mud from her legs.

"I've been franticly running from one to another, getting nowhere. Johnny the knife, Peg-leg Pete, Blind

Joe, Mary at the gin house, Sniffer, all the usual gang you'd talk to, but none of them knew what you were up to."

"Well, you can both relax now can't you? Let me finish cleaning myself and you can make me a nice hot drink and something to fill my belly, and then I'll tell you what's happened. It's been a good night."

I was curious and went to pick up the book that lay on the chair by the bowl of water Pru was using to wash in, but she snatched it away. That book wasn't leaving her custody.

Lottie made herself busy boiling the kettle again on the open fire and cutting thick slices of beef from the joint she'd roasted overnight. I think we were all ravenous and wolfed at our food. When she felt ready Pru sat herself in comfort and took Chika on her knee. Earlier the child appeared to have picked up the mood of concern and had seemed quiet and withdrawn. Now in Pru's arms she was clinging tight as though she was never going to release her grip.

Pru held the book aloft with what appeared to be a triumphant smile on her face. It was a tatty looking thing that had been well used, with greasy finger marks staining the brown leather cover.

"This is worth all the effort it's taken." I couldn't resist the question,

"What is it?"

"It's my little piece of revenge; it's my insurance."

Chapter 4

"These last two nights I've spent watching Finkelstein's hovel, just as I've done the other times I've come down to London. He always had his minders hanging around him and I began to think I'd never get the chance – but you know me, I never give up. Well, last night it was different. The minders cleared off in the early hours, he must have thought he was safe. I got close enough to see through those grimy windows and I watched him fall asleep in his chair."
Pru hesitated in her tale whilst making Chika more comfortable on her knee.

"It was easy to prise the window, the wood was quite rotten, and I climbed through. I had to be very careful avoiding all the clutter, but stealthily I tiptoed to his side. He was sound asleep, snoring like the very devil he is, and he never realised he had company. I knew exactly what I wanted and where it would be – the book. I'd seen plenty of it the last time I'd been there pretending I was Lady Bouverie, with your letter of administration forcing him to divide the spoils he'd hidden from the Excise for Lord Bouverie."

I realised she was talking of the night I'd spent waiting for her and then the morning when the men had come hammering at the door.

"This book..." and she held it aloft, "...holds the account of all those dealings he had with Bouverie and where he'd salted everything away. It was his bible, it never left his side – but there it was, lying in front within reach on his table." She laughed, with a hint of hysteria, obviously enjoying the escapade all over again.

"I was half out of the window again when he suddenly awoke, but he's getting old and decrepit now and he just wasn't quick enough. I dropped into the alley and ran for all I was worth because I knew he'd soon rouse his watchdogs. I wasn't sure whether he'd recognised me and if he did he'd know I had to get back to this side of the river and the bridge was the easiest place for his bloodhounds to intercept me. So, instead, I made for the waterfront. There was a lot of shouting with the hue and cry behind me and they were getting closer and closer. In the swirling mist I spotted an old wreck of a lighter lying on its side, half submerged just off the end of the quay. They were nearly on me and I'd nowhere else to run so I jumped and just trusted to luck. I couldn't see what lay before me but they always say 'fortune favours the brave'. I landed on what must have been the only bit of sound deck there was, and I covered myself with some old rotten and stinking sail cloth, and just waited until I thought it was safe," She wrung her hands, shook her head and blew a "phew" in exasperation.

"When daylight broke, I could see just how lucky I'd been, rotten boards and exposed rusty nails. There was so much activity on the quay, longshoremen, lightermen and colliers; I daren't stick my head out in case those searching for me were still about. I waited until I believed the chances were they'd gone and it was safe, then I got Jake, the old ferryman, to row me across"

"So, what are you going to do with the book?" I asked.

"Hide it..." she answered, "...where no-one else can get their hands on it."

"I still don't understand why it's so important to you?" I questioned.

"Let me explain. Finkelstein quickly found out the 'Letter of Administration' was a forgery, and realised he'd been had by a con trick. By that time I'd got away with the trinkets and the jewellery. He'd still got half the proceeds of Bouverie's smuggling, but it was a matter of injured pride to him, he couldn't let it be known that he'd been tricked by a woman. He set his bloodhounds to work to find who this fictitious Lady Bouverie really was and it didn't take long."

It was what I'd feared all along and I wasn't at all surprised by what she was telling me. She continued,

"As time went by I think what upset him most was that I'd turned the fortune I'd made into a viable venture with the Lady Ester, and from that point onwards he did everything possible to ruin it. It must have been him that informed the Excise people that I was smuggling. What they were looking for I don't know but Tom Blood was given a rough time. Every time he docked the Excise were all over the ship, but of course they never found anything because Tom was extra careful which made it appear we were running a clean enterprise."

"So, what was his next move?"

"His thugs paid Tom a visit down at the wharf and threatened to set the vessel alight, but they were dealing with a tough bunch in Tom and his crew. The next things were the threatening messages passed on to me. First of all that I was going to be murdered, just done to frighten me – because I knew that was hardly likely as Finkelstein would achieve nothing by it, he'd never get the gold and jewels back, nor would he obtain the Lady Ester. So his latest threat was that I was going to be kidnapped and held until I signed everything over to him."

"You knew that and you've been putting yourself at risk each night? Out there alone where only villains and street walkers would normally dare to go – actually venturing into the viper's back yard?" I asked,

"Jack, you of all people ought to know me by now. When I'm threatened I go on the offensive."

"So, when you've hidden the book away what purpose will it have served?"

"Can't you see? Insurance – Finkelstein knows that I've got enough in this book to send him to prison for the rest of his life, so surely he'll give up now."

"And if he doesn't give up, what then?"

"Oh he will. He knows that if he does anything now, I'll give the book to the Excise or the Peelers. I don't think there's anything in it that can incriminate me, so he's the one with everything to lose. The one thing he might do is he might try to recover the book so we just have to be careful."

Chika was still clinging tightly to Pru and she looked adoringly on the child as she said,

Sweet Retribution

"That's just one more reason why Chika's coming home with us. I don't want to give him the chance to snatch her as a lever to use against me to get the book." I'd listened to enough and said,

"Right, there's nothing more to keep us here let's get the stage – go home to the cottage up on the moor." The next morning we said our good-byes and I hailed a hackney carriage that took us to the outskirts of the city and the Blue Boar staging post. There were a few tears from Chika as we set out and I confess I felt a little emotional too leaving Lottie, but I was sure we'd be back when the Lady Ester returned. The child was in awe of the clamour around the stage and horses, but the excitement didn't keep her awake too long.

It was a long and somewhat uncomfortable journey as usual, but we took the opportunity to alight at each stage-post and obtain refreshment. We were tired and our bodies ached with the buffeting of the coach ride, but my spirits rose as we headed through the beautiful jewel of Matlock in the heart of my home county. Travelling beside the river Derwent, beneath those awesome cliffs, I really felt I was back in my element. We were on the last leg of the journey, content that at last we were far enough away and safe from anything that Finkelstein might do. We were all weary and the cold, damp and empty moorland cottage wasn't exactly welcoming, but with a fire in the grate and food in our stomachs, chances were that Pru and Chika would settle.

I didn't realise just how much of a shock it would be to poor Chika, vast open spaces, solitude and such frightening animals as sheep and red deer – she'd never seen the likes before in her short life. I was confident that she'd soon adapt, appreciate and begin to love this new environment as I did.

The autumn days were getting shorter and the weather more inclement, but whenever there was the opportunity we wrapped up warm and walked the woods, moors and grit-stone crags that surrounded us.

25

Sweet Retribution

As winter approached we spent more time around the hearth with log and peat fires to keep us warm. It soon became obvious that Chika was finding the solitude, the lack of other children to play with, a little depressing. It wasn't good for the child and it played heavily on our minds. We both tried to occupy her with stories.

I was surprised, and just as intrigued as Chika, with Pru's stories, especially about the Lady Ester. She'd obviously done her homework about the clipper and the tea trade but it appeared she'd bought the American built Baltimore Clipper by chance, at a bargain price when the previous owner died suddenly leaving huge debts.

Fortunately Lottie introduced her to Tom, Lottie's boyfriend at the time, who had spent years aboard the East India Company ships as first mate. Those 'East Indiamen' as the huge ships were called took forever to sail to China and return, so when the Americans began to build these sleeker, faster ships they called 'Baltimore clippers' Tom signed on aboard them. He got to know clippers like the Lady Ester inside-out, knew their foibles, their speed, how reliable they were and what weight of cargo they could carry. He also knew the tea trade and the side of the business that the Excise didn't. Crucially, he was experienced in the maelstrom of the Southern Ocean around the Cape and the South China Seas, an ideal man to captain the Lady Ester.

Pru told of ships visiting India and taking on a cargo of opium which was then carried to China where the demand exceeded supply, and tea became the cargo for their return. Although it had been a lucrative trade, opium addiction was becoming a major problem and the Chinese authorities became opposed to its import. In addition not only were there very real problems with them, there were also the pirates, and perhaps most dangerous of all, the heavily armed Dutch East India ships to contend with. They were slower but at times created a virtual blockade of British ships.

China tea always became available at the height of summer, which also coincided with the Southwest monsoon season, which meant fighting fierce head-winds to reach China and square rigged clippers weren't capable of sailing close to the wind, which meant continually sailing on a tack across the wind, lengthening their journey. They could often take twelve months to return home from such a journey.

On Tom's advice they'd decided to forego the opium trade and concentrate upon the less profitable but considerably less hazardous tea trade with West Bengal, India. That would mean a quicker turn around and, with luck; he could be back in port in seven months.

Pru told of Tom's earlier sea crossings of the Atlantic Ocean to the New World, and the British Colonies whilst sailing with the East India Company's tea ships which led to an incident in Boston harbour, Massachusetts. A revolt against British taxes saw tea to the value of £9,000 (a fortune) thrown overboard into the sea. That was the beginning of a fight for independence by the colonies and with it, the end of the trade.

These stories of faraway places had an exotic and mystical ring to them but I think I was probably more in awe of Pru's knowledge, all induced by this venture, but I think Chika found more interest in hearing about uncle Tom.

Chapter 5

Christmas was approaching fast and I was determined to make it one that Chika would enjoy. It was a considerable distance but I'd walk into town and buy presents – perhaps a pretty doll for Chika but what should I get for Pru, I'd have to give that more thought. I was hoping for snow – something Chika had never experienced – I'd build her a snowman and we could throw snowballs, but the weather just brought incessant rain. It was beginning to look as though we were in for a miserable time.

My efforts to melt into the back-woods of oblivion in my small moorland hideaway was making Pru miserable again and her discontent was unsettling Chika. It was approaching three years we'd occupied my little idyll but as much as I loved the high moors, the wild-life and the solitude, I knew in my heart that it couldn't possibly last. Pru was never going to be truly happy until she was back in London and Chika would fare better there. Perhaps such a move would be the best Christmas present for them both.

I only had to mention it to Pru and her face lit up like a beacon. Within the fortnight we'd gathered together the belongings we were taking with us, made fast the doors and windows of our home and we were off. Pru still had the cottage she'd occupied when I first entered her life. It was basic and the area wasn't exactly charming either, but it was a starting point. The only concern I had was that we were moving right back into Finkelstein territory and within his clutches again. Hopefully, he might have given up on efforts to hit back at Pru?

The journey took forever once again but Pru and Chika never once complained. Again our adopted daughter slept a good deal of the way despite the shaking, the bumps and the sway of the carriage on the uneven thoroughfare, and Pru was bright and light-hearted.

Sweet Retribution

It was evening as we reached the Blue Boar again and Pru ordered a chaise to take us and our luggage to the cottage. I must admit I'd lost all sense of bearing but I recognised the cottage immediately. There were some memories tied up in the place. I'd hardly say I entered with trepidation but certainly there was a queer feeling in my stomach.

Pru immediately set to giving the place some warmth and atmosphere with a roaring fire. The night was going to be another 'make-do' experience until fresh bedding and other essentials could be sourced in the morning.

I remembered the hard bench where I'd first settled before Pru took me to her bed – that was still there – the stone flagged floor of the kitchen, the secret escape route through the wainscoting onto the roof, and I wondered if the loose floorboard still existed in her bedroom where our 'escape fund' had been hidden. There was the table where I'd diligently performed my forgery; it was just as though somehow I was turning back time.

Whilst I was reminiscing and Chika was excitedly investigating every nook and cranny, Pru busied herself with preparing food she brought along. That night was spent, all three of us huddled together before the fire, but nothing seemed to matter. It was all very jovial and almost like an adventure spirit, we'd buy everything we needed the next day.

With bedding, blankets, food and provisions carried back to our cottage, and a thorough clean of everything; it began to feel so much more comfortable. Chika stayed with me whilst Pru went off for the afternoon, presumably renewing acquaintances. It seemed life had returned to normal for her.

I awoke early next morning to wash and shave before Pru and Chika arose. My heart sank as I opened the front door to find a dead rat on the doorstep, with a note that said 'Welcome Home'. It hadn't taken long for the word to have got around and it didn't take much of a guess at who might have sent the message and all it implied.

With a dustpan I picked up the rat threw it as far as I could into the thoroughfare where it could rot away; the note I burned in the fireplace. I said nothing to Pru, but the longer I left it, the more I wondered if I should tell her, to warn her for her own safety. I eventually dismissed the idea, believing she'd only laugh at what she'd see as a derisory attempt at scare tactics. I wasn't so sure and vowed not to let her out of my sight.

With breakfast over I carefully secured the cottage and the three of us set out for Lottie's home to give her the good news that we'd now returned to London to live. She was ecstatic to see us and with a shriek of joy she picked up Chika and swung her around then cuddled her tight. The child enjoyed the fuss and being the centre of attraction.

Lottie and Pru were soon down to business; with an in depth discussion about young William Pitt being returned as Prime Minister, about the revolution taking place in France and Napoleon's march across Europe. What was more important to them was the reduction of duties to reduce fraud in the revenue, but above all, parliament had set up a new department called the Board of Control to supervise directors of the East India Company. Oh if only that could have been done whilst Bouverie and his fraudulent ilk were the fabric of that company. This all meant better prospects for their small enterprise with the Lady Ester and for others like them.

Pru was eager to learn what she could of the warehouse activity – the measures Lottie had undertaken for enhanced security, auction arrangements, and all her ideas regarding wholesalers; but to me it was a whole new world beyond my understanding.

Lottie was overjoyed that she wouldn't be on her own for Christmas and directly began listing what she was going to bake, what meats she was going to order, and what ale she'd obtain. It seemed we could all rely on the best Christmas we'd had in years, but inevitably, remembering the dead rat on the door-step, I simply hoped that nothing was going to spoil it.

I was anxious to get home before darkness fell but Pru wanted to stop off at the street market, not so much for food as for presents for Chika, after all it was Christmas and the child had little by way of toys or games. Chika had eyes for a doll with a painted face, and a stick, cup and ball game. Pru took Chika ahead whilst I stayed behind to buy the toys and secrete them under my jacket, to keep the surprise for Christmas Day

I don't know whether or not Pru even noticed but I certainly did, there were no untoward comments but everyone passing by turned to look at Chika. I could see they thought her somewhat unusual, such a dusky coloured appearance. I suppose I should have expected it, after all I'd reacted in much the same way when I first saw her. People needed to see what I saw, the warm, happy loving child that lay within.

We settled down to a quiet evening but I couldn't put the dead rat out of my mind and every noise that I heard brought me to my feet to check. Pru couldn't understand what was unnerving me so.

That night I lay awake for some time, listening, before tiredness finally overcame me, but I was up next morning before the sun rose to check if the culprit had left another deposit. I was relieved to find to find the doorstep bare of any foul surprise and allowed myself to relax and wonder if my fears were misplaced, it having been a jape played by local children.

Christmas morning we dressed in our best and headed to Lottie's. After breakfast our little party visited the nearby Church of St John the Baptist, none of us were regular church goers but it seemed appropriate to go, and seeing Chika's enjoyment was well worth the effort. We all sang our hearts out.

After the service it was straight back to Lottie's where the joint of beef was slow roasting in the fireside oven. All the vegetables were ready prepared and were soon set to boil. I was kept busy carrying the coals and fetching water from the pump in the back yard, in fact doing anything I could to help.

We all sat down to a very exceptional meal and I couldn't help but enquire how Captain Tom and his crew would be spending Christmas? Lottie gave a rather rueful chuckle and almost with the glint of a tear in her eye she said,

"Chances are Christmas will be like any other day – they may just break open another keg o' rum, but I think it'll be ships biscuits and perhaps just a bit of fruit they've picked up in India. I'd hazard a guess that they'll be close to rounding the Cape now, and if I'm right they won't have time or energy for celebrations..." and she had another chuckle before saying, "...they'll more likely be praying hard that the seas calm down for them." She painted quite a picture in her tale of stormy seas that were frightening to me. I could only imagine those gigantic waves and horrendous winds. I asked,

"When do you expect him back?" and she replied,

"There's no telling. They could be stuck in the Doldrums without a breath of wind for ages from what Tom's told me, but with luck and a following wind, they could be back by April, and then we can celebrate." We tucked into our Christmas dinner and I, at least, felt grateful that I had not been destined to be a sailor.

With dinner over it was Chika's time to be spoilt. She loved the wooden doll with the painted face, and we each in turn played with the cup and ball game, until the ale began to take its toll and I began to fall asleep. It's dreadful what mischievous women will do to a sleeping man for the delight of a child. With soot from the chimney they gently painted my face, careful not to wake me. When I did awaken Chika screamed with delight but of course I had no idea what the hysteria was all about – until I was given a mirror. I decided that Christmas was a wonderful time with a young child.
Eventually it was time to make our way home. It had been a wonderful day thanks to Lottie's hospitality. As

Sweet Retribution

we walked home the dark didn't seem to hold the same foreboding, after all it was Christmas. There were lots of people about the streets and an air of merriment – until we reached home and then the mood changed as we saw the dead cat on the doorstep with the note 'Merry Christmas'. Pru was angry and immediately turned her wrath to the local street urchins, but I had to tell her this was the second violation of our home and that I felt there was a more sinister explanation.

Chapter 6

To me it seemed obvious that Finkelstein was behind these insidious moves but Pru wasn't entirely convinced, asking

"If he's behind it, what's he trying to do? He's hardly likely to be trying to drive us away. If he wants to get his revenge it's better that we're kept close at hand rather than driven away."

I agreed, that was common sense, but I asked,

"Is it just possible the message he wants to get over is that he's watching our every move and wants us to know the unfinished business between the two of you isn't over?

"It's possible but he knows there's a limit to what he can do because I've got the book."

It was almost as though she dismissed the whole issue as infantile and showed no further concern, but it still resonated with me and I still kept a weather eye open. Perhaps she was right as there was no re-occurrence. The New Year came and went without any further upset.

Neighbours in the close vicinity weren't particularly sociable – not deliberately unfriendly, but tended to keep themselves to themselves, it was a common attitude. Pru was spending more and more time with Lottie as January progressed, building their warehousing business, sourcing cargoes for the outward journeys to Africa and India, taking contracts from other shipping agents, and even local land based businesses.

Several times she voiced her worries about me having to care for Chika alone. It didn't particularly bother me but I understood when she suggested we hire a local girl to help with the domestic work and childminding. We decided to ask in the area, of anyone we came into contact with, and it wasn't long before a young woman presented herself to Pru.

Dina Carter informed us she was nineteen, a single mother and lived only two streets away with her widowed mother in a one-room rented abode. She was eager to take the job to help support her son. Uneducated but rather sharp in a street-wise fashion, she wasn't the ideal to fit Pru's ideas of a domestic or child-minder for Chika, but with no other prospects Dina was given the job at five shillings and six pence per week.

Chika was quite happy with Dina's attention, finding new spirited games to play and continuous company which she'd lacked before. Although I was on hand most of the time, I was taking advantage of the situation to practice the calligraphy and art work that I'd unfortunately been forced to abandon as an apprentice. Lottie had also inspired me to learn more of those foreign lands that had wetted my appetite and I buried myself in books. Dina quickly gained our trust and approval, and she appeared to like us.

She had quite an infectious laugh and as the days grew into weeks she became more relaxed in my company and me in hers. Pru was rarely at home until late afternoon when Dina returned home to her own family. Perhaps I should have been more careful and kept the relationship on a more professional basis but spending so much time together and in a relaxed atmosphere, I allowed the relationship to become more familiar. It's easy to see that now, in retrospect, but at the time I saw nothing wrong.

I think it all began with a playful tweak to my ear when I passed some jovial comment about her, and then the repartee began and seemed to escalate the situation. After a while it became normal to give each other a hug and next it was a peck on the cheek, all so very innocent.

That afternoon, Chika had fallen asleep after quite a boisterous morning playing physical games with Dina. With nothing to occupy her time Dina came and surprised me by depositing herself upon my lap. Although it took me unawares, I simply saw it as the usual playful Dina, but then she twisted herself around and with both hands holding my face she planted a kiss directly to my lips, which took my breath. As I recovered from the shock she settled herself down with her head on my chest.

I must admit that I was flattered but I felt rather embarrassed and pushed her away. I stood, hardly knowing what to say, and she looked at me crest-fallen. She pouted her lips, showing her disappointment by clasping her hands behind her and fluttering her eye-lashes in a most sensuous fashion. I was at a loss for something to say.

"Don't you like me?" she asked. It was a simple enough question but I hardly knew what to answer, after all she was an employee tasked to look after our child. I think I was embarrassed more than anything and said something like, "Of course, but..."   She stepped close and wrapped her arms around me, kissed me again, beginning with just a peck that developed into a passionate affair showing her full intentions. The embarrassment soon left me, ardour began to rise and we were soon draped together on the sofa. In my own defence it wasn't my hands that were doing the wandering, but that same old burning fire in my loins was at work again.

She unbuttoned her blouse and pulled my head to her naked breast. Her skirt rose to the top of her thighs revealing chalk white skin and I ran my hand up the inside of her leg, when suddenly we heard Chika awake and walking to the head of the stairs. We quickly adjusted our clothing and parted, fortunate that Chika had seen nothing. My face was burning and I felt rather foolish.

Dina had left before Pru arrived home. I'd quickly washed my face and cooled down, hopeful that nothing showed of my dalliance. Whether she suspected anything I don't know, perhaps it was just my conscience, but I thought I detected a chill in the air but she made no remark until after dinner. I sat down and opened my book and Pru casually remarked,

"Have you been upstairs?"

I could truthfully say "No" but my self confidence quickly drained away as I mistakenly thought there was an inference in her question. She hesitated as though considering my answer, and her face bore a puzzled expression, so I asked,

"Why, what makes you ask?" and she replied,

"Well someone has been in the drawers of my dresser."

Somewhat relieved that her question had headed in a different direction, I asked,

"How do you know?"

"Oh I know. There's nothing out of place but the drawers have been opened."

"I suppose Dina would have been in to straighten the bed but why should she open the drawers?"

"Exactly; why should she open the drawers?"

"Well if nothing's out of place, how can you tell?"

"Because before I left this morning I tied a head hair to the drawer, almost invisible, and it's broken which means someone opened the drawer."

"Well, the only other person in the house was Chika. I don't think she would have opened the drawers, but we can ask."

"No. I don't want to alarm her, but we must be careful, something is happening and my suspicions are that Dina has been searching through my cupboards and drawers. We know almost nothing of her background other than what she's told us, which may all be a pack of lies..." she hesitated with a frown on her face, but then continued, "...It may be nothing but it's best to be on our guard."

The following day Dina arrived once more in buoyant mood and nothing was said about Pru's discovery but it was enough to make me cautious. During the morning whilst Chika was occupied with the games, Dina approached me in that same familiar way but I must have seemed 'cold' to her advances. She asked, "What's wrong. Surely you haven't gone off me so soon," and I replied,

Sweet Retribution

"No, I'm not feeling quite myself; perhaps a fever coming on." It was enough to quell her ardour but although I made an effort to appear engrossed in my calligraphy I cast a wary eye upon her activities. I was able to report to Pru that evening that I'd seen nothing to indicate Dina wasn't to be trusted, and things settled down to normal once again.

It was probably a couple of days later, I was standing at the table, examining and admiring the calligraphy I'd prepared; the capitalised heading to the manuscript with its surrounding scrolls and patterns, all embossed with reds, blues, and greens of glossy inks. I was surprised by Dina approaching from behind, stretching her arms around my waist and resting her head on my back in a very affectionate manner. That's when the familiarity really began again. I admit that my weakness allowed it to develop, probably boosting my ego.

Dina didn't neglect Chika, in fact there was an obvious bond between the pair, and she would often take the child out walking to get fresh air. In the home she would play endless games and keep Chika interested in childish stories. It was when Chika fell asleep that Dina came to me and the sexual frivolities began. I say frivolities because that's what the dalliance amounted to, I wasn't falling in love with the girl; it was just raw sex. I don't think it meant anything to her either.

Chapter 7

I'd allowed my caution to wane, but not so with Pru, she'd said nothing to me but had secretly set out items in drawers in specific order so that it would show if they were disturbed. She came home early, whilst Dina was still out with Chika. I knew instinctively by her attitude there was something wrong. Of course the immediate thought came to me that something had warned her of my infidelity. She wasn't aggressive in her speech or in her mood but to me it was evident she was mulling something over; preparing herself.

When Dina arrived home with Chika there was a quiet, controlled atmosphere as she confronted Dina.

"Dina, you're an exceptional girl and I have no complaints as far as your work – looking after Chika – is concerned, but I'm puzzled."

"Puzzled?" she replied, "Why, what's wrong?"

"I'm puzzled, first of all why you've taken this job? You see I've been doing some checking and you're not the single parent mother that you told us you were, nor do you live with your mother in a one room abode. You're a married woman living with your husband..." Dina's face drained of colour and she stuttered to begin a denial, but Pru carried in the same quiet vein. "...Secondly, I've noticed, you've been searching through drawers and cupboards – don't deny it because I've been setting little traps that you haven't noticed."

Dina went very quiet and I'm sure tears welled up in her eyes, but surprisingly she didn't shout and storm as if affronted by such allegations, perhaps because of the quiet, authoritative manner in which Pru had handled the situation.

"Dina, I'm not accusing you of stealing, I just want to know why?"

"I suppose you want me to leave."

"No. I just want to know why; what you're searching for and why you've lied to us?" Dina sat down with her elbows on her knees and held her head in her hands.

"I had to do it. I was made to."

"Made to? By whom?" Pru persisted.

"I can't tell you that, it's more than my life's worth..." she began but then looked at us with pleading eyes and continued, "...I'll get hammered when I get home, when I tell him I've slipped up."

"Well, just tell me what you were looking for because you can see there are no valuables here."

"A book; I was told to look for a little brown book."

Pru looked at me and said, "I thought as much. You needn't tell me who's behind it all – I can guess."

Dina rose to leave but Pru placed a restraining hand on her arm and said,

"I don't want you to leave in fact I'll raise your wages to six shillings if you'll just do as I ask?" She turned looking astounded and asked,

"What are you asking me to do? I daren't do anything against them."

"I don't want you to do anything. I just want you to carry on as normal. That book you were searching for, you would never have found – it's in safe hands, but I don't want them to know that. I want you to simply let them think you're still trying to find it. I'm more interested in knowing what their next moves are, so if you could agree I'd like you to tell me what you overhear. If you do that there'll be good rewards. What do you say?"

"I still get to keep my job?" she asked with tear streaming down her face,

"Yes, with benefits."

I hadn't given Chika a thought and I don't think Pru had either, in confronting Dina in her presence and I noticed her standing with a woeful expression on her face and the glint of tears in her eye.

"Oh thank you" and Dina made an affectionate show of cuddling Chika before turning to embrace us. I turned away in embarrassment as Chika clung to her.

Sweet Retribution

That evening whilst Pru and I sat talking, and Chika was in bed asleep, I said,

"You knew didn't you; knew that all wasn't as it seemed with Dina?"

"No, not exactly, let's just say I suspected. I wondered from the moment I saw her why a good looking young woman like her wasn't married. When I saw bruising to her face I guessed she was being abused. Because she was prepared to take a miserably paid job convinced me she was being put up for it. I asked myself who would want her to be in my home and for what purpose, and there could only be one answer, Finkelstein. Dina's husband is obviously in his pay."

"And yet you're still prepared to have her in our home."

Pru smiled that hint of a sly, confident smile that I'd become used to and said,

"I can't remember who it was that said it, or what the actual quote was, but the general idea was that it's best to keep your enemies close so that you can see what they're plotting. I wouldn't exactly say that Dina is my enemy but all the same she's in my enemy's camp."

I couldn't help but think what a shrewd woman Pru was and I'd had a nervous moment or two when she'd confronted Dina, not knowing what Dina was going to throw back at her in defence or pique about our activities, whilst she was absent. I felt sure I'd had a narrow escape and this had been a warning. I made a pledge to myself that there'd be no more cheating no matter what encouragement came my way. I quite understood my own failings and that infidelity was a weakness, but I resolved to keep my pledge.

In the days to come Dina continued to prove her worth as a nanny but she wasn't the same ebullient, outgoing, sexy, familiar young woman as before. It would take some time before she regained her confidence. Pru continued to pay her the increase to her weekly wage of a shilling, which in itself was good money, but she also gave her the odd few pennies extra from time to time, as an incentive to bring her snippets of news of what was happening in the Finkelstein camp. There was really nothing that held any significance in her reports but encouragement was a small price to pay.

March came with its biting, blustering winds, bringing yet more miserable weather, morning frosts and a desire to stay wrapped up inside. Lottie explained that the northerly winds that still carried the prospects of snow, also meant that the Lady Ester would find it difficult to make headway, delaying Tom's return with his eagerly anticipated cargo of Darjeeling. We planned a celebration party for when he returned.

The days dragged until April when, if the proverbs proved true, March that had entered as a roaring lion would exit as a lamb. Unfortunately April, that carried so much expectation, actually brought little relief from the weather, and Tom's return looked so much less likely. There was a lot riding upon this cargo – crew members' families would have had a hard time whilst husbands were away, and although Pru wasn't hard hearted, her benevolence would only stretch so far. Gradually the weather improved and anticipation grew once more, but April was slipping by.

Finally on the seventeenth day of the month to the enormous relief of everyone concerned the Lady Ester tied up and furled her sails. She had a work-worn appearance having weathered so much but the crew and the dock workers were in a buoyant mood. We were all excited and if there had been bunting and fireworks the clipper couldn't have had a better reception.

Lottie and Pru had laid trestle tables with cooked meats and pastries in the warehouse with kegs of ale enough for a small army. It was a real celebration. One of the deck hands produced a squeeze box and played. There was raucous singing of shanties and dancing. Whilst we were enjoying ourselves, Tom and Pru opened up the Lady Ester's hatches to inspect the cargo. The chests of tea were fine, all sealed to prevent water damage and packed tight to avoid movement which could unbalance the ship. Unknown to me or the remainder of our party, one tea chest bore a mark, and when the cargo was unloaded and stored in the warehouse, that marked tea chest would, for the time being, remain sealed and buried deep under the pile, until the port authorities and excise people had examined everything.

The devastating news would come later.

Chapter 8

After the welcome home, the following day was taken with stevedores and derrick operators unloading the Lady Ester and storing the cargo, all under the watchful eye of the excise men. Pru was arranging the sale of the tea with the auctioneer when word came.

"Get down to the warehouse, quickly. There's trouble," said the lad.

She left the auctioneer at a run, wondering what disaster to expect, but all became apparent as she approached to see the Port Authority and Excise people busy putting their seal on the warehouse doors. Her heart was pounding as she enquired what was happening.

"Your whole cargo is impounded, which means you must not interfere with anything. Guards will be mounted to ensure nothing is touched until we're able to make a thorough examination," said the officious man nailing the notice to the door.

"Why, what's wrong? Surely your agents were here to see it unloaded?"

"It's normal procedure, you should know that."

"No it's not normal procedure. Something has happened tell me what's going on. This is a cargo of tea."

"We've received reliable information that contraband is being smuggled amongst this cargo."

"Contraband, what sort of contraband? What's your information and who's given it?"

"I can't reveal our sources..." said the rather pompous man that seemed to be in charge, "We'll be back in the morning and carry out a thorough examination. Until then the guards will prevent anyone from interfering with the cargo."

Pru arrived at Lottie's home where we were enjoying the remnants of the previous day's celebration. She had the concerned look of someone facing some deadly peril.

"What's wrong?" said Tom jumping to his feet.

"It's the Excise, they've impounded the cargo. You know what that means? They're going to find that tea chest."

I could see the fear etched on Pru's face and hear it in her voice. I said,

"What are you talking about? What are they going to find?"

Tom laid his hands on Pru's shoulders and calmly said,

"Calm yourself. They'll find nothing. I've made sure it's buried underneath the whole shebang."

"I wish I had your confidence. They said they'd had information that we were smuggling contraband. Who could have given them information – as if I didn't know," said Pru.

"I'll go down there and sort things out," suggested Tom grabbing his jacket.

"How are you going to sort things out?" I asked,

"Oh leave it with me..." and turning again to Pru he said "...I know a few people. Don't worry." And with that he'd gone.

The celebratory mood had fallen flat. The cargo was worth between five and six thousand guineas at auction and the small shipping enterprise couldn't take a loss like that. We were wondering what the devil Tom could do about the situation. Was he going to make matters worse?

Tom was gone rather a long time and when he returned he approached the house, with heavy footsteps, trudging along with shoulders bent and head down, looking thoroughly dejected. We went to meet him full of pessimism, expecting the worst. As he reached us he lifted his head and smiled – a beaming smile.

"What's happened?" Lottie asked. His face then took on more sombre look and he replied,

"Well, it's cost us dear..." he replied shaking his head, "...I hope I've done the right thing." Lottie took his arm and looked enquiringly at him.

"I was dealing with the harbour master and the Excise so they drove a hard bargain between them. They took a case of best Jamaica and five guineas apiece. It was the best I could do."

"So are we clear?" Pru asked.

"Yes. They tore down the impound notices as I watched. It perhaps seems a lot but we'd have lost so much more if they'd found it."

"Found what?" I asked, but Tom just grinned and slapped me on the back. Lottie and Pru looked at each other and smiled. I was totally dumbfounded and getting rather annoyed at being left in the dark. I just knew it had to be something illegal and they were running a risk with high consequences otherwise there wouldn't have been such panic. I said with a sour edge to my voice,

"Don't you think you can trust me? Why can't you tell me what it's all about?"

Tom said,

"Don't take it to heart Jack, it's something a bit special and I want it to be a surprise when you see it. I think we should all get down to the warehouse and sort things out because now I've paid them their bribe they know we've got something in there worth having. They don't know what it is but they'll think it worth breaking in there during the night."

"Yes, I'll get some lanterns it'll soon be dark," said Lottie.

Chika couldn't be left alone and so, with the four of us, we set out for the warehouse. Tom slipped the old watchman a few pennies to keep him sweet and turn the other way.

The chests of tea were surprisingly heavy and Tom and I took the brunt of the heavy lifting. He knew exactly where the marked chest had been hidden and it took a couple of hours of sweat and toil before it was uncovered.

Carefully Tom prized open the lid – carefully because it had to be replaced as though never interfered with. After delving deep amongst the tea he pulled out a leather satchel that for its size appeared very heavy. With satisfaction etched all over his face he handed it down and began the task of re-sealing the chest.

When we left during the early hours of the morning no-one would have known we'd been there – just in case the Excise changed their minds. The Lady Ester stood silent and ghostly with only the watchman aboard, enveloped by the morning mist and washed by a dark, stinking river that to me looked so malevolent.

The whole scene seemed to carry a heavy sense of unbridled criminality; amply reflecting whatever it was I was involved in. I still didn't know what we'd been skulking in the night to recover but I knew well enough that Tom's 'surprise' was something for which we were all risking our freedom.

Chika, excited to be out with grown-ups on some strange enterprise that she didn't understand, had grown tired and had to be carried home. Tom, despite his night's toil, willingly carried her on his back, and the moment we arrived at Lottie's she was put to bed. I couldn't contain my curiosity any longer,

"What's it all been about? What's in the satchel is someone going to tell me?" I blurted out. No one said anything but Tom looked at Pru and after some hesitation he took the satchel and passed it to me with a gesture that said, '*Here, look for yourself.*' It was heavy and when I opened it I found what appeared to be lumps of something heavy like metal, wrapped in linen cloth, together with a small linen draw-string bag. I emptied it all out on the table and unwrapped it.

"GOLD, Is this gold?" I asked, and Tom just smiled and said,

"It is. That's my surprise, and worth all the effort too." I then took the draw-string bag and looked inside. Its contents didn't have the breath taking excitement as when I saw the gold. It just appeared to be lots of pieces of dull glass. Tom caught my puzzled look and said,

"Diamonds; they're un-cut diamonds."

I'd never seen the likes before and although I realised the contents of the satchel must be valuable I'd no idea of their worth. I guessed it must be a fortune to have caused the distress it did when the Excise people impounded the cargo.

"Where's it from?" I persisted.

Tom looked at Pru again and raised his eye-brows in a questioning look, as much to say, '*Can I tell him?'* and Pru nodded her head. It was most unusual for her to divulge information remembering that her usual maxim was '*The least you know, the least you can tell',* but I suppose she thought he's in it up to his neck now so what harm is there.

"West Africa..." he answered, "...a place called Accra on the Gold Coast."

Lottie caught my blank expression and said,

"Can you remember the map I drew of Africa when I was explaining the Lady Ester's journey?"

"Yes," I replied, but in truth I only had a hazy recollection, and she continued,

"It's on the under-belly of that big bulge of Africa I showed you."

Tom took up the story again,

"Some years ago we were becalmed. The trade winds just stopped blowing, it's what they call the Doldrums, an area near the equator where sometimes the sails hang limp and it can last weeks. We just drifted until we saw land off the starboard bow. The captain lowered a boat and sent two of us to get fresh water and provisions. We found we were in this small port they called Accra. The place was under British administration. We obtained our fresh water and provisions, returned to the ship and when the wind picked up we were on our way again. That piece of ill luck, being marooned, actually acted in our favour and Accra became a port of call in the following years, as it was a deep water harbour." Tom stopped to take a drink of beer from his mug before continuing.

Sweet Retribution

"I was second mate at the time on an East Indiaman, running opium into China and trading for tea. We regularly called at other ports for provisions, but Accra became a handy port of call. We were sometimes there for a week or more depending on the weather. I got to know one or two people, Nabobs who were always looking to strike a bargain and they were eager to get hold of opium they could sell on to the Accran natives. They were pretty cute and you just had to have your wits about you." Tom supped more ale before continuing. I think we were all engrossed in his tale. He continued,

"I soon learnt it was a gold producing area, Ghana it's called, and it wasn't long before I was being offered these 'ere nuggets. All very hush-hush because it was very dangerous for them if they got caught, One or two had been executed by the authorities. Anyway, our opium was in great demand – it was cheap to us, India was producing tons of the stuff, and we could always spare some for a trade. Well, as I say, you had to know who you were dealing with and keep your wits about you because some had managed to pass off fool's gold – that's iron pyrites – to the unwary. Well there we are – I've done pretty well in the past and long may it last.

"What's to be done with it now, how can you sell it?" I asked.

"Oh, that's no problem. I know a jeweller who'll use the gold and cut the diamonds..." answered Pru, "...you know everybody's looking for a bargain."

"Let's all get some sleep, we've deserved it," said Lottie.

Chapter 9

It felt good to be home again in our little cottage, our family of three together as Pru took a day away from warehousing. Dina still came to take care of Chika and it was strange to see the easy going relationship between the pair, knowing how Dina had been caught out so recently on her underhand activities. Almost every small task such as preparing food, cleaning and laundry, they undertook together. I wondered how long it could last. Chika was under their feet the whole time demanding attention, wanting games. The day went well.

Dina was preparing to leave when she took Pru aside, and spoke in a hushed voice,

"Is there an auction soon?"

"Next Saturday. Why do you ask?" asked Pru. Dina bit her bottom lip and pondered for a moment then said,

"Oh, I don't know it may be nothing."

"Come on; tell me what you've heard. If it's enough to set you wondering it may be important."

"It was just a snippet of conversation I chanced to hear. It may be absolutely nothing but Finkelstein's bullies were talking with my husband, and they mentioned your auction. It probably means nothing but knowing how Finkelstein feels about you, I thought I ought to mention it."

"Is that all you heard, nothing more?" asked Pru.

"That's all, nothing more. It perhaps means nothing but I'd hate it if I hadn't said anything and they did something nasty."

"That's good, thank you Dina. I promised you there'd be a little reward if you learned anything useful, and if this turns out to be some diabolical scheme on their part, there'll be a guinea for you."

After Dina had left Pru told me what had been said, and continued,

"I must talk to Tom. If those thugs are scheming to disrupt the auction we shall have to have enough men to drive them away."

"What if they're planning to do more than disrupt the auction? What if they're planning to break into the warehouse and destroy the whole cargo of tea; maybe set fire to the warehouse?" I asked.

"That's just what they would do and It's five more days until the auction. We must protect the tea. It's time to have a word with Tom and see what he can fix up."

There was no time to waste so we were off to Tom and Lottie's home once again, to discuss what should be done.

Tom was undaunted and laughingly, said,

"My boys'll be up for a bit of rough and tumble. We'll all wait for 'em and give 'em the surprise o' their lives. I've got enough clubs aboard the Lady Ester for everyone. We keep 'em handy in case o' pirates."

The scene was set, Tom brought along his crew, all armed with their wooden clubs. I volunteered too. I didn't really relish the idea of a fight but I'm sure it would have looked a little like cowardice if I hadn't. The old watchman wasn't going to be much use and so he was encouraged to find a safe corner and look the other way if anything kicked off

"Monday night, Tuesday night and Wednesday night passed without incident and it began to look as though it was all for nothing. There was an air of disappointment that lingered amongst the lads.

Thursday arrived and we gathered again but now the expectation was waning a little, although we hoped that there might still be the chance of a little fun. We waited until dark for the rendezvous, secreting ourselves inside and outside the warehouse as we'd done on previous nights. We looked the part of a villainous gang prepared to wage war – which is exactly what we were about. We sat drinking ale, and telling whispered tales of exploits past, prepared for another fruitless night, but at about two of the church clock, I heard the hoot of an owl and that was the pre-arranged signal from our lookout. Immediately the excitement built to fever pitch. I grasped my club, nerves tingling, preparing for the worst.

Tom's crew were much more eager than I was for the melee, and I thought that if the opposition were as eager and prepared for what was about to happen, there would be a lot of blood and cracked heads. It's a frightening prospect, knowing what's about to happen; the tension builds, bladder weakens, and then suddenly all hell breaks loose. There's no time for worrying now, it's every man for himself, and that's just what happened. Tom's lookout spotted four rough looking men creeping towards the warehouse and keeping to the darkest shadows, obviously intent upon mischief.

We'd agreed to hold fast until we were sure just what they were about – before the trap was sprung. The men observed one of the miscreants with a lantern concealed under the folds of his coat, and when they smelled oil being splashed around, it was enough. We'd later find lantern oil soaking the wooden fabric of the building, and wads of gun cotton, confirming their intent. With the tar waterproofing of the timber it would have quickly become an inferno.

Little did they know a reception party was about to turn their evil intentions into a blood bath. The fury of hell was unleashed upon them by Tom's crewmen. The awful problem was that in the overcast, moonless night, there was no way that we could identify who was friend and who was foe and sadly some of us were receiving blows from our own party. No-one had given any thought to this before-hand or we could perhaps have worn a coloured patch or neckerchief.

I was lucky; reluctant to split heads with my club I joined the melee but kept rather to the back.

Three of the raiding party managed to flee with varying degrees of damage – mostly about the head and shoulders – but one lay motionless on the quay, blood pouring from his head. I was convinced he was dead and I wondered what trouble this would bring down upon us.

Tom and his crew dragged the body inside and lit candles.

"Is he dead?" I asked.

"No, but he'll soon wish he was."

"What are you going to do with him?

"Wait until he recovers consciousness then we'll have a nice little conversation with him and he'll tell us all we want to know," and Tom chuckled.

It was nearly daylight when the man recovered, still bleeding and shirt soaked in blood. Whether it was a pretence or whether he genuinely couldn't speak properly, I don't know, but we were getting nowhere. Even with a knife to his throat it didn't help his memory or his ability to say anything coherent. It was decided to let someone else take care of him, and who better than Finkelstein himself.

With support either side he was dragged through the deserted streets to the Bread Street hovel of East Cheap where Finkelstein lived. As Tom kicked and smashed open the locked door, Finkelstein's henchman sprang to his feet, but confronted by so many he wisely hesitated to intervene. The despicable, lank haired, greasy money lender froze in his seat. The injured youth was flung unceremoniously through the doorway at Finkelstein's feet and Tom's party simply turned to walk away. Tom looked back over his shoulder and said,

"He's yours – bear this in mind for the next time."

Dina arrived as normal but apologised saying,

"I'm sorry, I can't stay, I have to return home to tend my husband." Pru's response was to ask,

"Why, is he ill?" but Dina replied,

"No. He's been involved in a fight somewhere and he's come off worst. His scalp has been split and he seems to have fractured ribs." There was no response from Pru other than to press a guinea into Dina's hand.

Dina looked down at the coin and then at Pru, and a realisation spread across her face.

"What has he done?"

"It sounds most likely that he was one of the gang that tried to burn down the warehouse last night, but we had men waiting for them."

"So, they didn't manage it?"

"Oh no, they didn't manage it. Another lick of tar to the building, and you'd never know they tried." A smile spread across Dina's face as she turned to go, saying,

"Well, at least he won't be able to treat me like a punch-bag for a while, will he?
I think we all thought the guinea had been well spent and it proved where Dina's loyalties lay."

The day of the auction came without further ado and the tea was split into lots, each bought by different wholesalers at a fair price, which worked out at five pence per pound weight. Lottie did a quick calculation on 150 tons x 20cwts x 112lbs = 336,000 lbs at 5pence = 6,666 guineas. We'd hoped for that extra penny, but we were satisfied. When the auctioneer had been paid Lottie and Pru drew up their account. With the wages of the crew, Tom's stipend, the provisioning of the Lady Ester and the ship's chandler's costs, there was still sufficient to finance the next enterprise and take a reasonable dividend.

Lottie was forever trying to persuade Tom that she should go along too but Tom steadfastly refused insisting that all mariners regarded a woman aboard ship as unlucky and there were some members of the crew who'd refuse to sail. I'm sure Pru was pleased that she wouldn't be losing her friend for six or seven months. Lottie was crucial to the enterprise as agent,

As dry-docking need not be considered for re-caulking and barnacle scraping for another twelve months, the Lady Ester must set out again soon if the enterprise was to remain viable. Provided the voyage could be underway within the next few days, there would remain a reasonable chance of a return by Christmas.

With need to maximise profit Lottie managed to source a cargo of wool bales for India, which were loaded, overseen by Tom to ensure the weight distribution was precise and there could be no movement to upset the ships balance. Activity aboard ship increased day by day. Sails would be unfurled, checked and patched, spares checked likewise, ropes, shackles, pulleys, marlin spikes and all the paraphernalia of ship-board life stowed aboard. Food, fresh drinking water, medicines and liquor supplies were sourced and loaded; it was the second of May and finally the Lady Ester was ready to set sail.

As always there were clinging, tearful goodbyes as families gathered on the quay; husbands, fathers, and boyfriends, kissed and hugged those most dear to them before they embarked. Lottie and Tom were no exception, seven months was a long time apart. Pru and I were there to wave goodbye as the tide turned to carry them away from their moorings

Chapter 10

With the sailing of the Lady Ester there was a feeling of relief amongst us once more, as though we'd emerged unscathed from some catastrophe. It felt good thinking that there was little Finkelstein could do to us now the tea cargo had been auctioned and the Lady Ester had set sail. Life could begin to settle down again.

I returned to my calligraphy, not that I needed to practise the art for our financial well being, I simply enjoyed it. Chika was Pru's pride and joy and we still enjoyed Dina's company. We were a happy little band. Discussion about Chika's education was constant. It seemed to us that most people regarded a girl's schooling as totally irrelevant – a woman's place was in the home with children at her knee, what education did she need to clean and wash clothes? We wanted something better for Chika.

We were happy to teach her to count, the letters of the alphabet and the structure of simple words. Dina, as street wise as she appeared, was illiterate and sat with Chika, as eager to learn too. On certain days Lottie would visit and I took the opportunity to encourage her to teach what she knew of the geography of the world. I found her fascinating, her wealth of knowledge, and her drawings, were a window into another world.

With Lottie, geography would often drift sideways into a history lesson, telling of the British East India Company sanctioned under Queen Elizabeth the first, that had its own army and navy; its domination of the world's spice trade and its corruption with the Moguls of India that was leading to the present unrest. She told of its involvement in the opium trade and of China tea to New England where the unfair trade had led to the recent War of Independence and overthrow of British rule. It was no doubt too much for someone of Chika's age to absorb it all but to me, and obviously to Dina it was fantastic. Lottie was eager to point out she was no academic, all her knowledge had been acquired at the hands of Captain Tom, her sea-faring husband who had witnessed these world events first hand.

Chika was quick to learn and showed intelligence at such an early age, that we thought above normal, but what parent wouldn't believe so of their own brood? It sparked some deliberations upon how we could proceed with the education of our precocious child. Should we consider sending her away from home to a seminary for her better education that would fit her for some superior position, perhaps in the church?

Of that idea Pru was most definitely not in favour. It was clear to me she'd longed for a child for far too long than to now send her away in the best formative years of her life. Nothing was said by either of us but I suspect we both secretly worried that in such an event, Chika might well be bullied because of her ethnicity. No, Pru wanted her home where she could enjoy her love and adoration. Eventually it was mutually agreed that we'd search for suitable tutors for a home education. In the mean time we'd continue as we were, helping Dina too.

It was quite obvious to us that Dina's married life wasn't at all happy. Since her husband's attempt to fire the warehouse she'd received no physical harm, such as she'd grown used to up to that point, but the aggressive mental abuse was getting steadily worse. She was glad of the respite she gained each day caring for Chika. She feared that as her husband regained his strength and the fractured bones healed, the physical trauma would begin again. In the late summer of that year, her spirit finally broken, she ran from the torment of her home, but with no-where else to go she came to Pru.

Pru couldn't possibly be considered soft hearted, but by this time Dina had become both a friend to us and reliable carer for Chika. Although there were only two bedrooms, one occupied by us and the other set aside for Chika, we couldn't turn Dina away, and so it was resolved that another bed would be purchased and she would share the room with Chika, after all she was like an older sister.

There was always the worry that Dina's husband would target our home as he'd know exactly where she'd run to, but perhaps he'd had enough retribution to last him for a while, and so our little family – for family we regarded ourselves – had grown to four.

Dina was learning to bake too; bread and pastries. Pru was imparting all her knowledge and Chika was keen to be involved in the mixing of eggs, flour and yeast, a rather messy business but enjoyable for her. I confess I was enjoying a life of excess whilst others in the slums were probably finding it hard to avoid starvation.

Our new family member settled quickly and gradually that ebullient, cheeky nature returned to her, which was fine when Pru wasn't around but it could be a slight embarrassment when she was home. Pru didn't seem to give it much notice. On one morning Pru had decided to go to the market and take Chika along too. Dina had some washing to do so stayed behind. I'd completed some highlighted cards for the church and felt rather tired. I sat down in my favourite chair and before long I'd fallen asleep. I woke to find Dina at my side gently stroking my face. She'd covered me with a blanket. It was a little disconcerting as I thought Pru might return at any moment.

As I gathered my senses, Dina stayed at my side, smiling and brushed my hair back from my eyes. It was almost as though I'd suddenly developed a paralysis, I couldn't move and perhaps Dina took that as my acquiescence. She pressed her cheek to mine and it seemed we were back to that same sexual relationship that had begun earlier. I had to explain that Pru would be back at any moment and it wouldn't be wise to allow her to catch us in the act. When Pru did return the washing hung on the line in the back yard, the cottage was tidy, and to all outward appearances, Dina had fully occupied her time.

Sweet Retribution

As much as I loved Pru, the temptation Dina was posing was too hard to resist. Every opportunity that arose she took to stimulate those basic instincts in me and weak as I was, I began to succumb. Pru, as cute and aware in all other respects, seemed to have no mindfulness of the situation that was building between Dina and me. Whenever Pru had left, for whatever reason, especially if Chika was with her or occupied elsewhere, Dina would come to me and our encounters would become more physical. The bedroom would become our playground. She was so confident, often standing naked at the head of the stairs, beckoning me, her voluptuous breasts a magnet that drew me to her.

My previous encounters had done little to steady the rampaging sexual demands that took me to ecstasy, often much sooner than satisfied Dina. She would often take the initiative and the more physical role to satisfy her demands. I often remembered Pru telling me that sex was like an artist painting a masterpiece – anyone could brush paint on a canvas but the finer, delicate brush strokes only came with practise. It didn't appear to have worked in my case I was still that over-eager artist.

The inevitable finally came about when Dina took me aside to say she had missed her monthly bleed, she was understandably concerned. The news hit me like a punch to the stomach as I worried about the consequences. I convinced her to wait and say nothing for the moment. It was at this point that I noticed a livid mark upon her neck that she tried to conceal. I was sure that I hadn't caused it. She hid it well so that Pru didn't see it and gradually it faded away. My worries grew as time progressed, our fears confirmed, Dina was pregnant. I spent nights lying awake, wondering what to tell Pru but, afraid of what would result I kept silent. Dina on the other hand didn't seem to be particularly concerned and carried on as normal. I knew that eventually it would become obvious but until then nothing would be said.

Sweet Retribution

I noticed that Dina was occasionally going out in the evenings but nothing was said as both Pru and I recognised she had her own life to lead, but it did make me wonder, was I the one responsible or could it be someone else to blame? One evening whilst she was out Pru remarked to me,

"I think she's got a boyfriend, either that or she's trying to mend her broken marriage." I asked,

"What makes you think that?"

"Woman's intuition, she's going out more and she's got that sparkle. It's strange but true women who've suffered physical violence find it hard to break away from a marriage where they're no more than a punch-bag. "

They were only passing comments and quickly forgotten but it was enough to make me wonder again about her pregnancy. Was it me or had she found someone new?

As September drew to its close and the days began to get shorter, one evening Dina left at about 7.30pm and by 10.30pm we were ready to retire. We realised that Dina hadn't returned but she had her own key and we went to sleep unconcerned.

When daylight broke, Chika came to our bedroom having realised that Dina hadn't slept in her bed. Referring to our previous conversation Pru remarked,

"I told you so she's spent the night with her boyfriend."

We didn't think any more of it until we reached mid-day and there was still no sign of her. By that time we began to think it unusual but we were still not alarmed. It was the following day, nearly forty hours since Dina left the house, that we took notice when tales circulated in the neighbourhood of a body discovered on the mud banks of the Thames. It was gossip, and there was always alarmist talk of a body being washed up in the river. We still didn't know whether it was the body of a man or a woman, or indeed if it was true. If they'd said another woman's mutilated body had been found in

Whitechapel, it might have been different, but
Whitechapel was some distance away.

Chapter 11.

It was quite unusual to see these new 'Peelers' strutting about in their coat tails and toppers, there was no denying they were causing quite a stir. It was certainly time that something was done to make the streets safe. The voluntary constable and the old watchmen had had their day and they were only paying lip service to the robberies and violent assaults. They might look dandies, these Peelers, but they were showing an iron fist and were quite prepared to use their batons to crack a few heads.

Pru had decided to take Chika to the street markets of East Cheap, renowned to be the best in the whole area, so I decided to tag along. It was as we reached the bridge that we saw the Peeler pinning the notice to a wooden post. 'MURDER' it proclaimed, and described a young woman washed up on the banks of the Thames, with her head bashed in.

My stomach turned over with a dreadful fear; we were now four days without word from Dina. I just had to ask the Peeler what he knew.

He actually knew nothing more than was there in black and white on the poster, so I decided to tell him about Dina and her traumatic marriage. I began to tell him that Dina had failed to return home – but I realised I knew nothing of where Dina had lived with her husband or what his name was. I could only remember she'd said her name was Carter – perhaps they would have his name on record?

We continued to the market with a heavy feeling that it was Dina's body they'd found, which spoilt the whole day, and so with our vegetables, bread, butter, cheese and eggs, we trudged home. A rather sombre mood persisted throughout the afternoon and at about four o'clock there was a heavy bang-bang on the cottage door. I opened it to see a tall, heavily built, moustachioed man, wearing a bowler hat and looking very sour faced. He introduced himself as Inspector

Sweet Retribution

Stone of the Westminster Police, and he was here to follow up information given regarding a missing female.

My face must have drained of colour, my nerves were shot and I was sure he could tell, as I stuttered to ask him into our home. Inspector Stone eyed me up and down and cast a glance around the cottage, obviously weighing up everything in his mind before he began. He could probably see that I was beginning to perspire, but Pru was as calm as though she was used to entertaining police investigators in her home, but then I would have expected nothing less of her.

The inspector listened carefully and made notes of everything we could tell him about Dina, but finally he wanted to see Dina's room. He entered the bedroom very slowly, his eyes everywhere.

There was little for him to find other than a very few items of her clothing that she'd left behind. He examined every surface, even the floor, and it was at that point I realised what he was looking for – blood. He was making sure that Dina hadn't died there in her bedroom and that I – or we – weren't the guilty party. After some considerable time he left without a word about whether he was satisfied with what he'd seen. I was just pleased to see him go.

"Oh dear, that was a bit uncomfortable," said Pru. I had to agree but she went on to say, "I was hoping he wouldn't go into our bedroom. He'd have found that loose floorboard and I've just hidden that satchel with the gold and uncut stones. I must go and see my jeweller tomorrow and dispose of it all."
It had been a close call and a timely reminder not to let our caution slip.

That night we lay awake for a considerable time discussing the day's events and everything we could remember about Dina. We didn't know much about her husband – but we did know that he was part of Finkelstein's set up because of the attempt to fire the warehouse. We were both convinced in our own minds that her husband was responsible, knowing of his ill treatment of her. We were going to miss Dina and probably Chika would miss her most. Pru didn't tell me until much later she'd made up her mind to find out who Dina's husband was. I think if she had told me I would have suggested she didn't get involved.

We heard nothing more from the police inspector and our stash of smuggled contraband was disposed of at a very good price, it seems even the most prestigious jewellers of Westminster are not averse to a little dodgy dealing.

Pru asked me to stay at home that afternoon and look after Chika whilst she visited a friend. A 'friend' meant only one thing to me, she was off to see one of her associates of the undesirable underworld of cut-throats and thieves, to whom I'd had the earlier introduction. I knew better than ask why, and couldn't begin to understand her continued relationship with these people now that she was a successful business woman.

My misgivings about Pru getting involved it Dina's murder was to prove all too profound as she returned home in a dishevelled state. Alarmed, I asked,

"What's happened to you?" and Pru replied,

"Forget it. All that matters is I got what I went for." But I couldn't leave it at that and said,

"I can guess what you've been up to – you've been getting yourself involved in the business of Dina's murder, haven't you? What's happened?"

"I went out to see some friends to find out Dina's husband's name and where he lives, that's all."

"No it isn't all. Something's happened to you – I can tell by the state of you, your hair and your clothes."

"Oh it's nothing, some people got a bit upset about the questions I was asking, that's all."

"You should have known you were playing with fire sticking your nose in where it wasn't wanted. You knew he was part of Finkelstein's mob that he sent to burn the warehouse. You should leave it to the Peelers."

"I wanted to make sure they knew who he was, so now I've given them a name and address. He's Bill

Carter and he's hiding away in a brothel on Bethesda in East Cheap. If they're quick they'll catch him there."

"But don't you see, he'll now know who's grassed to the Peelers. You'll not be safe. If he can't get to you his friends will."

"Stop worrying. He knows that I'm not someone to be messed with, and so do his friends. I owe it to Dina

"I understand why you've done it but I can't help thinking you're storing up trouble for yourself."

Pru was too self confident but I could tell that tensions were liable to keep rising between us if I persisted, so I decided to leave well alone. What remained of the evening we spent reading stories and helping Chika with her words. We still hadn't found a suitable tutor for her but we were pleased with the progress we'd achieved

I lay abed that night unable to sleep; dead rats and dead cats on the doorstep were nothing when compared to the atrocities that were happening around the locality. The Ripper was at work around Whitechapel which was only streets away from us. Rumours were running wild and the Peelers had no idea who he might be.

The victims all appeared to be street-walkers – prostitutes – but Pru was given to being about in the dark hours with a self assurance that she was safe amongst the criminals. What if she was taken for one of those people, how safe would she be then? There was talk about it being a depraved doctor and even royalty, but that was pure speculation, it might just as easily be one of Finkelstein's mob.

Our visit to Lottie the following day had several purposes, including division of proceeds from the contraband, updates regarding prospective export cargos for the Lady Ester, tariffs on imports, harbour charges and detailed accounts of shipping expenditure to date. I had my own agenda.

I had to speak to Lottie to persuade her to convince Pru to curtail her nocturnal activities, if anyone could dissuade Pru, it would be Lottie. Pru wasn't about to take my advice but she had to be warned by someone that if Bill Carter was the one responsible for Dina's dreadful injuries, and was prepared to murder his wife, he wouldn't have any hesitation in attacking her. Lottie didn't have the same amount of concern for Pru's safety as I had but she promised to do as I asked.

I began to wish we were back in the hills of Derbyshire, safe and secure, away from all this violence and criminal skulduggery, but I knew that was never likely to happen. It was Pru's life-blood and she thrived on it. I feared we might all come to regret it.

The grapevine of the criminal underworld apparently exceeded the resolve of the new Peelers, as word soon reached us that Bill Carter had disappeared from his bolt hole and unsurprisingly no-one knew anything about him when the police went to arrest him.

Chapter 12

Bill Carter was the topic of conversation on everyone's lips in the neighbourhood, sightings of him here, more sightings there, suggestions of where he might be hiding, how he might be surviving, not one word worth a candle. He'd obviously got somewhere he could lay low until all this feverish interest in him blew over.

Although Pru had spread the word again, nothing was coming back but speculation about him having been whisked away on some boat across the Channel. I was sure he was still local; he had no known contacts abroad and he wasn't a sea-going type – in fact he was from agricultural stock, a labourer who had moved into London for a better life. My intuition kept me very wary and watchful, anticipating that he'd be out for revenge. For some days my nervousness saw danger in every place we went and in every fresh face we saw. Pru, however, was still prepared to venture out alone and nothing I could say or do would stop her.

Gradually, as the days became weeks since Carter had escaped, life for us started to settle down again, normality began to return and my nervous tension began to subside. That's when things kicked off

The three of us, Pru, Chika and me, had spent the afternoon at Lottie's and were returning home about eight o'clock. It was still daylight but drizzling rain. We were hurrying as none of us had taken any rainproof clothing. I don't really know what it was, maybe a premonition, but as we approached our cottage I stopped suddenly and grabbed Chika. Pru looked at me, puzzled by my obvious alarm, and asked,

"What's the matter?"
I wasn't sure myself but, call it a sixth sense, I said,

"Just wait here. There's something wrong, I think the door's open."

I cautiously approached and could see splintered woodwork and the door standing ajar. I crept to the hinge side of the door and stopped to listen, back pressed hard against the wall. I couldn't hear anything but my pulse was racing and I looked around for something to arm myself with, but could find nothing. With no sound coming from inside I cautiously pushed the broken door further open until I could see inside. My stomach lurched and sank to my boots, the place was a mess, broken furniture and crockery everywhere. The wall was smeared with something disgusting in a crude illiterate message that with a little effort I read as, "I'll be back."

Pru followed me into the house with Chika one step behind, surveying the carnage whilst I carefully negotiated my way upstairs, avoiding broken furniture as I went. With a carving knife in my hand I searched our bedroom and then went to Chika's room. There was little doubt left to the imagination of who was responsible for this mayhem as all of the garments that Dina had left behind were torn to shreds in what appeared to me a demonic knife wielding frenzy of slashing and tearing.

Chika was afraid, consumed by sobs and a deluge of tears whilst Pru held her close to her bosom in an effort to console her. I wish they had waited outside but now there was nothing either of us could do to lessen the trauma she was feeling. As far as Pru's feelings were concerned, she hardly said a word or shed a tear, but with a stony-faced resilience, simply began clearing the debris. All I could do was try to secure the door as just a temporary measure until I could get one of the ships' carpenters from the wharf to fix a new door. We could replace the furniture and that which was broken could be used to fuel the fire. It was the invasion – almost a desecration – of our home that sickened me.

It was late when we finally straightened the mess and I suggested that Pru take Chika in our bed for the night. I thought it the best way to avoid the child waking with nightmares; I'd make a bed downstairs. I didn't sleep well knowing the door was hardly secure and having read the message, "I'll be back."

Sweet Retribution

I believe we were all awake at the crack of dawn and I prepared a meagre breakfast, intending to walk into the City to report the incident to the Peelers, but Pru was reluctant. She said,

"What good will it do? They let him get away in the first place. They're not worth the effort. Just let me take care of it."

Once again I found myself bowing to her wishes. I despaired of what it was all leading to. My perception was that she was determined to act by some sort of 'criminal code' which gave her the right to extract an eye for an eye.

Whilst the carpenter worked to fit a heavy oak door I occupied Chika with number puzzles and simple mathematics and Pru left with shopping bags over her arm. Mid-afternoon a horse drawn delivery van arrived with new furniture and bedding. By the time Pru returned, the cottage had a comfortable, homely feel once again – if only the memory of trauma was so easily erased.

On the surface life carried on as normal with no outward signs of distress but none of us had put it out of our minds. Chika had returned to her own bed but there were times during the nights when she would climb into bed with us, making me aware that the dark nights still held fear for the child.

Both Pru and Lottie renewed their efforts to find Bill Carter through their underworld contacts, and to enhance their chances, a reward of twenty-five guineas was offered. I know I was beginning to irritate them both by my continual warnings to be careful, but their over-confident manner worried me. I was forever expecting something untoward to happen; convinced that we were being watched, after all he did in his crude way write "I'll be back." I didn't consider it paranoia, simply being cautious.

It didn't take long to prove my worries correct. Pru was out with Lottie and they'd taken Chika with them to the market. I sat alone in the back-yard, reading when there was a sudden crash of glass. I rushed into the cottage to find smoke and flame billowing from an oil soaked rag, wrapped around a piece of stone. Shards of broken glass from the window pane lay everywhere. Fortunately a pair of fire tongues lay on the hearth-stone and I was able to grab the burning cloth and throw it outside, only slight scorching of the stone flagged floor remained. By the time I got out of the front door there was no-one to be seen.

When Pru and Chika arrived home I'd cleared away the broken glass and fixed a wooden board into the window as a temporary measure. I'd scrubbed at the scorch marks and there was little left to see, but the smell left by the burning oily rag still lingered. I explained what had happened and I made my feelings clear that Bill Carter had indeed been watching our movements and he thought we were all out. If I hadn't been there the cottage could have burned down completely. Perhaps now everyone would take the threat Carter posed as serious and begin to take proper precautions. Pru, as calm as ever, said,

"I take everything as serious and I'm watching every step I make. We can't let him frighten us though. This only goes to show that he's somewhere close by and that all our efforts to find him are bringing him out into the open."

"Don't you think it would be best if we returned to the cottage on the moors, away from Carter and his ilk?" The question was probably pointless as I was already sure of the answer I'd get before the words left my mouth.

"I've no intention of letting him drive us out. He'd raze the cottage to the ground if we left...." hesitating a brief moment as though considering what to add, then continuing, "...Lottie's managed to get a guard dog for the warehouse. He's an English Mastiff. If you're so worried, how about bringing him home for a few nights?"

I'd never had a dog and this sounded like a huge beast and my immediate reaction was to ask,

"Is he dangerous?"

"No. He looks more dangerous than he is. Lottie thinks he's a big cuddly softy."

I wasn't keen to have a huge dog in what was basically a small cottage but considering the threat I felt we were under, I decided to give it a try. The very next morning, whilst the local glazier replaced the broken window, the three of us went down to the wharf. Lottie was already there and introduced us to Atlas, a two year old English Mastiff who must have weighed as heavy as me. He appeared to be the size of a donkey, with a care worn furrowed brow, sleepy looking eyes and enormous jowls. He looked at me and I'm sure his lip curled as though making his mind up whether to eat me. He didn't make a sound but stood protectively between me and Lottie.

"Good boy..." said Lottie patting him on the head, "....He's a bit protective. He's been handled by a woman and he's a little wary of men, but once he's got to know you he's fine."

I don't know whether he took a dislike to me or whether he could sense my nervousness but I wasn't at all sure we were going to get along. Chika was totally without fear and put her arms around the dog's neck and hugged him. It seemed I was outvoted about Atlas and he'd be coming home with us. Of one thing I was certain; Bill Carter would have to be very brave or very foolish to tangle with this boy.

Chapter 13.

It wasn't going to work, this huge animal in a two up/two down cottage with only a small back yard. Much as Chika and Pru took to Atlas he was too big. He seemed to tolerate me but I didn't quite feel the same bond with him as they did. I admit, having him around did make me feel easier when I considered the alternative with Bill Carter still around.

Pru was never going to agree to a return to my little farm on the moors, and the stress of living like this, continually looking over my shoulder, watching Pru's back, and trying to make our little home a fortress, was very wearing to say the least. Watching Chika with Atlas gave me an idea.

"Pru, both of you like Atlas but it's unfair having the dog penned up in such a small cottage with no outside garden. How much are you attached to this place? Would you consider moving to a nice house with a garden – say, somewhere south of the Thames, perhaps down Jamaica Road, beyond Lottie's cottage? Wouldn't it make more sense, we'd be nearer to Lottie and nearer the wharf too?" She didn't immediately answer but I could see she was giving it some thought.

That was the beginning of the saga, and at every opportunity I pushed the idea forward, even getting Lottie into the persuasion. She was eager for the idea to work because we'd all be closer and the warehouse business would benefit too. Eventually Pru succumbed,

"I've been attached to my cottage and it's hard to think of leaving. It's held some pleasant memories for me but perhaps the time has come to move on. I'll still have those memories and I agree we need more space."

That final acceptance began the search for a house that would suit us. We discussed what we both would ideally look for in a new home. Most important was the need for a garden, not too far from Lottie's cottage, but with three bedrooms and perhaps windows with plenty of sunlight. Some of these places had piped water – a pump in the kitchen that didn't freeze up in winter, our ideas were probably running away with us. A house like that was going to cost a fortune but I could always sell the farm – it was only a small cottage and a couple of outbuildings, with about five acres of unproductive moor, so it wouldn't raise much, but it would help. The question of cost didn't appear to concern Pru.

There weren't many options in the immediate vicinity of Jamaica Road and in the following weeks we began to extend our search further afield towards Rotherhithe and the open area of Southwark. It was still easy walking distance of Lottie's and the chances of finding something suitable were increased.

Eventually, after becoming increasingly despondent, we alighted upon The Old Vicarage. It had several of the features we'd wished for, a substantial stone built house of two storeys, with three bedrooms, a living room and parlour, a kitchen with an indoor water pump and a fine outside privy with a covered canopy that meant we didn't have to venture out into the weather when we used it. What was more, there was a fair sized garden where Atlas could run to his heart's content. The one thing that some might find disagreeable about the house was its situation – next door to the cemetery, but this didn't cause us any concern, in fact Pru found it a bargaining instrument to bring the asking price down.

The agent handling the sale of Pru's cottage also dealt with the purchase arrangements of The Old Vicarage and within the month we had moved our furniture in and were settling down, all thoughts of Bill Carter totally forgotten. Now our attentions were turning to Christmas and the prospects of Tom's return with the Lady Ester. We were into the latter days of November and excitement was already building. We readied the warehouse with its store of export wool bales destined for Kolkata, and cleared enough space to receive the import cargo of tea chests. We could relax a little now.

Sweet Retribution

I'd shown Chika how to make paper chains and she was busy preparing decorations for the house – it was going to be a Christmas to remember; but not for the reasons we had in mind. Bill Carter hadn't managed to find where we'd moved to but he still knew all about Lottie and where she lived.

The night was overcast with little natural light entering Lottie's bedroom. She always slept with the curtains open relying upon the break of daylight to awaken her. Something had disturbed her, perhaps a slight noise, but she felt no disquiet. It could have been the wind against the window pane or a draught up the chimney. She lay hoping to go back to sleep and heard the church clock strike two. Turning onto her side she pulled the bed covers tighter around her and buried her head into the pillow. Sleeping alone in the cottage had never bothered her and since Tom was so often away she prided herself on her self reliance. It was that self reliance that prompted her to always keep Tom's cutlass by the bedside, never thinking that she would need to use it; just a precaution, a morale booster

As she lay there, eyes becoming heavier, on the edge of drifting back to sleep; she felt a strange movement as though someone had stumbled against the bed. Now she was alarmed, there was someone in the room, she could hear their careful movements and smell a faint odour of ale.

She fumbled for the cutlass and quickly swung her legs out of bed, turning to face the intruder. Before she could clear her drowsiness and distinguish who or what was in the bedroom near her, or raise the cutlass to ward off any form of attack, she received a shattering blow to her right eye. Flashing lights blinded her as she sank into oblivion.

When she regained consciousness daylight was streaming into the room with a blinding light that made it impossible to keep her eyes open, and her head ached as though she'd been trampled by a herd of horses. She realised she was spread-eagled on the bed and her nightgown was around her neck. Lottie was knocking at the Old Vicarage door in a distressed state by mid-morning. Pru took a bowl of water to wash the blood from her face and neck and placed a cold compress to her eye which had obviously bled internally; the white of the right eye having become bright red.

There was swelling and bruising that would become more obvious around the eye and the cheekbone as time progressed. As the story unfolded Lottie and Pru spoke in hushed terms obviously describing the sexual assault and deciding what to do about it. Lottie was hugely embarrassed and pleaded with Pru not to report it to the Peelers or to tell Tom when he reached home.

I took it upon myself to go to Lottie's home to investigate how the intruder had gained entry. It took no time at all to figure out that sash window at the rear of the house had been forced with some form of flat instrument about an inch and a half wide. It was the illiterate writing scrawled on the wall that told me who we were dealing with, "Slagg ey b bak." Identical to the filth scrawled on our cottage wall intended to read 'I'll be back' – Bill Carter without a doubt.

I obliterated the scrawled message and after nailing the window shut I returned home. I couldn't help feeling we'd escaped just in time and poor Lottie had suffered the consequences. Knowing who we were dealing with was one thing, finding him and doing something about it was another thing altogether. I wanted to go out and physically search for Bill Carter but none of us had the faintest idea of what he looked like. I wished I still had the pair of pistols but I'd disposed of them long ago. They lay in a deep lake somewhere up in the hills, and with nothing else for protection, I took to carrying a knife in my belt.

It seemed that Lottie was emphatic in that she wouldn't involve the Peelers the embarrassment and humiliation would be too much, so there was little more we could do. The tactics gave Bill Carter the upper hand and all we could do was await the next incident and hope that we could overcome him. I thought long and hard to find some strategy that would bring him out into the open, but nothing would come to mind.

Chapter 14

Bill Carter was a wife beater, he'd had his head split open on the night of the attempt to burn the warehouse, he'd forced his wife, Dina, to take a job in our household, and when she turned against him she was found dead on the mud bank of the Thames. It didn't take a genius to figure out who was responsible for her murder. Pru had felt morally obliged to inform the Peelers about him, even giving information of where he was hiding out, but either through being slow to react or ineptitude on their part he'd escaped. Now, wanted for murder, he was evading capture and taking his revenge; trying to burn down our cottage and then this dreadful assault on Lottie.

Why oh why wouldn't they report this to the Peelers and get some protection. Tom, Lottie's husband, was bound to find out when he docked with his ship, only total silence on our part could prevent that. Had Lottie even considered that she might be pregnant – how would she explain that? How would Tom react?

Someone was bound to know where Carter was; where he was laying his head, where he was getting his food. Pru and Lottie had their criminal underground contacts who would spread the word far and wide through Cheapside, Shoreditch and out through all the slums of Whitechapel and Limehouse, but no information was filtering back.

I didn't have the same faith in this grape-vine as they did. Who knew where the loyalties of these people lay? Had they a foot in either camp? The twenty-five guinea reward for information Pru offered produced nothing of any use, only speculation that led nowhere.

The only solid lead we had was Carter's association with Finkelstein but how could we possibly approach him and persuade him to talk? Pru had had the good fortune to get to Finkelstein and steal his book. THE BOOK – that was the lever we had, but where was it? Pru was never likely to let that slip from her grasp, but if she could be persuaded to let me get my hands on it, it might contain something that we could use.

Lottie was persuaded to stay with us for a few days but she was determined the experience wasn't going to drive her from her home and she made it quite clear her stay would be a brief affair. She remained surprisingly sociable and strong minded considering what had happened to her.

Whilst she was with us she took quite a shine to Atlas. She'd originally obtained him as a guard dog for the warehouse but now, seeing him in a family environment, she began to think in terms of a dog of her own. Her predicament was the same as we encountered; a small cottage and a large dog, but she had the advantage of working at the warehouse each day where a dog would have ample scope to exercise.

Pru was a little more reticent, and when I broached the subject of the book she said,

"First of all let me make it clear that the book is not an option to trade or use as a bargaining tool. It's in safe hands, locked away securely in a vault where it will stay. Secondly, before we decide to take any other action I want to introduce you to someone who has something that's held my interest for some time. He supplies goods to the government through the East India Company and he has something we should consider. He'll remain anonymous to you and you must observe his conditions for secrecy."

That was intriguing and even more so to be left without further explanation.

"Tell us more Pru, what are you asking us to consider?" I asked, but she simply answered,

"Wait and see. I'll arrange a meeting tomorrow," and with that the subject was closed no matter what other questions were asked, there was to be no answer.

It was four in the afternoon and we were all gathered in the warehouse. The wharf was gradually growing quiet as lightermen, stevedores and dock hands ceased their work. Inside the warehouse oil lamps were lit and tension amongst us was growing as we heard the hackney carriage halt outside. Pru opened one of the huge doors and greeted a cigar smoking, imposing man in his fifties, dressed in an immaculate suit and overcoat. On his head he wore a fascinating covering of beautiful animal fur which he later explained was beaver. Intriguingly, he carried a small polished wooden box, which at a guess, was the reason for our meeting.

There were no formal introductions as we'd been emphatically told that his identity was to remain anonymous. We were invited to gather round as he placed the box on one of the bales of wool. It reminded me of the presentation box of flint-lock pistols I'd 'rescued' but which I'd finally thrown into the lake.

He opened the box to reveal a green baize cushioned lining and a pair of pistols the likes of which I'd never seen before. They were not much bigger than the size of a grown man's hand. My immediate thoughts were that they were too small to be real, more like a toy.

Lifting one of the pistols he held it in the flat of his hand and almost ignoring me, said,

"Ladies, I present to you the latest weapon of personal protection from America. It's going to be produced by the Derringer Company of Philadelphia. As you will see each pistol has two barrels, one above the other, and they can be easily turned over to fire two shots in rather quick succession."   He demonstrated how the barrels rotated. He then continued,

"The wonderful thing about these beauties is that they can be hidden in a pocket, or in a lady's muff, and kept ready primed. They don't require the old flint lock, only one of these..." and he produced a small capsule, "...it's called a percussion cap."   He handed the pistol to Pru, and as she examined it, he continued

"They are only for close encounter and at distance they wouldn't have great accuracy, in fact you'd be extremely lucky to hit the warehouse door at fifty paces, but with a calibre of this size at close quarters you'd certainly cause a lot of damage. Kill or seriously injure an attacker."

Lottie asked,

"Can you demonstrate?"

"Certainly madam, but I'd advise you to stand well back."

He then proceeded to prime one barrel and place the percussion cap.

"As you will have noticed I have not loaded a projectile." and he held aloft a lead ball to show the weapon was safe to fire.   Holding the pistol at arm's length he proceeded to demonstrate how to fire. Chika and Lottie dramatically put their fingers in their ears in anticipation. He pulled the trigger, the hammer fell and there was sharp retort that rather echoed inside the warehouse although it was nothing ear shattering.
The man turned to his audience and said,

"Well ladies, I understand that you're looking for some form of protection and I would suggest you'll find nothing better. I'm privileged to be able to offer these wonderful weapons for a ridiculous price. They're not yet in full production and you'll not be able to get them elsewhere."

"What price?" asked Pru.

"Well, I should be asking a hundred guineas, but because you're well recommended, I'll offer them to you for...a rock bottom price...ninety guineas."

"Too much," said Pru.

"Oh come now, what price safety? I'm offering them for a song at ninety."

"Let's be straight with one-another. They're stolen property, you know that and I know it. What's more they've been smuggled into the country," countered Pru.

The man became a little flustered and with some hesitation he said,

"Alright, then name your price."

"Fifty," snapped Pru.

"Oh no, I can't sell for fifty. I'd be losing money on them. There are people willing to snap my hand off for them at ninety."

"Alright then, sixty. I'm sure you'd be making a profit at sixty," counter Pru,

"Be reasonable, please."
After more haggling they finally shook hands at seventy-five guineas, and he left, I suspect, feeling a little brow beaten. I had to admire how Pru had handled the matter. The pair of Derringers was worth far more than seventy-five guineas. I was eager to handle them myself. Pru and Lottie had the protection they needed and Bill Carter was in for a big surprise when he next tried something, as he surely would.

Pru and Lottie were eager to try out the weapons and be comfortable about handling them and what better place than our garden, away from other homes and prying eyes. I set up a make shift target and we each fired the weapons – not with much accuracy, but I think we all slept easier that night.

Chapter 15

There was a huge reception for the Lady Ester as she tied up at the wharf. Her sails looked a little tattered and her paintwork wasn't looking at its best but she'd made excellent time with the trade winds in her favour. She was booked in for the dry dock and paintwork, caulking, and any damage all to be attended to. For now, all was focussed on the homecoming. Every crewman's family had been keeping a weather-eye open for the clipper and now we were all gathered in the warehouse for the celebration. Once again, Pru and Lottie had excelled themselves with the food and drink. As would be expected there was a great outpouring of emotion.

Tomorrow the cargo would be unloaded; for the moment the Excise people were clambering over everything, convinced they would find those items that were never likely to appear in the ship's manifest. Tom winked and gave a sly smile at Pru as if to say 'They won't find anything, it's too well hidden.'

Someone else had noticed the Lady Ester's arrival too. Pru stood apart, talking to a rather important looking man who I took to be someone of the Port Authority or Excise. All that I could perceive was a vigorous shaking of Pru's head as though in denial of something. It was much later that I thought to ask her who he was and she answered,

"The agent for Dorsey and Sons, they're a big set-up operating out of London and Portsmouth, trading with China. He wants to see our trading accounts, I've told him to get lost."

"What does that mean?"

"They'd like to buy us out but I've warned him off."

It was much later that Pru admitted to me that Dorsey and Sons' offer had caused her some serious consideration. She was astute in business and had an eye to the future. The first steam-boats had already appeared on the Thames and she could see that it was only a matter of time before steam would replace sail.

Steam ships wouldn't be delayed by the lack of wind or vagaries of the weather. But she had dismissed the offer as at that moment trade was still good – but for how long would that situation last? For now we had a cargo of valuable tea to auction.

The partying went on into the late afternoon then one by one the families began to depart. We stayed behind until the watch party came to guard the ship and cargo overnight. I decided to warn them about Bill Carter, that he might seize the opportunity to strike once again.

Christmas, with the Lady Ester safely home was going to be a fantastic time, if only what had happened to Lottie didn't spoil things. Lottie was still intent on silence about the whole matter but I could see that Tom was bound to find out about Bill Carter being on the run and trying to get his revenge. I wasn't about to divulge everything but I thought it best to warn him about what was happening with arson attacks and so on. Nothing was said about the attack on Lottie but that same night he discovered the Derringer hidden beneath the bolster of their bed. The fact that Pru had given it to her 'for protection' had seemed reason enough.

The following day was taken with unloading and storing the cargo of tea chests, all watched over very carefully by the port authority and the excise people. All went well and by mid afternoon the paperwork had all been signed off and everyone went away well satisfied with a bottle of rum each as a 'thank-you' token – there was always spirit of some description to be had cheaply on the docks.

As we walked home together, Tom asked me,

"I noticed the window was nailed shut. Lottie say's you must have done it."

I was taken a bit by surprise, and a little flustered I replied,

"Yes. I think someone tried to break in and with Bill Carter on the rampage I thought it best."

Tom continued in a not-too-concerned manner,

Sweet Retribution

"I noticed the marks the jemmy made when they tried to force it. They wouldn't have found anything worth stealing if they'd managed to get in."
My face must have gone red and I was thankful of the fading light not to have disclosed my embarrassment. Knowing of Tom's volatile temperament I was fearful of letting slip any indication of what had really taken place. Nothing more was said.

Two days until Christmas, the house decorated and festivities prepared, excitement was building and I think even Atlas was getting in the mood. His usual dower expression seemed to lift as he rolled around the hearth with Chika. My biggest problem was getting him out of my favourite chair to which he'd laid claim.

Down at the wharf everything seemed to have caught the Christmas fever, no-one appeared to have any appetite for work and the dockside workers were looking forward to the holiday. Tom and a select few of the crew were the only ones showing any enthusiasm for work, making the vessel ready to enter dry-dock as soon as Christmas was over.

Loading the cargo of wool bales couldn't be done until the Lady Ester had emerged from dry-dock; which meant the warehouse was full to capacity. An ideal time for any would-be arsonist to attack and in view of recent attempts we decided to employ watchmen and to take turns to guard the premises ourselves. Bill Carter was on our minds all the time but still no-one would recognise him if he showed his face. Tom was a bit more confident than I, doubting whether Carter would be prepared to risk an attack on the warehouse after he'd had his head split open at the last attempt, but he accepted that we couldn't take a chance.

Confident that interference with the cargo was unlikely, Tom decided to leave the trinkets he'd smuggled, hidden until a more leisurely time presented itself to manhandle the tea chests.

Sweet Retribution

As Pru and Lottie were busy preparing food, Tom persuaded me to walk down to the Angel public house. It was a rowdy bar that rang with laughter and singing. There was a roaring fire which added to the Christmas jollities and the intake of ale. We found ourselves a corner seat and the inn-keeper poured us each a tankard of foaming ale. I took my time with mine as I wasn't a regular drinker, whereas Tom finished his in just a few gulps. That set the scene for the evening, me being very slow with mine and Tom putting his away with alacrity, and slowly getting more and more maudlin as the evening went on.

"Jack..." he said in a hang-dog way, "...Jack, tell me straight...tell me...has Lottie been, y'know... having it off with somebody whilst I've been gone?"
The beer was really talking and he caught me at a moment when the beer I'd consumed was making me feel tipsy too. I still had the sense to be careful and not let my mouth run away with me,

"No Tom, most definitely not. Whatever makes you ask that?"

"Oh, she just seems different. I can't put my finger on it."

"Different? In what way is she different?"

"Quiet. That's it quiet."

"She's just the same old Lottie she's always been. She's loyal Tom, very loyal."

We'd had enough, both of us, and reluctant as he was, I had to get him home.

Meanwhile, Lottie was having a heart to heart talk with Pru whilst they prepared the food.

"I don't know what the devil to do. I think I'm pregnant. I've missed my monthly. I wondered for a while about going to see an old woman I know, but to tell the truth, I'm afraid. I've heard so many tales of how it's gone wrong." She wiped her hands and sat down on a kitchen stool, wiping a tear from her eye with her pinafore.

"I'd hoped I'd got away with it but no such luck. It'll break Tom's heart if I tell him. I've tried slippery elm but nothing's happened. There must be something else I could try. "

Pru put her arm around Lottie's shoulder in sympathy saying,

"Oh Lottie, I don't know what to suggest. You were not to blame. Surely Tom would understand if you told him what happened, that you were unconscious and couldn't fight back?"

"I don't know. He's a proud man and I don't want to risk him leaving me. I've been thinking, he's home now and he might accept the baby's his when he looks back and sees it's about nine months.. The timing would be about right."

"It's an awful risk to take. If he finds out – and it need only take a word slipped out in the wrong place – he might turn against you and the child.

"But there's only you and Tom that knows the truth."

"You must ask yourself, could you bring the child into the world and love it, knowing it was conceived in rape and knowing the violence of its real father?"

Pru poured them both a large brandy as Chika joined them. She hadn't heard a word of the conversation but somehow sensed the mood. The perception of the child was incredible and without a word she went to each in turn and hugged them tight.

When we were on our own Pru asked,

"You haven't said anything to Tom have you?"
I knew immediately what she meant and despite my tipsy beer head I was quick to deny.

"I've had to ask because Lottie thinks she's pregnant."

"Oh dear Pru, Tom's been quizzing me, he's thinking Lottie's got another man. He realises that she's changed somehow. I've said nothing but he says she's very quiet, brooding about something. I'm worried he might work it out. He's already discovered the Derringer and quizzed her about the window being nailed shut. He's an intelligent man he's bound to keep asking questions."

"I agree. We're going to carry as much guilt about this as Lottie if it all goes wrong. Tom's too good a friend to have us keep this from him, but if we tell him we're going to lose Lottie."

"Why won't she go to the Peelers and get them involved?"

"Because she fears the muck raking that it'll bring with it, and she says she isn't going to have them pawing over her body as though she was a piece of meat. I've told her it wouldn't be the Peelers it would be someone medically qualified. Anyway, it's all too late now, it happened days ago and as she said, they'd probably think the story made up when she didn't report it straight away."

Chapter 16

Christmas morning and we awoke to a dark, damp morning, but that didn't dull the enthusiasm and excitement for Chika. I think, like many more, we would have stayed in bed and enjoyed a relaxing lie in, but of that there was no chance, when Chika jumped onto our bed the moment she awoke. She wanted to remind us Tom and Lottie were coming early to take us all to church and she was looking forward to the singing, just like last year. I wasn't sure what Chika would actually make of the service. We'd done our best to explain our Christian beliefs, but would her tender mind have understood and absorbed everything?

We'd considered going to the midnight mass service to welcome in Christmas Day but with so much preparation for our festivities and our concern that Chika would be too tired, we'd opted for the morning service.

Tom and Lottie arrived for an early breakfast. Tom looked as though he hadn't recovered from last night's visit to the Angel – either that or he'd been awake half the night. It was a brisk walk to the Church of St.John and dressed in our best the slight drizzle didn't dampen our spirits – or so I thought.

The vicar was at the door to welcome everyone and we went inside to join the growing congregation. We occupied seats towards the back of the nave that were clearly for the occupancy of anyone. Chika ran forward toward the chancel where a decorated Nativity scene with a baby Jesus lying in a manger, Mary and Joseph, together with a donkey were alongside. Along with other youngsters she stood in awe until Pru gently took her hand and led her back to where we sat.

The genial vicar rose to the pulpit and surveyed the congregation acknowledging the large number of parishioners who'd gathered there, and undoubtedly wishing that all Sunday services were as well attended.

"Welcome everyone to the Church of St.John and Latter-day Saints. We're gathered today to celebrate the

Nativity – the birthday of Christ that we call Christmas Day, and what better way could there be than to begin our service with a rousing carol Joy to the World."

There was an uplifting participation from young and old, and Chika tried her best to read from the hymn sheet and join in. It wasn't a carol she'd heard before. Everyone seemed to be enjoying it except Lottie, she seemed a little subdued.

The vicar, lighting the fifth Advent candle, began again once the congregation had regained their seats,

"Almighty God, who has given us thy only begotten son...." and he continued with the Collect to its Amen. I looked again at Lottie thinking she was showing signs of distress. When it came to the Epistle and the vicar read from Hebrews,

"Thou art my son, this day I have begotten Thee, and again, I will be to him a father, and he shall be to me a Son..."

Lottie, slid from her seat, excusing herself saying, "I must get some fresh air."

Tom followed her out into the porch and said,

"Lottie, it's time we sat down and talked about whatever it is that's troubling you."

She dissolved into a flood of tears and Tom took her in his arms saying,

"Whatever it is Lottie, I'm here for you. I'll do anything for you. Come on, we can work through this. Let's go home, I'll light a fire and we'll sit and talk with no-one to disturb us."

Pru and I knew only too well what was wrong and decided to leave them to themselves. We'd be there for them both whatever the outcome. We never saw them again all Christmas Day. We tried hard to show a brave face for the sake of Chika who understood nothing of the dilemma facing everyone. Although we ate well and tried some party games to keep the spirit of Christmas alive, Tom and Lottie were always at the back of our minds, and it took the edge off the festive season.

Sweet Retribution

The following morning, Boxing Day, Pru decided she must visit Lottie; perhaps she needed support. She related to me later that morning what took place. Invited into the cottage there was an unusual air of calm as though Tom and Lottie were keeping their feelings subdued, and Lottie said in a quiet manner,

"Tom knows. I've told him."

Tom raised his head to look at Pru and said with a sad note in his voice,

"I can't believe that you were all going to keep it from me."

A lump formed in Pru's throat and a tear came to her eye as she said,

"Tom, we've been racked with guilt, but we were sworn to secrecy. Lottie was afraid you'd blame her – and that you wouldn't understand. It's caused us all a lot of anxiety and Lottie's been torn apart by what's happened."

He said in sad but sincere manner,

"It's upset me sure, but I don't blame Lottie. I'm more upset that everyone decided to keep it from me."

"I can only apologise and ask you to forgive us. Will you both come and join us – there's so much food, we can't possibly eat it all ourselves."

"I think I'd rather stay at home with Lottie today. Don't think I'm being ungrateful but I think we just need time to ourselves. We'll all meet up tomorrow at the wharf to begin the transfer of the Lady Ester to the dry-dock."

Pru returned home and related what had been said, adding,

"Tom's been affected quite deeply by what's happened but I think everything is going to be alright between them."

"This Christmas is going to be remembered for all the wrong reasons. Even Chika has perceived the mood."

I wondered what Tom was going to say when we met but I felt relief that it was out in the open.

Sweet Retribution

Whilst the tide was high Tom's crew attached the winches and with the harbour crew's expertise the Lady Ester glided into the dry-dock. After the tide's ebb the gates would be closed and as much of the water pumped out as possible, allowing the clipper to rest in the cradles and on the piles of timber. Yet more timbers would be put in place to prop the ship upright. With everything in place men would be able to work beneath the hull in relative safety.

With Tom occupied so, Pru, Lottie and I toiled with the tea chests to reach that one with the special markings. It was heavy work and despite the season we were all three wet with perspiration by the time our objective was reached. I carefully opened the chest, using the same careful technique Tom used last time, in order that it could be re-sealed and remain as though never opened. I dug deep into the tea until my fingers touched the box I searched for. It was remarkably heavy for its size but I eventually recovered it and carefully resealed the chest. I wasn't prepared to open the box until Tom joined us.

Pru later told me that whilst I was busy extracting the box, Lottie had taken the opportunity to tell her that Tom had been understandably upset about the whole affair but had shown great sympathy and affection. She thought initially that he'd probably go into some deep depression and perhaps isolate himself, but he actually became very angry with himself for not having made better provision for her safety whilst he was away. She told him about the scrawled writing on the wall and how it matched the writing left in our cottage which identified Bill Carter as responsible. Tom threatens to tear him limb from limb if he can find him – and he will. He's intent on finding him.

When Tom eventually joined us I quite expected some rebuke for having kept Lottie's secret, but although he wasn't the same old gregarious and jovial Tom, he was surprisingly social. He eagerly prised off the lid of the box to reveal a hoard of golden trinkets, Buddhas, male and female gods. He laid them out on the chest and proceeded to identify each one. About four inches high they were a beautiful array of a goldsmith's expertise.

"This one is a gift to Chika. It's the goddess Sarawati, goddess of wisdom, music and learning. There's only one other that I've brought as a gift, and that's for Lottie. It's this one, Varuna, god of sky and oceans, and I thought Varuna would be there to look after the two of us, especially whilst we're apart." He then separated three others from the remainder and said,

"These three are the holy trinity of the Hindu religion. This one is Brahma – the creator, this is Vishnu – the preserver, and this is Shiva – the destroyer. They're highly sought after by Hindus and the immigrant population of Hindus in London is growing. They should fetch a good price." Careful to replace them in the fibrous packing to avoid damage, he said,

"The others are all gods or goddesses, there's Durga, Parvati, Agni, Surya, Ganpti, but I can't identify which is which. The only other that I can identify is Lakshmi the goddess of wealth, abundance and fertility. That I thought might be appropriate for Pru. They're all solid gold and must be worth a king's ransom."

He packed them all away and looked at the astonished faces around him, and said,

"I was expecting you to ask me how I'd got them and at what cost. It was most fortunate in one way but rather cruel in another. As you know the East India Company rules West Bengal with an iron fist. Gold smuggling has become a serious issue and those caught are summarily dealt with by hanging. My contact has unfortunately been arrested and his fate is fairly certain which means his wife and family are also in danger. I have made a bargain with her; I've taken this hoard to avoid her arrest too. I've given her the equivalent of one hundred guineas – I don't know what that amounts to in Rupees – but I've promised her another one hundred when we return. We've know each other for a considerable time and she trusts me. If, for some reason I cannot return, I shall honour my pledge and get someone else to deliver the money. Unfortunately, unless I can make another contact this will be the last for some time. I have to be careful too because I stand the same risks as everyone else."

I was left speechless. What beautiful trinkets, but what a risk.

Chapter 17

As we walked home with our trinkets Pru kept her Derringer handy, fearful of losing such a valuable haul to footpads. Lottie suddenly bent double and grabbed at her abdomen. Sharp stabbing pains consumed her. She grimaced at Pru who immediately went to her aid. I learned afterwards that Lottie had confessed she'd continued taking the slippery elm and had purposely done more heavy lifting and jumping down from the stack of tea chests than would normally be advisable to someone in her condition. They were both hoping that her efforts had done the trick.

Sure enough the spasms increased and by the time Lottie reached home the 'monthly curse' had begun in earnest. She was never sure whether the abortive substance she'd been taking, the excessive physical exercise, or – which was just as likely – the relaxing of tension and worry had allowed nature to follow its natural course. Suddenly she was our old Lottie once again.

The relief was felt by all of us, and we were ready to resume our Christmas festivities. That was when Tom dropped his bombshell.

"I'm considering stepping down. I've been training the first mate, he's got his papers, and he's quite capable, I need the partnership to agree but with what's happened to Lottie, I've decided that I'm needed ashore."

That came out of the blue, none of us – not even Lottie – expected it, and we realised that Tom needed time to reflect on his decision and we needed a serious discussion, involving the four of us to determine where the business was going. None of us, including Tom, felt that we wanted to break up the partnership but could we carry on without Tom at the helm of the Lady Ester? It was at that point that Pru reminded us of the interest of Dorsey and Sons.

As the New Year began the auction of our tea brought us 8,000 guineas before the auctioneers took their cut.

Sweet Retribution

Pru sat with the accounts and with a healthy nett balance, the business showed a profit that obviously justified Dorsey and Sons interest. We spent long evenings talking over the advantages and disadvantages of carrying on as we were; of carrying on with an additional partner in a new captain for the Lady Ester; of splitting the business and selling off the lady Ester but retaining the warehousing side; or selling off the whole lot. It was at this point Pru told us of her considerations in seeing the future in steam ships, and I think that had a huge part to play in our deliberations.

There were sensible views that carried the conversation in different directions, as emotion pulled in one direction and common sense in another. Eventually it was decided that Pru should enquire whether Dorsey and Son still had an interest in purchasing our business wholesale, and if so, what offer were they prepared to make?.

Pru had shown herself a capable negotiator and with a sound knowledge of the worth of the ship, the warehouse, and current contracts; she would know when the offer reached consideration point. They weren't likely to come with a sensible offer to begin with, they'd just 'test the waters', and it would be up to Pru to push up the ante.

There was a very restrained acknowledgement from Dorsey and Son's agent, especially as he'd made the initial approach. It was a slow progress with attempts to lay ground rules by him which would be to his advantage, but Pru was wise to his manoeuvres. Soon they were talking sensible prices that Pru could take back to her partners for a decision.

We were gathered around our kitchen table in eager anticipation of what Pru had to tell us.

"Eight thousand guineas for the Lady Ester alone and twelve thousand guineas for the whole. The whole will include warehouse, docking facilities and contracts."
Tom asked with a questioning frown,

"Eight thousand guineas? Considering she's just been in dry-dock and had a re-fit, is that enough?"

"She cost me ten to buy, and bear in mind she'd been built in America four years earlier and I've had her nearly four years, I think eight thousand is a fair price. She'd been on the China trade before I bought her and she's done five voyages to India since, so she's bound to be feeling her age, you should know that Tom."

"Aye, you have a point."

"Well, we've got four days to decide. Let's sleep on it and we can vote on it tomorrow. To save any concern, I negotiated that if we sell, Dorsey and Sons will take on the whole of the present crew so their futures are secure. I suggest that out of our shares we give each of the crew a ten guineas loyalty payment.   I'm probably the biggest stake holder in our partnership but I'm going to suggest that if we do decide to sell, we split the monies four ways – equal shares. There'll be legal fees to take care of but our accounts show a balance of six thousand guineas. When added to the twelve thousand of the sale, that's eighteen thousand guineas. After all debts are paid we each benefit by roughly four thousand five hundred guineas.

It had been an exciting episode to our lives and I was afraid there were going to be regrets in letting go of the Lady Ester, but after lengthy discussion, Pru and I decided that providing Tom and Lottie were of the same mind, we'd sell.

A formal vote was taken and we all agreed the sale would go ahead. The final handshake with Dorsey and Son's agent came on the fourth day, and now it was down to the lawyers, dotting the i's and crossing the t's.

This was the point at which the hunt to root out Bill Carter intensified, with Tom leading the charge. An offensive is perhaps the best way to describe it. After some thought he took me aside to explain his ideas I can't say that I was enthusiastic about his proposals.

"OK, we can't use the book but Finkelstein doesn't know that. Jack, you and I are going to pay him a visit." Tom announced.

"He'll be well guarded by his henchmen." I countered. Tom smiled saying,

"It'll be a nice little surprise for him won't it?"
I hardly relished an encounter with Finkelstein or his thugs, I didn't have a liking for violence but Tom wanted support and it would have been churlish, even cowardly, to turn my back on him.
Evening would be best when there were not so many people about.

Nervous, and trying hard to hide it, I joined Tom for what promised to be a testing time for me. When we'd had the encounter at the warehouse it had been their intention to burn it down but we'd surprised them. I'd been able to hang back behind the others so that I was hardly involved, but now I had to go side-by-side with Tom.

It was a good walk to the bridge, about three-quarters of a mile and Tom was striding out purposefully. I still hadn't the same enthusiasm. The mist was gathering over the river and what boats were moored, were gently rocking to the sound of the lapping water.

Tension was beginning to build as we headed for Bread Street, East Cheap. Finkelstein's place was easy to recognise from Pru's description of when she'd gained the book. Tom hesitated a moment to draw a lethal looking knife from its sheath on his belt. It was almost a touch of reassurance in handling it before we went into action. He wiped the blade on his sleeve before replacing it in its sheath – but he left the clip unfastened, ready for a quick draw. I began to tremble at what seemed likely to happen.

Through the grimy window I could see the flickering candle on a cluttered table but everything else was so indistinct. Tom tried the handle but the door was obviously locked. That was going to be no obstacle to him and he simply put the sole of his boot against the door and kicked out. The old flimsy door stood no chance against Tom's weight, and flew open. Tom strode inside and I followed. I could see a figure huddled in blankets in a chair beyond the table, but I hadn't seen the burly figure emerge between Tom and Finkelstein. He faced up to Tom and I thought the blows would begin but Tom stood very still, poised but controlled. He said to the man facing him,

"Don't force me to tear you apart. I'm here to talk to him," indicating Finkelstein, who appeared to be trying to protect himself with a tray, held across his chest. The burly minder looked at Finkelstein and lowered his fists but he stayed barring the way to Tom and watching him intently. Tom just laid a hand lightly upon the man's shoulder without showing any physical aggression and gently pushed him aside so that he stood facing Finkelstein,

"What do you want?" Finkelstein asked in a cringing way.

"Information," said Tom.

"Who are you? asked Finkelstein.

I perceived the thug manoeuvre around the back of Tom and with confidence building I tapped him on the arm and said,

"I wouldn't if I were you. We're prepared to raze this place to the ground if you start anything."
It seemed to subdue any intent of aggression and he stepped back.

"Who are you?" Finkelstein asked again. Tom answered,

"It doesn't matter who we are, just accept that I'm feeling very aggrieved at one of your sewer rats."

"Well my dear, tell me what you want and I might be able to help you."

I recognised that smarmy, slimy way of Finkelstein that Pru had described so many times. His manner of addressing grown men – "my dear" – typified the greasy rogue for what he was.

"Bill Carter – he's one of yours. I want him and if I don't get him I'm coming back here to rip your heart out."

"Oh please my dear, don't let our little conversation turn to such violent threats. If I can help you I will. This gentleman... Carter... you say he's one of mine, but the name means nothing to me."

"Oh, don't give me that; you know the weasel. I've come here with an offer, a little brown book. I'm sure you know what I'm talking about? Bill Carter for the book that's the offer."

"Show me."

"Don't take me for a fool. Do you honestly think I'd bring it with me?"

"My dears, I think you must have me confused with someone else. A little brown book, now what could that be? You'd have to show me. Now this person, this man... Carter did you say? I may,...I say I may,...be able to help you. I do have means of locating people that are difficult to find. Come back in...let's say, a week...and bring this intriguing little brown book with you. We might have something to talk about."

"Oh be sure of that, we'll be back. Don't let this matter turn ugly," and with that Tom withdrew his knife from its sheath and, despite Finkelstein shrinking back in fear, Tom sliced off a lock of that straggly, greasy hair that protruded from beneath his Kippa.

"That's just to show you we mean business," he said letting the hair fall into Finkelstein's lap, and with that we turned and walked away.

As we did so, Tom confided,

"That didn't go too well. He wasn't as frightened as I thought he'd be and without the book I'm not so sure he'll give Carter up. He'll certainly be better prepared for our next visit."

My heart sank to think we were going to have to return.

Chapter 18

Both Pru and Lottie renewed their efforts around their old haunts, calling in favours from amongst their thieving friends, and again pushing the twenty-five guinea bounty they'd placed on Bill Carter's head.

Tom moved amongst the crews of ships in the docklands, amongst stevedores and lightermen, but no sound word was coming from any of these sources, but at least the three of them were keeping the search alive and on everyone's conscience. Wherever Bill Carter was, he was lying deep under cover with some solid protection.

As night fell we were glad to close the door on the bitter wind that howled outside. The oil lamps were lit and Chika lay on the hearth before a roaring fire, rolling about with Atlas in a playful game. I think Pru was in the kitchen and I was on the verge of falling asleep in my favourite chair, when suddenly Atlas jumped to his feet and ran to the door. He made low growling noises, deep in his throat, clearly ready to attack – he'd obviously heard something that I had not.

The next moment there was a hammering on the door. I jumped to my feet and took hold of Atlas's collar. Before I ventured to open the door I asked,

"Who is it?"

"Police," was the reply.

Pru hurried through from the kitchen to my side and we looked at each other wondering why they were here. With all that had happened involving Carter and Finkelstein, I wasn't disposed to open the door until I was sure who was there.

The hammering on the door was repeated and the voice shouted, "Police – Inspector Stone."   I shouted,

"Wait a moment. I must deal with the dog."

Eventually, assured of who was at the door, and with Atlas in the parlour with Chika, I opened the door and recognised the same surly features of Inspector Stone who had visited us at the cottage. He removed his bowler hat as he entered the hallway and looked me in the eye, frowning as he did so. The muscles around his eyes tensed and produced a squint and without saying a word, his facial expression was casting a severe questioning look. I do believe it was a practised manner of approach to instill as much discomfort to his opposition as he could before he even spoke. I must say that it was very effective; I was almost dumb-struck.

Pru, quite unaffected, said,

"What brings you out on such a cold wet night, Inspector?"

"I want to know what's going on," he answered.

"What do you mean – what's going on," she enquired.

"I mean exactly what I say. What's going on? Reliable information has reached me that you're acting like an unofficial police force, searching for the murder suspect, Bill Carter, and you've even offered a very substantial reward. What game are you playing?"

"Well inspector, it seems you aren't trying too hard to find him and so we took it upon ourselves to catch him."

The inspector's face began to show signs of embarrassment as I joined in, feeling a little braver,

"We told you exactly where he was hiding but you let him get away, and as far as I can see you've done nothing to apprehend him since."
I thought our defiance had put him on the back foot but I was wrong. He countered,

"You're obviously well known amongst the vermin I deal with; I have to ask myself why? They're a strange choice of friends for business people such as you. It makes me wonder if you're the upright citizens you appear to be?"

"You're quite offensive when you choose to be, inspector. 'Vermin' is your choice of description, my choice is 'disadvantaged," Pru said with obvious needle.

"I didn't come here to argue with you about your friends, but to find out just what drives you..." he said looking directly at me again, "...you see, my undercover men observed you paying a rather forceful visit to a Mr

Finkelstein on Bread Street, East Cheap, the other evening – kicked the door in I believe. I have to ask myself what purpose you might have with someone of such a dubious nature as Mr Finkelstein?"

I decided that nothing was lost in telling the truth, or at least so much of the truth as suited our purpose,

"Bill Carter is one of Finkelstein's villains and he must know where he's hiding out but he refused to acknowledge that he knew him."

Just at that moment Chika decided to open the parlour door and Atlas took the chance to push his way out too. His lip was curled as he made towards Inspector Stone. Chika grabbed his collar but the huge dog just dragged her along. I stepped in front of the inspector, in an attempt to shield him, but Pru simply said "Cease Atlas" and miraculously the dog stopped. She placed a hand on Atlas's head and said, "Enough. Friend." I think even the inspector was impressed, yet quite obviously shaken by the episode – his face was quite white – he tried his hardest not to show it, and returned to his questioning without even a stutter.

"What makes you say he's one of Finkelstein's villains?"

"Some months ago we believe Finkelstein sent a band of rough-necks to set fire to our warehouse but we intercepted them. Bill Carter was one of them – that is a fact – and he was injured in the attack. His wife, Dina, was working for us and she pre-warned us about the attack. That's what led to her being murdered. Now, perhaps, you can understand why we have such a vested interest in finding him."

"Right, now we understand each other, I'm going to suggest that we work together; I want to see Bill Carter apprehended as much as you and your knowledge of the...er... 'disadvantaged'...could be of considerable use to me."

The change of attitude was considerable and the inspector began to show a little more of the mellow side to his nature. Pru offered him tea and he accepted. As we sat together Pru said,

"Have you considered Carter for the 'Jack-the-Ripper' murders around Whitechapel; we know he's extremely violent towards women, and associates with prostitutes?"

The inspector replied,

"I haven't personally been involved in those investigations but I understand the officers dealing with the murders have a strong suspect. From what I do know, they're not just violent killings; the suspect slices them open and removes body parts. I don't think that Carter fits into that profile but I'll put his name forward – just in case."

The description of what 'Jack-the-Ripper' did to his victims was gory to say the least whilst we were drinking our tea, but the inspector couldn't be criticised as Pru was the one who brought up the subject.

The inspector left but I was sure we were going to see a lot more of him. We still didn't tell him what had happened to Lottie.

When I told Tom of the inspector's visit he wasn't exactly enthusiastic about a liaison with the Peelers saying,

"I want to find Carter myself. I want to take the evil bastard apart. The Peelers can have what's left of him when I've done."

I could understand Tom's feelings but personally, it was good to know that they hadn't given up on Carter. Surely, with the police, the underworld, and us with the twenty-five guineas reward, all striving to find him, he couldn't stay hidden for much longer.

A week had quickly passed when Tom broached the subject of a return to Finkelstein. I couldn't think of any way to dissuade him but deep inside I had this premonition, or perhaps it would be better to say, a foreboding of a tragedy. Reputations of Finkelstein's mob weren't going to stop Tom. Thoughts of a ruckus were as nothing to him, whereas I dreaded the encounter. This time we were going to wrong-foot Finkelstein by going along in broad daylight. Tom's thinking was that they'd expect another visit after dark but by making it daylight hours he wouldn't have his thugs about him in readiness.

We set off for Bread Street, Tom with a grim determination and me, frankly scared, but I wasn't prepared to show my fear. I was going to watch his back even if it meant getting a good hiding – bravado if you like.

As we approached Finkelstein's lair I noticed the door had been repaired – it looked considerably stronger. Tom strode forward and opened the door; I followed inside. Finkelstein sat at the far side of the table, with a quill in hand and a list of figures in the book before him. He looked up with what appeared to be an unconcerned attitude and said,

"Ah my dears, I've been expecting you. Have you brought the book?"

Tom looked at him with a sneer on his face, and replied,

"What do you take me for? I want Carter before you get the book."

"Oh, well my dear, I fear we don't have any more to talk about. We agreed didn't we – bring me the book and I'll try to find the gentleman. A bargain is a bargain."

Tom's temper flared and he began to approach Finkelstein with clenched fists and said,

"You slimy toad, I'm going to...", but before he could finish the sentence men seemed to appear from everywhere. We were surrounded. Tom lashed out at the nearest one, felling him with a tremendous punch to the jaw, and it all developed into a melee. I don't know what happened but I was suddenly on the floor with one pinning me down and another punching my head. I instinctively kicked out catching one of them in the groin. I remember Tom drawing his knife but everything from that point became a blur. The next I can remember was

Tom with a grip on my jacket collar, dragging me out into the street.

My head felt as though several horses had kicked and trampled me and my ribs ached beyond description. It was as we quickly retreated that I noticed the blood on my hands and jacket and I couldn't see just where I was bleeding. It was some time before I realised it wasn't my blood, it was Tom. His shirt and jacket were covered and the blood was running down onto his breeches.

Chapter 19

Tom led me down to the bridge, pausing only to look down river toward the wharf, and then we carried on through Potters Fields, with him clutching his side as we walked. He knew exactly what he was about, making for a newly berthed clipper where he hailed the captain as an old friend. Explaining his predicament Tom lifted his shirt and revealed a six inch open wound on his side.

"Looks nice and clean..." said the captain, "....we'll get Bell to have a look at it." That was Tom's purpose in coming there, he knew Bell, the ship's carpenter, who also acted as the ship's surgeon whilst at sea. If anyone could fix him up Bell was the one, well experienced – removing limbs, pulling teeth, and suturing wounds.

Bell, a whiskery old sea dog, looking none too hygienic, appeared carrying a sail-cloth bundle of surgical instruments. He was hardly my idea of a surgeon but Tom seemed to have utter faith in the man and as he removed his jacket and shirt the captain appeared with a bottle of liquor; most probably rum.

The carpenter unwrapped his surgeon's instruments as Tom uncorked the bottle and drank a serious measure. I watched almost anticipating the pain this was going to cause. Bell chose a vicious looking needle bent in a 'c' shape and proceeded to thread a length of twine. His offer of a leather belt to bite upon was rejected by Tom as the wound was sutured and the edges pulled tightly together.

I was sweating just to watch but Tom remained steadfast with the liquor level within the bottle rapidly diminishing. I counted fourteen stitches, all less than half an inch apart, tied off and looking expertly done.

"Looks good to me," said Bell wiping the area with something that made Tom flinch, turning his skin a vivid yellow colour. He saw me looking puzzled and said simply,

"Iodine – kills infection."

Sweet Retribution

"As I handed Tom his shirt, Bell could see me looking at the amount of blood staining and laughed, saying,

"Looks a lot but believe me, that's nothing. I've seen men lose buckets of blood and recover."

I hardly believed that – 'buckets of blood' was surely an exaggeration, but even so his confidence was encouraging. Lottie was furious with us both when she learned what had happened and there didn't appear much sympathy for poor Tom. The wound was going to take some time to heal and he wasn't going to get into such violent scrapes for some time. I think we both got off lightly. Whatever the future held for us it wasn't going to be such a bull headed approach, we were going to have to find a more subtle means. It's certainly taught me a salutary lesson in dealing with someone as devious and vicious as Finkelstein.

For the moment our focus was diverted from Carter, Finkelstein and his thugs, to matters closer to home. We were doing our best to educate Chika but we really needed a tutor capable of more than basics, and it was then that Tom introduced us to Sandra Chung. Sandra, a second generation British lady of Chinese descent, was a widow on hard times, living in the Chinese quarter of Limehouse that had become a ghetto.

Normally I wouldn't have entertained the idea of engaging with someone from this area, notorious for its enclave of Chinese sailors, its opium dens, gambling dens and the 'Puckapu' numbers racket that brought poverty and misery, to most who existed there. However, Tom assured us that Sandra Chung was exceptional.

Just how he came to know her wasn't disclosed. It was quite possible that he'd encountered her deceased husband either on one of the ships or in the West India Docks; but I wasn't about to enquire too closely.

She spoke English, albeit with a Cantonese accent, and impressed us with her mathematical genius, using only a system of wooden beads on a frame. I think I would have engaged her immediately if it wasn't for the fact that Chika would be exposed to the degradations of Limehouse. However, Sandra assured us that she would be prepared to come to our home if I would agree to pay the ferryman. It was only a brief row-boat journey across the river from Limehouse Basin, and so began Chika's tutelage two days each week.

Chika was excited and eager to learn and a rapport quickly developed between pupil and teacher. The child was inquisitive to learn about Sandra, where her forebears came from, how they travelled here, why they left their homeland and how they felt about living in a foreign land. To Chika it was a geography, history and cultural lesson, all in one.

As I listened to her stories it became quite obvious to me that Sandra was living amongst poverty and discrimination, and I began to understand why the opium dens flourished openly and why crime was so rampant around Limehouse. It amazed me that she had such high principals, but she assured me that despite the poverty and the despondency that it brought, the average Chinese held self-respect very high in their lives. Sadly, the minority, usually those who had succumbed to opium addiction, brought their society into disrepute, as did the youth who were increasingly drawn to a gang culture.

Despite her self-esteem I was intrigued at how much she knew about the criminal aspect of life around her and where the influences were coming from. It transpired that for some time she'd been operating as a one-woman-welfare nurse and mid-wife amongst the Limehouse community, and all the unsavoury news was picked up in those visits.

Feeling that Sandra was totally open about her life and the Chinese people around her, I ventured to ask,

"Is there any truth in what we hear about a white-slave trade – young white girls being lured into opium dens, never to be seen again?" She shook her head and grimaced, replying,

"It's a terrible slur, just stories made up to sell newspapers."
I could understand the antipathy the rumours were causing but Sandra was adamant it wasn't true. I wanted to know more,
   "What are Triads? I've heard the name but never understood what the word meant." The question seemed to take her aback, and she hesitated before answering,
   "What have you heard?"
   "Only that they're supposed to be a criminal organisation. I don't even know that they exist."
   "They do exist but they have a fearful reputation. I don't like to talk about them."   I waited, giving her the opportunity to expand on her answer, and she began,
   "They do exist but it's kept very secret. It all began in China many years ago with a society called the 'Heaven and Earth Society' or the 'Tiandihui' which was a fraternal society that spread all across China. Eventually it broke up into smaller groups of which three became the main societies. The principal one of the three was 'Three Harmonies Society' or the 'Sanhehui' and they adopted the triangle as their emblem. Triad evolves from triangle. Initially, on the surface, their purpose was to help immigrant Chinese to settle in their new homeland but they soon became that organised crime organisation that we've all heard about."
   An embryo of a plan began to form in my mind but who were they and how dangerous were they? I pursued the questions,
   "Do they exist here in London?"
   "Please don't ask me anymore. It's not wise for anyone to talk openly about them."
   She was genuinely afraid to talk about them which made me convinced that they must exist in Limehouse. I'd heard of the street gangs and the violence but I'd had the impression they were youngsters fuelled by drink and drugs. I was sure Triads were on a different level to teenage gangs.

Sweet Retribution

That evening, I called on Tom,

"I've been talking to Sandra Chung, and I had this wild idea that I thought I'd run by you. Finkelstein runs a criminal organisation doesn't he – with Bill Carter a part of it? Sandra's been telling me about the Chinese Triads, and they're also criminal organisations. They're bound to be in opposition to Finkelstein. What if we could get them at each other's throats? Surely that would be better than us trying to fight Finkelstein?"

"Jack, I don't think you realise what you're contemplating. You don't mess about with Triads. I've seen what happens with them in Hong Kong. They take no prisoners. They control organised crime and when they meet opposition, it's all out war."

"Yes but surely to have them against Finkelstein it would finish him forever?"

"I've mixed with the Chinese sailors around Limehouse basin for a long time and I'm pretty sure that if triads operated here, I'd have heard. Forget it, you don't want to see a war involving triads – it's frightening."

At that moment Lottie entered the room and asked,

"Have you heard about the body taken from the river this morning?"

Neither of us had heard tell of it, and I asked,

"No, what makes you ask?"

"Well I heard you talking about the Chinese. If it's true, they fished a body from the Thames this morning it was caught up in mooring lines of a ship down-river towards the new West India Docks."

"Well, what's that of interest to us? They're always pulling someone from the river," remarked Tom.

"I don't know much about it but I understand she was Chinese and with you talking about them, I thought I'd mention it," answered Lottie blithely.

Why my mind should immediately associate a body found in the river with Sandra Chung, I don't know, but then I realised she'd been to teach Chika that day, so it couldn't be her, but the fact that she used the ferry did cause a flutter in my chest. No more was said about it but it did bring our conversation regarding Triads and Finkelstein to an abrupt end and I returned home. My idea probably hadn't been sensible anyway.

I didn't give the matter anymore thought until Sandra next visited and she came with the news that it wasn't a drowning but a murder. A young Chinese woman had been bludgeoned to death and thrown into the Thames. She was understood to be a Limehouse woman associated with an opium den and a brothel. There were three things that immediately resonated in my mind; bludgeoned to death, brothel and thrown into the river. All three things had the hallmark of someone like Bill Carter – his wife had been bludgeoned and thrown into the river, and he'd tried to avoid capture by hiding in a brothel. What were the chances they could be connected?

Chapter 20

After talking with Pru it was realised that Limehouse was a little outside of the area covered by her friends. It was more likely that Tom might have contacts amongst the Chinese, apart from Sandra Chung, and he'd more cause than anyone to delve into the seamier side of that community to try to find Bill Carter. Surely he'd have some sort of rapport with the Chinese sailors?

Next morning I was knocking on his door soon after breakfast.

"Tom, the young Chinese woman they dragged from the river that Lottie mentioned yesterday, was actually murdered. She'd been bludgeoned to death and thrown into the river. It's a long shot but that's exactly what Bill Carter did to his wife. The more I think about it the more I'm convinced there could be a connection. Not only did he kill his wife and dispose of her body in the river, he was hiding in a brothel, and apparently this Chinese woman worked in a brothel. Does that not seem a coincidence? Do you know people in Limehouse who might talk to us?" Tom eagerly grabbed his jacket, saying,

"I think I know someone who'll help us."
Lottie was less enthusiastic, and warned us both not to get into any more fights, adding that Tom's wound was still tender and wasn't fully healed.

Jake the ferryman was idling his time talking to another boat owner as we reached the landing stage and immediately took our shilling to row us across. Tom took the opportunity to ask what he knew about the murder but it seemed he knew less than we did. When we reached Limehouse basin I was in a totally strange environment and I was in Tom's hands. He obviously knew the area and made straight for the Bunch o' Grapes public house on the riverside Narrow Street. And then on to the Shipwright's Arms on Garford Street near to the West India Docks that were still under construction.

Tom was quite liberal with offers of beer to those he engaged in conversation which paid dividends when he talked to an old salt. We learned that the body was indeed that of a Chinese prostitute called China Lily, who was from the Guangzhou opium house on Limehouse Causeway.

I anticipated that we'd head straight to the Guangzhou but instead I was led to the Christian Mission and the Confucian temple where Tom knew he'd find Sandra Chung. When I asked why we needed to speak to Sandra, Tom replied,

"Sandra has worked amongst the prostitutes in this area for a long time. If anyone will know about China Lily, Sandra will. If we go straight to the Guangzhou and start asking questions it's unlikely they'll tell us anything, but if Sandra goes there they just might open up because they know her."

She was on her hands and knees, cleaning the floor as we walked into the mission. She looked up and saw us and as there were others in the room she left her cleaning and beckoned us to follow into a small anti-room. I let Tom do the talking,

"Sandra, the young lady that was taken from the river, was probably someone known to you – she went under the name China Lily? I understand she worked from Guangzhou the brothel and opium house."

"Yes, I heard it was Lily. She was a nice girl – didn't deserve to die like that."

"Have you heard anything that might give us a clue as to who did this to her?"

"No. No-one has said anything."

"I don't like to ask this of you, but would you do me a favour by paying a visit to the Guangzhou to see what you can find out?"

"Oh Mr Tom, I don't like the idea. I've worked hard to build up a trust with these people and I don't want to jeopardise it now."

"You'd be doing it for Lily. It's unlikely they'd talk to us but they know you and all we want to know is who she was seen with before she was found in the river."

"You have to understand what opium does to them; their minds will be just a haze. It's unlikely anyone would take any notice of the clients visiting the girls."

"Well, perhaps if you spoke to some of the other girls there, they might remember a particular man – maybe a regular. I'm sure they talk to one-another especially if one of their clients was particularly violent. Please try."

"Alright Mr Tom. I don't like this but I'll do it for you and for Lily. Is there anyone in particular you have in mind?"

"Thank you Sandra, No, no-one in particular but a name – even a first name – or a description, any bit of information would be useful. I'm sure Lily would thank you too if only she could. Jack and I will go down to the Bunch o' Grapes and wait for you."

Sandra, a familiar figure at the Guangzhou, walked into the smoky, sweet atmosphere and understandably no-one took any interest in her. She'd entered this brothel many times before in her role as substitute mother figure to the girls working there, especially when troubles surfaced. She made her way through the recumbent figures on their cushions and mattresses, with their yen-tsiang opium pipes; the typical long bamboo stemmed pipe with the porcelain bowl attached, held over the individual oil burners to vaporise the drug. There was no point in trying to engage any of them in conversation, their glazed expressions showed only too well that such an attempt was pointless. She made directly for the stairs. It was where the hazardous encounters, the lecherous pulling and mauling always took place, as the drunks and drug affected males, tried to proposition any female as she'd learned to her cost. Over time she'd had to steel herself to develop means of rebuffing their advances. Fortunately, today, there were fewer customers hanging about. The madam sitting at the doorway to the boudoirs, controlling the girls and their customers, looked up, recognised and acknowledged Sandra, but then paid her little further attention. Making her way from cubicle to cubicle she looked for those girls who were not occupied.

As Tom and I walked down to Narrow Street, he remarked that he knew Sandra would go to the Guangzhou for us, even against her better instincts. He didn't exactly enlighten me but I gathered that she was somehow in his debt. He hesitated outside the pub looking at the river and was obviously puzzling over something in his mind. I asked what it was and he said,

"I'm just thinking about the tide and slack water. The old chap at the Shipwright Arms said the body was pulled from the river at first light Tuesday morning and she'd not been in the river very long. The tide must have been on the turn for her to be caught up in the mooring lines otherwise she'd have been carried much further down river. I'd make a guess the river was at low ebb when she was thrown in. That tells me two things: one is that who-ever did this couldn't have reached the water because of the mud banks other than at a wharf or landing stage, and the second thing is the time – it had to be somewhere around four or five in the morning. I'm asking myself who apart from the murderer would be about at that time of the morning?"

"There'd be watchmen of the Port Authority and there'd be the musketeers and special constables of the West India Docks, but would they have eyes on the waterfront along Narrow Street?" I ventured.

We entered the Bunch o' Grapes and the landlord brought us a jug of ale to fill our tankards. Time began to drag and my senses began to swim with the ale as we waited for Sandra to appear. I wondered if she had decided against the task but Tom had the utmost faith in her. I'd guess we'd been there about two hours when Sandra eventually arrived. She said,

"I've spent some time with the girls at the Guangzhou. They're frightened that's clear, and more than one has talked about a particular man they're afraid of. He's menacing, threatening and very physical but no-one said they had been injured by him. There's no name I can give you but he's scarred on the left side of his face – not a knife scar, more like a burn that covers his cheek and runs up to his eye. Apparently he's not what you might call a regular but he does use the place from time to time. The girls try to avoid him if possible."

Scar face, perhaps we were a little closer to identifying Bill Carter – if it was him, and I felt the day had been worthwhile. Tom, on the other hand said very little as we were rowed across the river again by the ferryman.

That evening there was a knock at the door and again it was greeted by the deep-throat growling of Atlas as he rushed to defend his home. I took a firm hold of his collar and without opening the door I asked the caller to identify himself. It was Inspector Stone. I bid him wait whilst I secured Atlas out of harm's way and I'm sure the inspector appreciated the situation. When I eventually opened the door he was stood well back until he saw that he was in no danger. I still had that uneasy feeling in the pit of my stomach to see him but his attitude was perceptibly less confrontational.

Pru invited him to sit with us at the kitchen table and take a cup of tea which he accepted. Chika released Atlas from the parlour and he eyed the inspector with indecision, whether to bite or not, until Pru spoke to assure him and he ambled away to lie before the fire. Pru opened the conversation with,

"Have you come to tell us you've found Bill Carter, inspector?" and he replied,

"I wish I could answer yes, but I'm afraid he still evades us. I've come to ask what your activities have revealed? I understand from my men that someone paid another visit to that rogue Finkelstein – a little conflagration apparently took place and I'm presuming that it was your men, so I wondered what had transpired?"

"You're very astute inspector, but I know nothing of such a conflagration. However, I will say that nothing of any value has reached my ears. I'm sure we understand one-another?"

"We do, madam. We do."

I asked, "Inspector, I presume you know of the body taken from the river near the West India Docks on Tuesday; a young Chinese woman?"

"Yes, what of it?"

"Well, I was told that she was murdered, is that so?"

"I'm not dealing with that incident but, yes, it's being treated as murder. What makes you ask?"

"I wondered if you'd realised the similarities of that murder with the one for which we believe Bill Carter is responsible? The woman was apparently bludgeoned to death, she was thrown into the river after death, and she worked as a prostitute at the Guangzhou, a brothel. Bill Carter's wife was bludgeoned to death, she was thrown into the river, and he was hiding out in a brothel. Does that not make him a suspect for this murder too?"

"As I say, I'm not the investigating officer, in that incident, but I'm sure the similarities won't have gone unnoticed." His brow furrowed and he looked inquiringly at me, and said,

"How do you come to know so much about it?"

"Because news travels fast around here inspector. When we heard about it we began to make our own enquiries amongst the Chinese in Limehouse, wondering if there was a connection with Bill Carter."

"What did you find?"

"We found that the girls at the Guangzhou were afraid of someone you might describe as a client. A man who used the place infrequently, who had a threatening and what was described as a 'very physical' way of treating the girls. Most of them tried their best to avoid him. It was someone with a distinctive scar to his left cheek. A scar that might be a burn scar that runs up to his eye. Do you happen to know inspector, does Carter have such a scar?"

"I'm worried about you; you know so much about this murder, why should I not consider that you may be a suspect?"

"Because you know that I'm trying to help you. I've a vested interest in seeing Carter caught..." and mid sentence I realised that I was about to reveal Lottie's secret, so I tried to change direction, "...and you didn't answer my question, does Carter have a scar to his left cheek?"

"I don't recall such a scar having been recorded on his descriptive form when he was last arrested, but that doesn't mean he hasn't got such a scar – it might be a more recent acquisition."

"Has he been ruled out of the Whitechapel murders – they were all prostitutes too?"

"I think I told you, I'm not investigating them either, but I'm sure nothing has been ruled out. I probably mentioned the last time we met; those killings seem to be of a different category. The killer cuts them apart – probably has the skills of a surgeon – and removes body parts."

The inspector pushed his empty cup and saucer across the table and prepared to rise with a view to leaving, but I didn't want him to leave until I'd exhausted my questioning, and said,

"Before you go inspector, we've been considering the state of the river and the position where the body of the Chinese prostitute was found. Limehouse to the West India Docks is only a short distance, which suggests the body was thrown into the river at slack water – otherwise she'd have been carried further down river. At the turn of the tide, whoever threw her in must have thrown her from a wharf or landing stage to reach the water otherwise they'd have had to struggle down the muddy embankment. By our reckoning that means she must have been thrown in somewhere about four in the morning. There wouldn't have been many people about at that time, maybe the odd watchman or the musketeers guarding the West India Docks. Perhaps you have the resources to make enquiries amongst them?"

"Hmm" Inspector Stone murmured as he turned to leave, offering no commitment. Atlas followed him to the door as if to ensure he left the house. I didn't feel as though we'd made much progress but at least it had shown that the police hadn't lost interest.

Chapter 21.

Chika was wrapped up warm against a rather chilly March wind and the occasional flake of snow, enjoying the freedom of the garden with Atlas. Pru had gone on her usual weekly shopping expedition to the market, which gave me the opportunity to empty and thoroughly clean the oil lamps. The wicks needed trimming and the glass globes needed to be cleaned of the smoke haze that reduced their illumination. With no-one to take my attention, my mind was apt to wander to the memories of youth; roaming the moors, care-free times swimming in the lakes, fishing for trout and grayling, searching for birds' nests – I realised how much I missed it all.

A sudden scream brought me out of my reverie, surely that was Chika. I left everything and rushed outside just in time to see a figure running off through the grave-yard, and Chika standing watching. Atlas seemed very excited; growling, and standing on his back legs up against the garden wall, watching the running figure. I'm sure if he could have climbed the wall he'd have chased after him.

"What happened?" I asked running to her side.

"Atlas bit him."

"How could he bite him if he was over the wall?"

"He was a nice man and he just wanted to talk. He climbed over into the garden – that's when Atlas went for him. I tried to stop him but he wouldn't listen to me."

"Did the man touch you?"

"No, he just wanted to talk but Atlas went for him."

"Have you seen him before?"

"No. He said he was a friend of yours and he asked where you were. I told him you were busy. He seemed very nice."

"What made you scream?"

"I Thought Atlas was going to kill him, he'd got him on the ground. I grabbed his collar and tried to pull him away but he went at him again. Luckily he only bit him once and tore his trousers but he managed to scramble to his feet and get away over the wall."

Chika was frightened, but only frightened for the man's sake. She was scolding Atlas, but I was quietly patting and praising him – I didn't want Chika to be afraid for her own safety but in my own heart and mind I was sure that a terrible crime had been averted.

As soon as Pru arrived home I quietly took her to one side and explained what had happened. Thankfully she didn't go into hysterics and agreed that we kept the issue low key for Chika's sake, but we agreed that this was a serious attempt to either kidnap Chika or worse.

That afternoon we sat before the fire and in a quiet conversational way we talked Chika into revealing exactly how the man had approached her. She gave precisely the same story over again for Pru's benefit. I'd not thought to ask her to describe the man, but Pru proceeded to draw out of her little snippets,

"Was he in workmen's clothes?"

"I don't know."

"Well, did he look as though he'd been digging a grave – were his clothes dirty?"

"No, I don't think so, not until Atlas got him on the ground. He tore his trousers and I could see blood where he bit him."

I asked, "He said he was a friend of mine didn't he?"

"Yes, he asked me where you were and I told him you were busy in the house."

"Well what did he look like? Did he have a beard or whiskers?"

"No. I don't think so because I remember his face was all red on one side and his skin looked as though it was stretched tight – a sort of scar."

A Scar – that was enough. A shiver ran through me as I realised how close we'd come to losing Chika. I looked at Pru and I could see from her horrified expression that she'd made the same connection. Thank goodness for Atlas.

Sweet Retribution

It might not be conclusive proof that it was Bill Carter but in our minds it was proof enough and meant that he'd found us. Now he knew where we'd moved to and he was out to settle the score. It was perhaps our nosing around in Limehouse and by the river that had stirred him into action. On the one hand I was pleased we were forcing him to come out from his cover, but on the other hand I felt a heightened degree of concern as to what it might lead to. Pru made the Derringer readily available, just in case.

Next morning we called on Tom and Lottie to let them know what had happened and then we walked to Westminster to try to find Inspector Stone. He wasn't available so I tried talking to another plain clothes man, telling him about the attempted abduction of Chika, but he didn't accept that it was an attempt to abduct her. Never-the-less he promised to pass on the information to Inspector Stone. I felt the matter had been dismissed out of hand and it was highly unlikely that Inspector Stone would ever hear of our visit so I told him I had some valuable information that I would only disclose to Inspector Stone if he would visit me.

Sure enough, that evening there was that now familiar knocking at the door and this time Pru had Atlas firmly under control as I opened the door. Stone was standing well back, wary that the huge dog might rush at him, but seeing no fearful Atlas he stepped forward and said,
"You wanted to see me?"
I asked him inside and again he took his place at the kitchen table whilst Pru administered tea. Atlas gave him no more than a glance after Pru had given the 'all clear' but I think the inspector still remained a little cautious.
"What was it you wanted to see me about?" he asked.
"Didn't they tell you? I told them all about it this morning." I answered.
"They said something about the dog having bit someone. I don't deal with that sort of thing."

Sweet Retribution

"Obviously they didn't tell you what had happened. The dog did bite someone but it was because he tried to take Chika." I then related the whole story to him and related the information I'd given him the previous evening regarding the scar on the face of the man who'd frightened the girls of the Guangzhou.

"Surely inspector, there's a good chance that this is Bill Carter. He's tried to burn down the warehouse, he's murdered his wife, we think he's the murderer of the Chinese prostitute and he's threatened to get even with us. It's got to be more than a coincidence that he's tried to abduct Chika after we'd been making enquiries about him around Limehouse?"

"Well, we're doing our best to find him but I can't have a man hanging around just on the off-chance. Anyway I doubt whether he's likely to show up again after being bitten by the dog," and he looked again at Atlas who was putting on a show as a big cuddly softy."

."Oh, I'm sure he'll show up again. He's made his intentions quite clear. He's left his message scrawled on the wall and this is his third attempt to cause us harm." I suddenly realised I'd come very close to revealing to him about the assault on Lottie, so I quickly changed tack and asked,

"Did your officers find anyone amongst the musketeers or the watchmen around West India Docks who might have seen anything in the early hours of last Tuesday morning?"

"I believe I told you, it isn't my investigation so I can't say exactly what's been done. I will make it my business to find out though. One thing more, be very careful not to allow the dog to accept treats from others. I've known incidents where poisoned meat has been fed to dogs that have been an obstacle to burglaries."

With that advice the inspector finished his tea and left, again Atlas followed him to the door. I must admit I'd never considered the prospect of poisoned meat but Pru was confident that Atlas's training had been to reject food from strangers.

Sweet Retribution

Next morning Sandra Chung came again to tutor Chika, bringing with her a small present. It was a wooden framework with beads that slid along wires that she called an abacus. She explained in very simple terms that she intended to teach Chika an ancient Chinese method of counting and solving complex mathematical problems with the beads. I was intrigued; I'd seen her using the device when we initially interviewed her and I was astounded how quickly and easily she was able to give answers to problems that would take me a considerable time with pen and paper. I was hopeful that I might learn too if I paid attention. Sandra also had other teaching aids; a folder of hand drawn maps, lists of ancient kings and queens, historical figures and their achievements, and world events. I think both Pru and I both felt Chika was in good hands.

Before leaving she said,

"I've not seen mister Tom but I've kept my ears open whilst I've been at the Guangzhou and I overheard two of the girls talking about the scar faced man that frightens them so. One girl was convinced he was working at James Mitchell's foundry near the rope walk. Perhaps you'll tell mister Tom?"

That was hot news and I went straight to Tom.

"What do you suggest, Tom. Shall we wait and inform Inspector Stone?"

"No, you know what happened last time we told them where he was – they let him flee the nest. No, they'll go blundering in and we'll lose him again. We'll go and make some pretence of ordering rope, or even pretend I'm looking for a job, and see if we can surprise him."

"Of course, why didn't I think of it before? His burn scar – that's where he got the burn scar," said Tom.

"Well, what do we do? We can't just go into the foundry and start asking questions, can we? He's bound to realise those questions are about him and he'll just disappear again," I said.

"Leave it to me. The foundry manager's someone I've done business with. I've not seen him for a while but he used to take a jar or two in the ale-house on Narrow Street," he replied, but I insisted in going along too. The ale-house was bustling with people, dockyard workers, colliers, rope-makers and people of all the trades associated with sailing craft and the river, and I wondered however they could hold a conversation with all that noise. Some were sat around a table playing bones, others playing cards, and amidst it all someone in the corner was playing a squeeze box and attempting to sing. It seemed everyone was raising their voice to be heard above the racket.

Tom stood surveying the throng then moved amongst them obviously searching for the manager of the foundry – I simply followed. Eventually he spotted his quarry in a small alcove. There were inaudible words of greeting and handshakes before being interrupted by the grubby-white- apron-wearing publican with a huge jug of ale and tankards. Tom and his friend went into a huddle and although I could guess what the conversation was about I couldn't hear a word. I couldn't contribute anything so decided to carry my ale outside into the fresh air, watching a game of skittles whilst I waited…and waited. Eventually Tom appeared, very red faced and clearly a little inebriated. The walk and the ferry across the river helped clear his head as he began to disclose what he'd learned.

"The man with the burn scar working at the factory has given his name as Billy Wheeler. Apparently he's a good workman but he's fond of drink and an aggressive braggart. His scar came as a result of deliberately refusing to heed warnings about safety; it taught him a painful lesson. He keeps himself to himself and he isn't well liked by fellow workers because of his attitude. He's kept on because he works hard. He was away from work one day recently because of illness – could that have been a dog bite?"

I agreed with Tom, it wasn't conclusive that Billy Wheeler was actually Bill Carter but he wasn't likely to use his real name – being wanted for murder. The terms 'aggressive', 'attitude' and 'braggart' certainly fit his character, but how were we going to prove this was Bill Carter?

The problem was that we couldn't positively identify him, only Chika had ever seen him up close, and I was reluctant to use her. According to the foundry manager Wheeler's shift would end at two in the afternoon and if we waited near the foundry entrance we'd see him leave and observe what Wheeler looked like. We had to acknowledge that Wheeler might not be the man we were looking for.

The following day Tom and I waited as the shifts changed, watching as the men left the foundry gates. Of the six men we observed leaving the premises it was difficult to determine which one was Billy Wheeler as they were all covered with foundry grime, dirty faced with ash and dust. Just one stood apart from the other five who left in a bunch. We remembered that Wheeler was not well liked which was good reason for him to leave alone.

Tom suggested that I should follow at a distance to discover where he was living whilst he went into the foundry to find the manager. He was bound to have some record of his employee's addresses.

Billy Wheeler was acting in a furtive manner, continually looking over his shoulder. It gave me even more reason to believe he was our man. I kept well back, taking advantage of yards and alleys to shield me from his view. He made straight for the Bunch o' Grapes which I should have expected knowing his propensity for drink and after the heat of the foundry he'd be eager to slake his thirst.

I settled down to wait a short distance away in the rope-maker's field from where I had a good view of the ale-house. Fortunately, the waiting wasn't too long and he emerged from the pub and stood looking about him, to my mind he was checking to see that all was clear. He continued through the back alleys, occasionally pausing to check if he was being followed. Finally he entered a dilapidated terrace house with a dirty, neglected appearance. There were broken window panes and not a trace of paint on door – quite typical of the slums I'd seen around Limehouse. Two women were hanging about the street corner, undoubtedly soliciting a customer. Just the type of area and abode suited to Bill Carter.

I waited again, just in case he was only visiting this property, and kept a steady watch on the door I'd seen him enter. I was wondering how long to stay there because Tom wouldn't know where I was, when suddenly an arm came around my neck from behind and held me. It took me completely by surprise. I didn't have time to think, it was just an automatic impulse to scrape the heel of my boot down his shin and stamp on his foot. It was enough to break his hold on me and I swivelled around to see his scarred face. Billy Wheeler had obviously realised I was following him and had left by a rear door or window and crept round behind me to take me unawares. He lashed out at me with clenched fist but fortunately he delivered only a glancing blow and I took the opportunity to bring my knee up into his groin. He doubled up in pain and just to be sure I kicked him there again.

I looked around, hoping to see Tom approaching and unsure what to do. Billy Wheeler lay on the ground curled up in a foetal manner, moaning and rolling his eyes, trying to cope with the pain. For someone with a reputation of violence he didn't convince me of his ability. I placed my foot on his neck and said,

"You're my prisoner Bill Carter and I'm handing you over to the peelers."

"What? What did you call me – Bill Carter? My name's not Carter it's Wheeler; Billy Wheeler. Why would you hand me over to the Peelers?

"Don't expect me to fall for that. I know you're Billy Carter – you killed your wife – the Peelers are after you."

Sweet Retribution

"Killed my wife? My wife's very much alive she's the one I'm running from. Her brothers are after me – I thought you were somebody working for them."
He was convincing in his denial and emphatic that his name was indeed Billy Wheeler, so much so that I was beginning to have my doubts; wondering if we'd got the wrong suspect. I said,

"OK, show me where you live and if you've anything there to prove who you are, then you're free to go."
He painfully rose to his feet and hobbled across the alley to the house I'd seen him enter, Opening the door to his room I saw just a pathetic jumble of detritus. Rubbish everywhere, discarded clothing strewn across the floor, a blanket in the corner that appeared to be his bed, and nothing much more to make it a home. I was still very apprehensive and wary, thinking it might all be a sham and that he might produce a knife and suddenly resume his attack.

He moved some items covering a small wooden box that he opened and withdrew a small folded paper that he handed to me – a baptismal certificate in the name William Wheeler. He said, "That's all I've kept. Wedding certificate and everything else I destroyed."

Chapter 22

Tom was anxiously waiting near the foundry and as I approached he rushed to meet me.

"Where the hell have you been? I'd begun to think something had happened to you." I shook my head and said,

"It's all been a wild-goose chase," and I explained what had happened."

"And you took him at his word – just on the baptism certificate? He could have picked that up anywhere. Come on, let's get back there quickly, I want to see this fella for myself,"

I led Tom back to the hovel where I'd left Billy Wheeler, feeling a little upset that Tom should question my judgement. I was convinced that I'd made the right decision. I pushed open the door into the lobby and began to climb the stairs towards Billy Wheeler's room, gradually feeling uneasy about the whole situation. The door stood ajar and I called out, "Billy, are you there?" but there was no response. Tom pushed past me and kicked the door wide open. Billy had fled leaving behind just a scene of squalor; rubbish and rags all over the floor. The small wooden box and its contents had gone too.

"Well, there's your answer; that was Bill Carter and you've been hoodwinked, you've let him go." said Tom, clearly annoyed.

"I'm sorry," was all I could say. Tom didn't respond and the long walk back to the ferryboat was taken in silence between us. Eventually, as we waited for the ferryman, Tom said,

"It's my fault. I should never have left you to follow him on your own. He's escaped us this time but our time will come; we'll find him wherever he goes to ground."
His attitude was beginning to lighten a little but I still felt stupid and remorseful about my failure. I'd had Bill Carter there in my grasp and I'd let him go. Somehow I was going to have to explain to Lottie and Pru. The more

I thought about it, the more I saw how stupid I'd been; the scarred face, the aggressive nature, the brothel, the squalor, everything about him should have convinced me that I had Bill Carter in my grasp and I'd let him escape – on the evidence of a baptismal certificate. For goodness sake, I'd forged a more complicated document than that and yet I'd never even considered it might be false in any way – how could I hold my head up again?

When I came to repeat the sorry tale to Lottie and Pru I expected some scathing comments but although I'm sure they felt disappointment they were understanding and supportive.

Tom returned to the foundry the following day but there was no sign of Billy Wheeler, and he spent the rest of the day trawling around ale-houses, brothels and opium dens throughout Limehouse, and enquiring of his friends and acquaintances. In each case he drew a blank; we'd driven Bill Carter underground again. Tom returned home in a depressed mood that I tried to lighten by saying,

""Well, he'll not be so eager to seek his revenge because he now knows what's likely to happen to him," but it didn't help. I knew I had let my friends down. He simply said,

"So close. So close."

Pru was equally disappointed and decided to spend some time amongst her old acquaintances of the disadvantaged and the criminal underworld, to refresh and double her twenty-five guinea bounty she'd placed on Bill Carter. I was as eager as Pru to encourage someone to pass on information that would lead to his capture, but I had an over-riding concern that there'd be unscrupulous people who'd make up false information just to claim the bounty.

Someone must know where Bill Carter was. The only sure thing we knew was that he was an associate of Finkelstein but why was he working in the foundry to support himself? Had Finkelstein washed his hands of him? I felt it was the time to re-examine the link with this obnoxious fence and money-lender. The rat obviously needed someone to collect his dues and to enforce his terms of borrowing; he was too old and feeble to act the enforcer himself. He needed others around him and he'd been astute enough to have Dina planted in our home; could we possibly turn the tables and get close to someone in his camp?

I was the person responsible for letting Carter escape so I felt that I must do something to rectify the situation. I decided to pay some attention to the comings and goings from Finkelstein's den. I didn't say anything to Pru, Tom or Lottie, knowing they'd only try to put me off. There was no way in which I could make a direct approach; I'd be recognised immediately after the confrontations that Tom and I had made with this slimy reptile. How was I to go about it?

Bread Street, East Cheap, was hardly a bustling thoroughfare at the best of times, and this morning there were only the odd one or two down-and-outs hanging about doorways and a couple of bare-foot children playing with a whip and top. The whole street, and Finkelstein's place in particular, was a scene of neglect and dilapidation that looked worse in daylight than I'd remembered from our last visit. Outside his abode, a pugilistic monster with a broken nose, was hanging about, obviously guarding the entrance. He was someone I'd never seen before and I was pretty sure he wouldn't recognise me, but still I kept clear of him.

I looked for somewhere from where I could observe Finkelstein's premises and the narrow alleyway that ran alongside. A seedy looking doss house almost opposite fitted the bill. As I stepped inside the open doorway I was confronted by an old hag who looked as seedy as the house she kept. She looked me up and down and I suddenly realised that my clothes stood me apart from her usual clients, but she made no comment.

Sweet Retribution

I asked if she had a room vacant and she beckoned me to follow. She led me through a dark passage to a room at the rear and opened the door to reveal what appeared more like a cupboard than a room with living space. There was very little daylight into the room and the smell of unwashed bodies was overpowering. I pinched my nose and shook my head, saying that it wouldn't do. She made a snorting noise that sounded like "Uh", turned on her heels and led me back to the staircase. As we climbed the stairs I was careful not to step too heavily on some of the treads as they looked rather unsafe. A small room at the front, overlooking the street was ideal for my purpose despite having broken glass in the grimy window. It held no bed or other furniture, only old rags presumably left by the last occupant. There was no lock on the door but I paid her the six pence she demanded. No identification was asked or given.

She left me to return downstairs and I went to the window. I wiped my sleeve on the remaining glass and looked out onto Finkelstein's den. The only activity was the broken-nosed pugilist who still hung about. It was going to be a tedious exercise with no seat to rest my wearying frame.

As dusk fell and vision deteriorated I decided to head home with nothing achieved. I managed to slip out of the doss house without the old hag noticing – or so I thought.

I faced a few inquisitive questions from Pru and Chika about where I'd been all day but I managed to placate them without revealing too much. The evening was spent quietly reading, however, with the book in my lap, the Finkelstein setup was constantly on my mind – wondering what if anything was going to be achieved by my observations. I was feeling a little subdued and disheartened believing that nothing was likely to emerge from it. Nothing was coming from any other source and I concluded that this negative attitude wasn't going to help so I had to continue.

Sweet Retribution

The following morning I set out again but, calling at the street market I picked up a discarded wooden box to serve as a seat as I watched from the window. The old hag was waiting as I returned to the rented room but no words were exchanged, just a steely suspicious look from her; I took no notice. Once again there was little activity along Bread Street and as the morning progressed I found it difficult to concentrate. I found myself counting cracks in the wall, holes in the wainscot and mouse-holes in the skirting. I vowed to bring a book with me the next time.

Time dragged and I craved food and drink and all I'd brought along was a couple of apples I needed better preparation if this was to continue. By mid-afternoon my resolve was weakening and I was just about to give up on what I was beginning to believe was a lost cause, when I saw the old hag shuffle across the street and enter Finkelstein's hovel. Alarm bells started to ring in my mind. I watched intently until she re-appeared and was disturbed to see her glance up at my window – or did I imagine it? What had she been up to in Finkelstein's den? Was she in cahoots with him? Had she warned him of my presence? Ought I to get out quickly? All these thoughts bounced around in my mind.

I could hear a tiny voice in my head saying, *"Don't lose your nerve – stick it out,"* and I began to look at it from a different prospective. If she was a trusted friend of Finkelstein then perhaps she could be of use to us. I stayed where I was.

As dusk descended I gave up my task and left my room. I walked to the end of Bread Street, looking forward to a decent meal when I reached home. Thoughts of Finkelstein, the doss house and the old hag had left my mind, but suddenly I realised I had company. Two rough looking individuals were following me close behind. My instinct was to run but my legs wouldn't carry me fast enough and they were soon on me. I backed up against a wall to prevent anyone from taking me from behind but it didn't save me. Blows came thick and fast to my face and to my solar plexus. I doubled up in pain and fell to the floor. I curled up in a ball with my hands and arms trying to protect my head and the blows from their fists changed to kicks to my ribs.

As quickly as it had begun it ended and my two assailants had gone without a word of explanation, leaving me blooded and in awful pain. Well, there was my answer – the old hag had warned Finkelstein and this had been his retribution.

The long walk home was as painful as the beating I'd taken. Pru met me at the door, shocked to see the state I was in. Bloodied nose, swelling and reddening around both eyes – they'd be black and blue by morning. I could feel the terrible bruising around my rib cage and feared there could be broken ribs. Of course she wanted to know what had happened and the truth had to come out about my ill conceived watch on Finkelstein. To say she was scathing in her remarks of the stupidity of my efforts would be less than truthful.

Chapter 23

As soon as Tom heard what had happened he was round to see me. I admit I wasn't good company. As predicted my eyes and nose were swollen and black with bruising. The whites of both eyes had turned crimson. I tried my best to be sociable but my head ached and my ribs were a torture every time I moved, coughed or attempted to laugh. Of course I had the same derision from Tom that I'd had from Pru,

"Whatever possessed you to go on your own? You'd had a dose of their welcome the last time we went there together."

"I never intended to confront them, just keep a watch to see if Bill Carter showed up, or to find a weak link – someone we could put some pressure on to reveal his whereabouts," was my lame response. Tom continued,

"Well, now you know it's dangerous to go anywhere near Bread Street on your own. They're all in his pocket."

"I suppose I knew I was playing with fire so I've only myself to blame, but I felt as though I'd let everyone down in allowing him to escape. I had to do something to flush him out."

"No-one is blaming you for what happened. I should never have let you follow him on your own, so if we're apportioning blame I'm just as much responsible. One thing is for sure, after this episode no-one goes alone."

Pru was listening and nodded her head in agreement. Tom stayed to take a glass of wine with us but left with an intriguing remark,

"Since learning what happened to you I've had the semblance of an idea. I'll not say any more about it for the moment. We must wait until you've recovered."
I pondered upon what he could have in mind but couldn't figure out what it might be.

Recovery was taking a considerable time, the bruising was fading to a yellow hue but my ribs were still painful.

Sweet Retribution

Boredom was another issue I had to contend with; everything I enjoyed caused me pain – playing with Chika or even a gentle walk with Atlas – and so I was reduced to sitting and reading. Even prolonged sitting in one position became uncomfortable and sleep was problematic. Days were long and miserable, wishing I'd had more sense than go alone into the lion's den. Pru must have been tired of my moaning and the burden I'd become but she made no complaint.

Gradually, as the days passed, my recovery improved. Chika, normally a typical rumbustious child, had learnt to be very careful about me and even Atlas, who loved to jump up and nuzzle me, realised something was amiss and was less inclined to rough play.

I think Sandra Chung felt sympathetic and to make things easier on Pru, began to take Chika walking as part of her education, showing her things we all probably took for granted. She explained the background, and history, of features all around us. Chika enjoyed it all and it was clear that she'd formed a close friendship with her tutor.

Chika stood at the front door and waved goodbye as Sandra left. She put away her books and equipment and went out into the garden with Atlas to enjoy the June afternoon sun. Pru was busy baking and I sat reading – keeping as still as possible to avoid those sharp pains from my ribs. Probably an hour had passed and Atlas wandered in and lay down on the hearth. I thought that Chika had probably tired him out but thought no more of it.

A short time later Pru called Chika to come in and wash before tea, before returning to the kitchen to tidy up after her baking. After a few minutes Pru realised that Chika hadn't responded so she went out into the garden to see what was keeping her, but there was no sign of the child. Panic gripped her, remembering the incident only three months earlier when the stranger had entered the garden and had been driven away by Atlas. She shouted for Chika thinking that she'd wandered out of sight but again there was no response. The panic was now turning to fear.

I realised something was wrong when Pru ran back into the house, her face white and strained. The shock and fear in her face was enough to make me jump to my feet, all consideration for the pain gone.

"She's gone. Chika's gone – she's been taken." Pru blubbered, her face contorted with anguish and tears streaming down her face. I lamely said,

"Calm down she's probably hiding somewhere – playing a game," and I went outside to search myself. Now the panic had reached me too, especially as I noticed several stones dislodged from the wall as though someone had climbed over from the church yard. My stomach felt as though it had become a whirlpool with the anxiety that was gripping me.

I climbed the wall and searched through the gravestones and around the church itself, all the time calling Chika's name but there was no sign of her. Why hadn't Atlas been there to protect her? I returned to Pru who had gone through the house and the privy, searching with the desperate hope that she'd slipped into the house unseen and perhaps fallen asleep. We were now frantic with worry – what had happened to her?

The natural thing was to rush to Lottie and Tom to get their help. Together we searched the streets, the alleys, the park, the ferry and riverside, anywhere that we could – but it was all taking time and the longer Chika was missing, the more desperate we were becoming. I was now convinced that Bill Carter or Finkelstein was behind this, but what more could I do.

I made my way to the bridge and on to Westminster to the Police station, leaving behind Pru, Lottie and Tom to continue the search. All the time I was thinking what dreadful retribution I would exact on Finkelstein if Chika wasn't found. At the police station I blurted out my fears for Chika but the desk sergeant seemed almost dismissive of my concerns, telling me that the child would almost certainly return home at her leisure, wondering what all the fuss was about. He promised that all the officers on duty would be alerted

When I reached home Pru met me on the street, absolutely distraught, her face awash with tears, and she explained that she'd knocked on doors and questioned passers-by but no-one had seen or heard anything. Tom and Lottie were still out searching. Time was fast heading towards dusk and pessimism was building. A knock at the door brought both of us rushing to answer. Although I didn't appreciate the significance at the time, Atlas remained sprawled on the hearth.

I opened the door to see Inspector Stone, careful as always to stand well back knowing Atlas for the guard dog he was. It was clear that he didn't come with good news just from his facial expression and I feared the worst but he quickly dispelled all thoughts that he was the bearer of bad news. There were none of the platitudes that I'd received at the police station he spoke with concern and clarity.

"This has the hallmark of a planned abduction, no spur of the moment thing. I'm looking at your dog. He's lethargic and showing none of his usual aggression. I think he's taken either poison or a strong sedative. Bearing in mind what you told me before about the stranger in your garden that your dog bit, I believe this was a planned abduction. I'd hazard a guess you'll be receiving some form of ransom note. If so, that begs the question, why would someone do this, and who knows your family and your home well enough to use the child in this way? Who hates you enough to do this?" He looked at us questioningly before he continued,

"You have to ask yourself who amongst your acquaintances or business contacts is most likely to do this, and why. What have you done to provoke it?"

I decided to tell the inspector everything, all that we'd previously kept from him. I began,

"I've already told you about Bill Carter who's wanted for murder; well it all goes much deeper than that. It all stems from the money lender, Finkelstein who lives on

Bread Street. You know him; you've said you had men watching his premises."

My brain was working feverishly as I spoke to explain Finkelstein's war with Pru without exposing her part in the confidence trick and my part as a forger. I continued,

"Some years ago a business transaction with him went wrong. That led to his men targeting my home, breaking in and causing extensive damage. There was also an attempt to set it on fire – a window was broken and a burning tar cloth was thrown into the room. Fortunately I was on hand to extinguish the fire. Then there were dead rats left to cause us upset.

"*About* that time Pru came upon a book that Finkelstein kept as a record of all his criminal dealings. He knows we've got it and he's desperate to get it back. He forced Bill Carter's wife, Dina, to obtain employment here as a home help and child minder, but his real intention was that once inside the house she would search for the book.

"We realised what was happening and confronted Dina and she admitted her real purpose but she wasn't a criminal at heart and she agreed to stay in the position we employed her and keep us informed of what Finkelstein intended next.

"It was through Dina that we learnt he intended to send men to burn down our tea warehouse. We set a trap and caught them red handed. I believe that Bill Carter was one of the gang and he was injured in the melee that ensued. I believe that Carter realised that Dina had given us that information and that's why she ended up in the Thames with her head bashed in." I hesitated to look at Pru who was pacing back and forth in the kitchen wringing her hands. I continued,

"We're sure it was Carter who broke into our friend's home during the night and seriously assaulted her. Because the police had failed to arrest him at the brothel we informed you about, we decided to try to catch him ourselves. We found he'd been working at the foundry in Limehouse and I followed him to the room he was renting. Unfortunately, he got away again, but now we know he's got a scar to the left cheek, the result of an accident at the foundry. I think it will be him that's taken Chika."

I was getting no input from Pru and I wondered just how far I could take this revelation to Inspector Stone, but I felt that the situation had become so serious that we just had to reveal everything. I continued,

"It's the book that's at the centre of all this. Finkelstein is so desperate to recover it that he'll go to any lengths to get it back. He knows that if it fell into your hands or those of the excise people he'd go to prison for a long time." The inspector asked,

"Where is this book now?"
I looked at Pru knowing how reluctant she was to let it out of her hands, wondering what she would say, but I think she realised that this was the answer to recovering Chika. She answered,

"It's in the hands of my bank, locked away. They don't know what it contains."

Chapter 24

The trauma of her abduction kept repeating in Chika's mind as she sat on the floor, alone, hands tied behind her and still blindfold. The tears streamed down her cheeks and her nose was running, she was unable to help herself. The threats to strike her made her afraid to call out. Wherever she was, it was so quiet, no sounds that she recognised; she shivered with fear of what was going to happen to her.

"I'd kicked and struggled against the scar faced man holding me and I'd tried to scream "*Let me go*" but he'd quickly stifled my shouts with a strong hand across my mouth, making it hard to breathe.

"He'd held me in a tight grip as he dragged me through the church yard only hesitating to put a rough sack over my head so that I couldn't see. Then he and tied my arms behind me, lifted me off my feet and carried me over his shoulder. How far he carried me I couldn't tell, but it didn't seem to take a long time. Wherever he'd brought me to was a cold place with the smell of mould and damp. I remembered the door making a scraping noise on the floor as he pushed it open. It must have been some sort of outhouse.

"I sobbed and begged him to let me go but he didn't answer; it seemed so quiet, not even the sound of his breathlessness from carrying me, and after a while I realised I was alone. He'd left me there tied up and hardly able to move. I tried to untie my wrists but with my hands behind my back, and whatever he'd used to bind me was so tight, I couldn't get free. I struggled to my feet but realised there was something holding me back – I was fastened to something solid. I began to wonder was I going to be left there to die? Oh Mama, Papa, get me free, please, please.

"I felt so cold, so alone and frightened, and time dragged on and on. Just being trapped and alone in this strange place, unable to see, made me want to scream but I was too afraid in case he heard me. It must have

141

been night when he came back. I'm ashamed to say I'd wet myself but I couldn't help it.

"He took that sack off my head but it was so dark I still couldn't see where I was, and before my eyes could get accustomed to the darkness he tied his neckerchief over my eyes. Dragging me to my feet he made me walk, blindfold, and still with my arms tied. We left the smell of the mouldy, damp outhouse and I could feel the wind and the fresh air on my face. He held me tight to make sure I couldn't escape and he pulled me along faster than my legs could carry me. I didn't know where we were going but eventually I heard the rush and splash of water. We were at the river and I heard the familiar sound of a small boat bumping against its mooring.

"Just to know I was by the river made me afraid that he might throw me in – drown me. I was shivering with fright, but he lifted me down into the boat and made me lie down on the bottom. I could hear the sound of the oars splashing through the water. I don't think there was anyone else there so he must have rowed the boat himself. It seemed to take forever until he lifted me out again. I had no idea where we were but I remember having to stumble up some stone steps from the boat.

"That's when I heard a woman – she'd obviously been waiting for us. She said, "What's taken you so long?" I didn't hear what he said. With him holding my arm on one side and her holding the other they made me walk a long way. I could still hear the swish of water but I'd no idea where I was or where I was being taken.

"They were talking to each other in whispers so that I couldn't hear what was said, but I did catch one word, I think it was the name of a bird, a 'Raven', but it meant nothing to me. The man picked me up and put me over his shoulder. He seemed a little unsteady as he carried me and I realised it was because he was stepping into another boat of some description. I could feel the gentle rocking beneath me as he put me down on the floor. He threatened me to keep quiet and said that if I began to shout he'd throw me into the river.

Sweet Retribution

"He took the binding from my wrists and the neckerchief from my eyes. My hands had been tied so long that I had pins and needles in my hands but I rubbed my eyes and looked around. I was in a small, narrow room, obviously a boat, and although I could smell the fumes of an oil lamp in the air, the flame had been extinguished so there was no light.

"When he left I rushed to the door but it was locked. As daylight began to break I heard footsteps aboard the boat. I quickly retreated as far as I could away from the door; afraid that the man had returned and of what he might do to me, but when the door opened it was a woman – the same voice I'd heard earlier.

"She scowled at me and warned me to behave or she said she'd sell me. I didn't understand who she was going to sell me to but I'd heard about slaves and I knew something like that had happened to my real mother. I began to shake and the tears began again. I didn't want to leave my Mama and Papa.

"The nasty woman gave me a cup of water. I hadn't realised how thirsty I was. She gave me some pieces of bread that were spread with something greasy, it didn't taste very good but I was just pleased to eat something, I was so hungry.

"She said she'd have to leave me locked in the cabin as she had to make '*some arrangements*'. I didn't understand what she meant but she warned me that the door would be locked and someone would be listening outside in case I tried to get out. If I made a sound like shouting to attract help the man outside was going to give me a severe whipping.

I was alone again. I frantically looked around for some means of escape, but there was no other way out other than the locked door. There were small windows with curtains, but too small to climb through even if I could open them. I looked out to see other boats on the river, but I was afraid to be seen and careful in case the man listening outside saw me.

Sweet Retribution

"Once again I was alone for hours with just my thoughts and fears for company. I cried so much I don't think there were any more tears to cry. I knelt down, put my hands together and prayed to Jesus but I don't think he heard me. I realised I was abandoned and there was no-one to help me. I was so miserable I tried to curl up in the corner and go to sleep but sleep wouldn't come.

"It was late in the afternoon when the stern faced woman returned. She said she been to see Mama and Papa and they didn't want me to come home so I was now hers to do with as she pleased. I couldn't believe what she was saying but even so it was so upsetting, I was reduced to sobbing again.

"She told me I was to spend the night there and the next morning she'd take me to my new home. I thought a '*new home*', that means she really is going to sell me. She gave me a blanket and told me to go to sleep but I think I lay awake, crying all night trying to convince myself that Mama and Papa wouldn't really give me away. What could I have done to make them want to give me away?"

I don't believe any of us had any sleep that night. Tom and Lottie stayed with us making endless cups of sweet tea throughout the night. I couldn't sit still and was out walking the streets, despite the pouring rain, hoping to hear the sound of Chika's voice calling. When daylight broke I'd walked miles, explored every alley, every derelict property, every thicket and every conceivable hiding place within a mile of home in each direction. What's more, the tide was low and I walked the river bank searching the mud flats in view of Bill Carter's past crimes. All that I'd achieved was to get a soaking and the prospect of pneumonia.

At about eight o'clock that morning Inspector Stone was back to give support and to explain that he had a team of constables searching the area and to shake up every criminal and every informant in the area. In view of the desk sergeant's dismissive attitude when I reported Chika's abduction I thought we were getting special treatment, after all who would normally give tuppence about a half-caste kid? Surely I could be forgiven for such thoughts knowing the attitude of the general public.

The first question he asked was whether there had been any form of contact from the abductor, but of course there had not. He assured us it would come at some stage. In the meantime he implored us to keep faith – she would return to us. It was his contention that wherever she was, and whoever had taken her, she would be treated well because she was the bargaining chip in whatever they wanted.

"We've told you who's behind it – Finkelstein. He wants that book. What are you doing about him?"

"Ah, Mr Finkelstein! We're enjoying the pleasure of his company at the moment. Of course he denies any knowledge of your daughter's abduction, and I wouldn't have expected anything less, but we'll see what a few days of incarceration do for his memory. Officers are currently examining his salubrious premises, looking for anything that might incriminate him. We're aware he fences stolen property but he's cute, it looks as though he keeps nothing on the premises. That brings me to the book. It's important that you hand it over to me. It might be the means of holding him in custody and the key to getting your daughter back."

Pru didn't respond immediately but stood looking at the inspector. I wondered if I'd done right by disclosing about the book before having discussed it with her. She looked quite helpless and drained of all colour, but then she said,

"I've been thinking about the book inspector. If we're correct in believing Finkelstein is behind Chika's abduction, that's the only thing that will keep her safe. If he knows the book is in your hands he'll no longer have need for her as a bargaining tool and he'll want to dispose of her. He'll know he can't just let her go because she'd be able to implicate him, so he'd probably have her killed. We know Bill Carter has no qualms about killing. Poor Chika would probably be found floating in the river, just like the others."

It wasn't the ranting of a distraught mother, but quite rational thinking at a time of such distress. However, the mere idea set Pru off in floods of tears again. Lottie was quickly by her side with an arm around her shoulder; she had almost as much emotion invested in Chika as we had. Pru dried her tears and then said,

"Inspector Stone, can I strike a bargain with you? If you don't find any stolen goods at Finkelstein's den would you consider letting him go free for the time being? That would give me the opportunity to bargain with him for the return of Chika. I could return the book to him and you could be hidden close by to arrest him with the book once Chika was released." He answered,

"The truth is that unless we find stolen property or something to tie him to the abduction, I'm going to have to let him go anyway, but I fear your plan wouldn't work because he wouldn't release her until the book was in his hands. At that point I wouldn't be able to arrest him with the book because he'd have to pass word to whoever is holding her for them to release her. We might just lose the book entirely."

"Wouldn't that be preferable, just to get Chika back?" I said.

"Let's not worry about that for the moment..." the inspector said, "...Let's wait to see what the day brings. I'm certain there'll be contact in one way or another..." he paused to look outside at the inclement weather and turned back to us, " I have a team of men gathered outside and they're co-ordinating a party of concerned volunteers from the neighbourhood, to make a concentrated search of the area. I know you've already searched but I want to go over everything in a more intense way."

Sweet Retribution

Tom and I donned our coats and boots once more and joined the search party. I was a little surprised that the vicar of the church next door was leading the volunteers. We hadn't yet introduced ourselves to him and I think the truth is that we weren't really a regular church-going family, but that didn't seem to matter. As far as he was concerned we were distressed and he felt it his Christian duty to help. The other volunteers seemed to look to him for direction which gave me the impression they must be his usual congregation.

The rain was incessant but the search continued regardless, encouraging home and business occupiers to search their own premises. I believe every possible nook and cranny that could be searched was searched, but of course nothing was found that related to Chika. I never thought that anything would be found because I was convinced she was being held somewhere out of our reach. At the conclusion of the day's searching Inspector Stone returned with us to speak with Pru and Lottie. He began,

"I'm not too disheartened by the fact that we've found nothing. It gives me assurance that she's being held by someone that needs her for bargaining power and we'll be hearing from them very soon."

Chapter25

Inspect Stone's views on Chika's abduction didn't instil the confidence in Pru that he'd intended. She continued to torture herself, accusing herself of neglecting her child. The inspector left saying he must return to Westminster to put more pressure on his prisoner, Finkelstein, and he left his sergeant with us – just in case there was contact.

Within moments of the inspector's departure, Atlas, now recovered, was first to hear another caller. I took hold of his collar and opened to the door to see the Reverend Jackson who had participated in the search. ....He explained that he felt it his duty to offer his condolence and perhaps help with spiritual guidance. Pru led him to the parlour where Tom and Lottie joined us. The reverend gentleman implored us to put our trust in The Lord and began a prayer for the safe return of Chika. His prayers were designed to give us strength and fortitude in this time of distress.

I was only half listening because I could hear footsteps in the room above and I realised that the sergeant was searching the upstairs rooms. I left the others and went to the stairs just in time to see the sergeant leaving Chika's bedroom.

"What are you doing?" I asked.

"I'm doing what I'm asked to do, searching to make sure the child isn't here, and looking for signs of foul play. That's my job."

"What do you mean, 'foul play'?"

"Oh you'd be surprised how many people report someone missing when they've actually done away with them themselves."

This took my breath away. I couldn't believe what he was saying. We were being viewed as possible child murderers. I turned and descended the stairs, leaving him to carry on with his search. Downstairs I kept the matter to myself, I knew it would further upset Pru and although I was offended and angry at what I saw as an accusation, I realised it was a consideration that the police had to make. It was a rather brutal truth that could have been put more tactfully, but then, I didn't associate any of these iron fisted Peelers with any semblance of tact. We just needed to show we had nothing to hide so I didn't complain or argue and what's more, I decided not to tell Pru about what the sergeant was doing.

The inspector returned again that evening and said that Finkelstein had stuck to his story that he knew nothing about Chika's abduction. Nothing had been found at his premises that warranted his further detention and so he had no option but to release him. I expected nothing more of the hateful money lender. No mention had been made to him about the book and so I felt that an advantage.

I discussed it that night with Pru. She was distraught and very tearful, but she was still thinking very clearly. Her view of the situation was that considering Tom's recent foray into Finkelstein's den when he received the knife wound, and more recently my attempt to spy on his dealings when I was badly beaten, it would be more sensible for her to make a direct approach to Finkelstein to strike a bargain, as she was confident his bully-boys wouldn't assault her in the same way. I objected to her taking such a risk and I'm sure neither Tom nor Lottie would approve either, but Pru was desperate for the safety of Chika and once her mind was set, nothing would convince her otherwise. I was sworn to secrecy.

We hardly slept again that night and we'd cried so many tears there could hardly be more tears to cry. I couldn't begin to imagine what Chika was going through. I found it hard to resist the temptation to going outside into the street hoping to see Chika running toward me. I knew in my heart that it was a hopeless idea but sense and reason didn't help me.

.... Before daylight broke, Atlas rose to his feet and gave a little growl that made me jump to my feet in expectation that someone was approaching, but he settled down again on his bed without his usual rush to the door. I couldn't help but to go and check. I opened the door but there was no-one there and I was closing the door again when my eyes caught sight of something on the doorstep. I bent down to examine it as in the dark it wasn't at all clear what it was; a shoe – a child's shoe. I picked it up and carried it into the light – it was one of Chika's shoes, surely, but how did it get there? My heart started to thump as I ran into the street but there was no sign of anyone.

Chapter 26

I needed Pru to tell me I wasn't imagining this, it was Chika's shoe. It was dry despite the relentless rain, and Pru actually held it to her nose and could smell the scent of Chika. Someone must have been watching the house and our activities to have found an opportunity to deposit the shoe. What were they telling us, because this was a deliberate act? Was it a message to tell us that Chika was alive or was this the mind of a sadistic person playing with our emotions?

Inspector Stone took it as an optimistic sign; something to grab our attention. He tried to bolster our spirits with his opinion that we were into the third day since Chika had been taken and we'd soon receive some contact with a ransom demand.

We hadn't thought to let Sandra Chung know about Chika's abduction but when she arrived that morning she told us that Limehouse was alive to the fact. There was intense police activity in the area, searching for Bill Carter and for Chika. Sandra was heartbroken to think that her little pupil had been taken from her family, and she had simply come to offer what help she could. She told us that waiting for the ferry this morning Chika had been the centre of conversation amongst the passengers and one woman in particular had suggested that she could help. "Help, in what way?" asked Sandra.

"The Lord blessed me with special powers. I'm what they call a clairvoyant. I don't talk with spirits beyond the grave or any of that mumbo jumbo. I have visions beyond what normal people see and last night I saw that child being held. The vision was over in a flash but I think I might see more if I could speak to her parents." Sandra told the woman she was coming to see us and that she would mention their conversation. The woman gave no name or address but said she'd be back at the ferry at seven o'clock that evening if anyone would like to contact her.

Sweet Retribution

I was very sceptical, taking the view that the woman was probably a confidence trickster and it brought to mind the gypsy Romany Rose with her crystal ball when I crossed her palm with silver at the fairground. Rose had later confessed to me that she couldn't see into the future at all, or read anyone's mind. She'd relied upon others in the audience to listen to conversations and pick up snippets of information that she could use to her advantage. That had been Pru's stock-in-trade too, she'd used her feminine wiles to trick Finkelstein into parting with the wealth he'd accumulated whilst trading with Lord Bouverie in smuggled gold, silver and precious stones. Surely she wouldn't be taken in by such rubbish; would she?

I was astounded to hear Pru ask Sandra to make contact with the woman again. I was sure that Sandra's meeting with this so called clairvoyant was no mere chance. My perception was that the woman somehow knew Sandra was visiting us and had engineered this meeting and was trying to use the situation to make money out of us. How could Pru be hoodwinked in this way?

Chika had endured a dreadful night of fear and the heartbreak of wondering, '*Is it really true what this cruel woman is saying – that Mama and Papa really don't want me anymore. Why? What have I done to make them feel that way?*'

She shrank into the corner pulling the blanket over her head and wrapping it tight about her as though making a cocoon to shut out the world and all the bad people. She felt a tug on the blanket and heard the harsh tones of the woman, "Come on, get to your feet. We're moving," but before we left she gave me a pencil and a scrap of paper and made me write, dictating, 'Mama, I want to come home'. I couldn't understand – she'd told me Mama and Papa didn't want me, but I just hoped it wasn't true."

Sweet Retribution

Daylight was entering the cabin through the small windows but it was another dismal day that did nothing to help Chika's feelings. There was no breakfast, just another cup of water. The woman hung onto Chika tightly, dragging her along rather than leading her. Stepping off the barge onto the landing stage, the motion of the boat almost caused Chika to fall, but the woman was irritated and just dragged her along. Chika had to quickly regain her balance for fear of reprisal. It wasn't easy to walk on the towpath as it was so muddy. Chika's insignificant little voice asked, *"Where are we going?"* The woman snapped back, "Keep your mouth shut. You'll find out soon enough." It was obvious she was trying to avoid being seen or heard and was keeping to back alleys where at that time of the morning it was unlikely that they'd be seen.

Chika remembered, "I didn't recognise anything of where she was taking me, I'd never been there before, but eventually we arrived at a big house somewhere. There was a sign outside that said, 'Rooms to Let'. The thing I remember most was the noise – I'd never heard anything like it before. It was a loud squawking noise and screeching as though something was in dreadful pain. I thought something or somebody was being tortured which frightened me even more, wondering what was going to happen to me.

"A big fat woman opened the door to us and the woman holding me said to her, "Here she is, and don't let her get away or you know what'll happen." The fat woman said, "She won't escape, I've got just the room. It's high up, too high for her to jump and the door's got good locks."

"The squawking and screeching made me look beyond the fat woman into the hall, down the passage past the staircase, and I could see a large bird with a long tail, with feathers of bright reds and greens, perched in a big cage. I'd never seen or heard such a bird before and I wondered could this be the raven that I'd heard them whispering about?

153

Sweet Retribution

The woman that brought me there took off my shoes saying, "There, she won't want to run very far without shoes on her feet," then she turned and left, leaving the fat woman to drag me inside and up two flights of stairs where she pushed me into a bare room and locked the door. I could still hear the squawking and screeching which made me think that it would be no use crying out for help – people would think it was the bird.

The following morning, the fourth day, Sandra returned to us with the clairvoyant. She appeared to be a woman in her mid-forties, rather overweight and suitably dressed against the weather. She wore gold ear-rings and seemed to have a swarthy facial appearance. I was sure she was a gypsy, but as she spoke I heard an unfamiliar accent, something like that I associated with the midlands. Atlas had recovered from what poison or sedative had been fed to him and was once again his usual protective self, watching her with distrust. I decided it best to confine him to the kitchen whilst we occupied the parlour. I noticed that she was looking about her as though trying to assess our worth. I was extremely suspicious of her.

She introduced herself as Mrs Marie Hope and asked Pru to tell her exactly what had happened and as much information about Chika that we could. She wanted to know Chika's age, what her interests were, even what food she liked – which to me seemed strange. The most important thing she needed she said, was something of her wearing apparel – best of all something she had worn quite recently. Pru appeared quite happy to accommodate her and brought forth the shoe that had mysteriously appeared on the doorstep.

Mrs Hope asked to be left alone with the shoe for a few moments and when we returned to her she said,

"This little shoe speaks volumes to me. Chika is alive and being well treated. She tells me that you should not worry about her." Pru's question was immediate and almost frantic,

"Where, where is she?"

Mrs Hope looked sympathetically on Pru and answered,

"She doesn't know where she is. It's just a room without a view outside."

"What can she hear outside the room?"

"People talking – just [people talking."

I was getting a little irritated, and said,

"Well, you're supposed to be a clairvoyant with this extraordinary vision and you've told us about this vision of Chika being held. If you're genuine, why can't you see where she's being held and who's holding her?" Pru grabbed my arm and said

"Calm down, let Mrs Hope help us in any way she can."

I shook my head in despair to think Pru was being hoodwinked, taken in by this fraudster. Pru, an accomplished confidence trickster, being so naive. She said,

"Take no notice Mrs Hope. Just tell us what we must do to get her back," and the clairvoyant replied,

"I'm not sure. There's something I really don't understand. I'm getting a clear impression that there's some disagreement behind all this. I can't put my finger on it but someone believes you owe them something – a debt? Or could it be that you have something they want?

That put a different aspect upon what she was saying, she had hit a raw nerve with me.

"Alright Mrs Hope, if it's money you're after, how much will it take to get you to leave us alone?"

It was a bit abrupt but I couldn't help it. I genuinely believed that all she wanted was to get money from us. She surprised me with the huffiness of her reply,

"Please don't insult me, money's of no concern to me. I'm trying to help out of the goodness of my heart."

Sweet Retribution

Pru tried hard to placate her and thanked her for her vision, shaking her hand as she left. Mrs Hope promised to return.

Pru followed me into the kitchen, patted Atlas on the head, then turned to me and said,

"I'm sorry I put you through that, I should have said something before she came. Look, she's as phony as they come. I knew that the moment Sandra mentioned about her. I don't know who she is or where she's from but I've taken the opportunity to tell Tom, and he's waiting at Limehouse basin for when she gets off the ferry. He's going to follow her because I believe she's the one who'll be delivering the message. Just think about it for a moment. She knows Chika's being held. She wanted an item of Chika's wearing apparel – not just any item but something she'd worn recently. She wanted to make sure we'd found the shoe, and she's made it plain that we have something that whoever is holding Chika wants rather badly. It all adds up, she's tied up in this. Hopefully, Tom can follow her and find out who she is and where she lives. Perhaps that will lead us to Chika."

My faith in Pru was restored immediately – I should never have doubted her. That crafty, scheming Pru was still on top of her game. It gave me more confidence that we were going to find our daughter. I said,

"If you're correct and she was here to deliver the message – a reminder – that we're holding something that's wanted, it confirms it's Finkelstein behind it all, but it doesn't deliver a demand as such and it doesn't help us to find Chika."
Pru replied,

"I think that was just a tester, she wanted to see our reaction. There'll be something more specific quite soon. Perhaps Tom will bring some good news.

It was well after dark when Tom appeared. He'd waited for the ferry and followed Mrs Hope. He reported that she'd tried to avoid being followed by back-tracking and going out of her way, but he'd persevered and followed her from Limehouse basin onto the canal tow path where she finally boarded an old barge.

After dark he carefully approached the barge and could hear a male voice but was unable to see who it was. He desperately hoped he was going to find Chika but he was disappointed. The only positive thing that came from following her was that the barge had the name 'Raven' painted in ornate black lettering with fancy gold edging on a white background, on the bow.

A decision had to be made now, do we tell Inspector Stone – and risk that he or his men go in ham-fisted and spoil things before we can learn any more – or, do we keep it to ourselves for the time-being on the chance that Mrs Hope will reveal more? On the one hand, Pru seemed to have the confidence of Mrs Hope and it could lead to finding Chika, but on the other hand there was no doubt that Inspector Stone was going to be seriously annoyed that we'd kept it from him.

Chapter 27

"There was always lots of noise from below in the house. I could hear the fat woman screaming and the bird seemed to be mimicking her, and between the two of them the noise was dreadful. I looked out of the window wondering if I could climb out and escape but it was too high and I hadn't any shoes. There wasn't much to see, only other roofs and a haze of smoke from chimneys.

For most of the time I sat on the floor with my back against the wall, wrapped in the blanket I'd been given, lonely and frightened that I was never going to see Mama again. I only saw the fat woman once or twice during the day, when she brought food and water, at all other times the door was kept locked and no-one came near me. With nothing more to occupy my mind I tried to think of other ways I might escape, perhaps slip by her when she brought me food, but I had no shoes. I realised thoughts of escape were pointless, the fat woman was very careful to make sure I couldn't slip by her and I was sure that if I tried she'd give me a hiding. I don't know what she'd been told about me but she said, "You're a wicked young wench to keep runnin' away, but I'll make sure you don't run away agen. Your mother's fed up o' your antics."

I'd cried and cried for so long that now the tears had virtually dried up and I began to accept that this was going to be my life from now on. I was alone and was going to remain alone.

I can't get over how empty the house seems each morning I wake up and there's no Chika to jump on my bed and hug both Pru and me. Even on the coldest of mornings when the window panes were covered with ice, Chika would raise the temperature with her joy and vitality. Here we were in the height of summer and yet the morning seemed cold and dismal without her. I rose and went to the window to look outside and the scene was just as dismal, rain beating down with some ferocity. The fifth day since Chika had been taken and the churning in my stomach seemed never ending, wondering where she was and how she was being treated. I yearned for her to be returned to us as the happy, bright, loving and outgoing child she had been. The feeling of helplessness was overwhelming.

Exhaustion had eventually overcome both of us and we'd finally slept, fitfully but slept never-the-less. I awakened with a band of steel compressing my brain, a headache that seemed to be with me most of the time. Pru and I had spent hours, long into the night, talking about Chika, Bill Carter, Finkelstein, and discussing what we should do regarding Mrs Hope the clairvoyant, and Tom's discovery of the canal barge.

The decision that we finally arrived at was that we should wait for twenty-four hours, expecting Mrs Hope to return, before informing Inspector Stone. Tom's inclination had been to return to the barge and take the offensive, threatening both Mrs Hope and whoever the unknown male was with physical violence forcing them to reveal where Chika was. Neither Pru nor Lottie was in favour of that – violence might jeopardise Chika's safety.

Sandra Chung arrived during the morning. We decided not to reveal to her what we thought about her introduction of Mrs Hope. Sandra took to doing small domestic tasks about the house such as tea-making, feeding Atlas and pot washing, just to relieve Pru of such tedium. She noticed that I was holding my head in my hands and enquired what was wrong. I explained about my continual headache. She said it was due to the pressure of dealing with Chika's abduction. I didn't really need her to tell me that, it was common sense and plain enough for me to realise. She bade me sit down and remove my shoes and socks. I frowned, failing to understand why I should do this, but then she took a small case from her handbag and produced an array of very fine needles the thickness of a human hair.

Sweet Retribution
I was apprehensive of what she intended but she explained she'd been brought up with a Chinese remedy which released pent up forces within the body. I didn't fully understand what she was explaining but she talked of 'Qi' or 'Chee', energy that flowed through meridian points. She began to insert those needles into specific points in my feet and hands. Surprisingly, to have the needles pricking my flesh didn't hurt at all and amazingly, after a short time the headache eased. I wished the problem of Chika could be solved as easily.

Inspector Stone called again in the afternoon. He had nothing new to tell but assured us that the search for Chika was still top priority. I looked across at Pru, wondering whether she'd stick to our agreement not to disclose about the so called clairvoyant, but I needn't have concerned myself. Pru avoided the issue.

That afternoon and evening we waited on tenterhooks for Mrs Hope to appear again but we were disappointed. Perhaps she'd realised we knew she was a fraud, or maybe this was part of the tactics to put us through as much heartache as possible. Tom had spent miserably wet, fruitless hours watching the barge but returned to us late that evening frustrated that we didn't want him to jump aboard the craft and physically drag the truth from her. I was quickly coming round to favour his method. It all meant another fretful and tearful night of waiting and hoping. Should we have told Inspector Stone?

Life for Chika hadn't varied, apart from the food. It had all been what the fat woman called 'soaky' which seemed to be bread in warm milk, but today there was crusty bread spread with something. The rain was splattering against the window panes and all the roofs looked wet and shiny, but nothing made the day seem better for Chika. The loneliness grew each day and she prayed morning and night that Mama and Papa hadn't really deserted her.

Morning broke on day six, another miserable prospect for us. I knew Pru hadn't slept well and so I left her to try to catch up on some rest. Atlas was whining as I descended the stairs and I presumed he wanted to go out into the garden to relieve himself. However, when I opened the back door he steadfastly waited by the front door, continuing to whine. I wondered if he was trying to tell me something and so I unlocked the door and peered out.

There was no-one about but Atlas pushed past me and went directly to the corner of the small porch. It was then I saw what had attracted his attention. Another small shoe, undoubtedly the other of the pair Chika had been wearing. It was dry, having been placed out of the rain. I raced out into the street but there was no-one to be seen. Whoever had placed it there couldn't have retreated more than a few minutes otherwise Atlas would have woken me sooner with his whining, and the shoe would have become wet.

Pru quickly joined me in the kitchen. She looked pale and drained of emotion; absolutely desolate. Breakfast was very simple as both of us had lost our appetite and gloom seemed to pervade the house. Pru picked up Chika's shoe and sat staring at it for several minutes without speaking, then suddenly said,

"What's this?" and she carefully extracted a piece of paper that had been pushed down to the toe. She opened it up and read aloud,

'Mama, I want to come home.'

She burst into tears as she exclaimed, "It's Chika, but what's this?" As she unfolded the last piece of the paper, she said, "There's another message. It's a scrawl I don't recognise,

'Bunch o' Grapes. Midnight tonight. <u>No Peelers.</u>

The last two words were heavily underlined; obviously a threat. It was a scrawl but perfectly legible which, as far as I could see ruled out Bill Carter. No sooner had we discovered the message but Tom was there to join us, almost as though he'd anticipated the contact. He read the message and said,

"I'll go there early, I'll sit and watch until after midnight – make sure you're safe, identify who meets you and then follow them afterwards. We'll perhaps find where they're holding Chika."

It seemed a good idea but I insisted that he didn't intervene. I didn't want things to go sour and lose Chika entirely. Pru questioned whether it should be me or her to go to the Bunch o' Grapes but I argued that we were dealing with dangerous people and insisted that it should be me. The hours seemed to drag as we waited for the time for me to make the rendezvous.

The rain continued to pour down and Jake, the ferryman lamented that the river was awash with debris that was being flushed in from the swollen streams and rivers. He rowed me across and into Limehouse basin as the last ferry-crossing of the evening. I knew that it was going to be a long walk to the bridge and home again in the early hours, and a good soaking if the rain persisted, but it was no real concern if only I could negotiate Chika's release.

I was at the Bunch o' Grapes on Narrow Street with plenty of time to spare. I stood outside in a gateway opposite, in deep shadow watching but only one person emerged, drunkenly staggering and holding on to anything he could to remain on his feet. There was no sign of Tom. As midnight approached there was no-one outside who could have possibly been the one I was to meet so I ventured inside.

It was a dingy atmosphere lit by a gas lamp and the flickering light of a fire that was now burning very low. The ash was spilling out onto the hearth. Just four men occupied the room, sprawled out in chairs around a table and in front of the fire. They all looked as though they were asleep or nearly so, their tankards three-parts empty on the table. The landlord, in his filthy apron, sat alongside, leaning heavily on one of the barrels of ale, fast asleep, with a large white enamelled jug at his feet. No one took any notice of me as I walked in, and I could see no sign of Tom or anyone else who was waiting to meet me. I could do no other than wait as instructed so I gently shook the landlord awake and asked for a tankard of ale.

I waited for what seemed to be an hour, slowly sipping my ale, and watching the door, but no-one came. I decided that whoever had sent the note had me on a wild goose chase, and I rose to my feet to leave. The landlord stepped between me and the exit and asked,

"I bin watchin' yer. Was yer expectin' t' meet somebody?"
I answered "Yes, I was," and he said,

"I thought so. I thought it must be yer. She said I was t' give yer this 'ere note," and he handed me a piece of paper. The message upon it read,

"This was to test you; to make sure you'd done as you were told – to come alone with no funny business. You'll be contacted again."

The landlord explained, "A woman gev it t' me an' paid me sixpence t' give it t' yer when you cum."
I left the Bunch o' Grapes feeling angry and disappointed; no nearer to getting the release of Chika, and also puzzled that Tom wasn't there.

Chapter 28

It was unusual for Tom to break a promise. He'd promised to be at the Bunch o' Grapes to watch when I met the sender of that note and make sure it wasn't a trap. Why hadn't he been there? Something must have happened to him. Soaked to the skin by the incessant rain, I walked towards the bridge, heading home, facing a trudge of some two and a half miles.

Uncomfortable and disheartened I began to think of poor Chika, imagining how distraught she must be, held against her will and separated from her loved ones. What disappointment Pru would feel when I explained it had all been a hoax. My thoughts swung back and forth, one moment wondering about Tom, the next imagining the dreadful conditions and treatment of Chika and then, what diabolical revenge I could exact on those holding her.

I'd probably only walked half a mile, deep in my own tortured imaginings, only half aware of what was going on around me. I could hear the river, a malevolent swish, swirl and splash, and also the continual drumming of the heavy rain drops on the ground, but something else had touched my senses. It was the sound of running feet behind me. I stopped and peered back into the darkness. Gradually the image of a heavy built man running towards me, appeared out of the gloom, surely it was Tom.

Out of breath and doubled up with stitch from his exertions, he took some time to recover sufficient to say,

"I thought I might catch up with you. Let me get my breath and I'll tell you what happened."
He sat for a minute on the keel of an upturned rowing boat that had been dragged up from the river. Through his gasps he managed to continue,

"I got to the ale house a long time before midnight and I sat quietly with my ale. It wasn't particularly busy and I was able to watch the comings and goings of all the customers and as time progressed the place began to empty. Only a few hard drinkers were left, none of them looked sober enough to be the person you were to meet.

"I was astonished to see a woman walk in – you don't get respectable women visiting a place like that at that time of the evening. She was quite intriguing, keeping her face obscured the best she could with a wide brimmed rain-wear hat, and turning her back to me she engaged the licensee in conversation. The light wasn't too good which didn't help so I rose and took my empty tankard to the landlord pretending that I needed a refill.

"As I approached I saw her hand a note to the landlord and she looked towards me with a contemptuous look, as though I was intruding in her conversation. I realised it was the same woman I'd followed from the ferry point to the barge on the canal.

Alarm bells began to ring in my head; this was the woman masquerading as a clairvoyant. There had to be some connection between her and Chika's abduction, what other reason would she have for being there?

"She immediately turned on her heels and left. I now had a dilemma, had she recognised me (I hardly thought she could have done, I'd kept my distance as I'd followed her that first night) and was she the person who had made the appointment in the note. It was obvious that she had no intention of waiting for you to arrive so I had to make a quick decision of what to do. Should I wait for you to appear or should I follow her? I decided to follow her.

"I think I made the right decision. I followed her, not to the barge as I'd expected, but to a gin palace close to the Guangzhou on Limehouse Causeway. I was careful not to be seen. Who do you think she went there to meet?"

I couldn't guess and just shook my head. He carried on,

"None other than Bill Carter, at least I think it was him. I deliberated whether to go in and grab him – I so wanted to beat the living daylights out of him – if only I could have been sure – but I realised it was more important to find Chika than risk being wrong."

Despite being soaked, I said,

"Come on, let go back to that gin palace, we can easily take Carter and force him to tell us where Chika is."

Tom was as eager as me to get hold of Bill Carter and I could quite imagine what terrible revenge he would take, but he said,

"We could go back and we could take him – if it is him – but what if I'm wrong, or what if he escapes; what if Chika isn't there? Then we've made the problem of finding her worse. Let's go back to the Bunch o' Grapes and find out what the note she gave to the landlord was all about."

"I can tell you that. She gave him sixpence to watch out for me and to give me the note." I handed Tom the slip of paper but without light he couldn't read it. I told him that it said the meeting was to test whether I'd come alone as instructed. They're purposefully putting us through more agony – just twisting the knife to make it more painful. It says we'll be contacted again."

With the prospect of another contact we decided to return home and await that contact, Bill Carter would have to wait for another day but our day would surely come soon.

I arrived home soaked and despondent to an anxious greeting from Pru. Only the warm glow of the oil lamp lightened the gloom. Even Atlas greeted me with expectation that quickly waned as he realised Chika wasn't with me. As I discarded my sodden clothing I explained,

"It was just a test to see if I involved the peelers. The landlord had been paid to give me this note," and I handed her the paper. I continued, "Tom was there early and mingled with the customers intending to watch and make sure I was safe. He saw a woman enter the ale-house and approach the landlord. She was obviously giving him the note with instructions to look out for me.

Sweet Retribution

Fortunately Tom recognised her – it was the woman who came here pretending to be a clairvoyant. When she left he followed her to a gin palace near the Guangzhou. He's not sure but he believes it was Bill Carter she met there."

Pru wiped her eyes and read through the note and remained thoughtful for a moment before saying,

"It doesn't say how we'll be contacted. If that woman calls here again what are we going to do?"
I'd thought of nothing else all the way home and replied,

"I've come around to thinking like Tom. It's time to stop this game, letting them dictate to us. I think we should go on the offensive. If we can get hold of her we can force her to tell us where Chika is."

"How do we force her?"

"Lock her in the attic until she tells us."

"What if she doesn't know where Chika is?"

"She's bound to know. She's mixed up in this as deep as she could be."

"Just think back to Dina. She was forced to work for her husband and only knew she was looking for the book. She didn't know why or what it was all about. It's possible that this woman is being used in the same way and only doing what she's forced to do. If that's the case where does that leave us?"

"Well, what about the canal barge or that gin palace, why can't we force our way in those and tear the place apart until they tell where she is?

"Jack, I'm afraid of what they'll do with Chika if we try anything like that. The book is what's behind it all; Finkelstein and the book. He knows the police are involved and he's got others to do the dirty work, hoping it can't be pinned on him. I've made up my mind – I'm going to confront him; no police; no strong arm tactics; just a straight forward face to face on my own."

"Pru, you can't. You know what his men did to both me and Tom. What makes you think they'll be any different just because you're a woman?"

"I'll take that risk. I think he'll be more intent on getting his hands on that book."

It was clear she'd made up her mind and nothing was going to persuade her otherwise.

It was almost daylight before we finally retired, only to spend hours awake, fretting about our child. Neither of us really slept and we arose to day number seven of our nightmare, feeling distraught and washed out. My inner thoughts were continually chastising me, telling me we'd brought all this despair upon ourselves. I know we'd been as guilty as one another in striving to become rich. Pru perhaps more-so in the initial stages, but her driving force was to exact revenge upon Lord Bouverie for his ill treatment of her deceased husband and in doing so outwitting and obtaining some of the ill-gotten gains of Finkelstein, but I'd been just as guilty in forging the document that made it possible. Then, when Finkelstein's mobsters had sought to intimidate us, she'd taken the book – his personal record of his illegal transactions – which was really at the heart of Chika's abduction. Oh, if only we could turn back time. Why not just give the book back or, better still, why not hand it to the police and let them deal with Finkelstein? Why was Pru so determined not to involve the police?

Chapter 29

After a miserly breakfast – our stomachs unwilling to take much – Pru set off for Westminster in determined fashion and by mid-day had returned with her package. She unwrapped the paper and threw that brown leather covered book down on the table before me, saying,

"There, that's what it's all about."
It was the first time she'd allowed me to have my hands on it. I opened it up only to be confused by the contents – page after page of scribble that appeared to me to be some sort of code. The only things that I could decipher were names – probably all of them hiding a true identity. It wasn't until I'd flipped through to the last few pages that I realised why Pru had been so reluctant to hand it over to the police. There, in plain print and underlined, was repeated reference to her. I must have had a frown of confusion on my face as I'd turned the pages and she said,

"Do you see now why he's so anxious to get it back?"
I shook my head and answered,

"Well frankly, no. It all appears to be in code. The only thing I recognise is your name."

"No, it's not in code – except the names – just think for a minute, he's Jewish isn't he? What does that tell you?"

"I don't know, just tell me."

"Well, I didn't understand what was written either but I took it to a Jewish friend and he told me what I should have realised from the start. It's written in Yiddish, the vernacular or idiom of Hebrew used by Jewish people widely throughout Europe. He explained that Jews, especially those from Germany, were known as Ashkenazi Jews and spoke this Yiddish idiom.

I still don't understand what's written here but he could see that it was a damning record that the Excise people would love to get hold of. He didn't read enough of it to reach the point where I'm mentioned. I've had it locked away in the vault of a bank ever since. Finkelstein's done all he could to get it back from me and abducting

Chika is the latest. It shows just how valuable it is to him and to what lengths he'll go to recover it."

"So, what's the next move?"

"I thought it was my insurance against him trying to do things against me – like burning down the warehouse – but that was before I understood that the book implicated me too. I still hung onto it because I saw it as a means of obtaining some of that fabulous wealth it contains, but now I've learned the lesson; Chika's life is more important. I thought about tearing out the pages where I'm mentioned and handing it over to the police, but Finkelstein is so wicked he might do something drastic like harming Chika. I can't bear the thought of her being found floating in the river so I've decided to hand it back to him providing he releases her."

Now, the panic in me was rising to an extraordinary level. I'd known fear before but this was something different, something I'd never experienced – fear for someone else – my Pru. She was going into Finkelstein's den – completely alone. No matter what I said to dissuade her or to let me accompany her; was dismissed with some determination. His band of thugs had already shown how violent they could be. They'd knifed Tom in the side; would they show that sort of violence to a woman? Would they hold her hostage like Chika? No matter how I pleaded or tried to convince her of the terrible danger she was putting herself in, made any difference. "I've got what he wants and he knows he's not going to get it if he harms me or Chika," was her response.

Within minutes of Pru asserting herself in her decision to visit Finkelstein alone, there was a knock at the door accompanied by a deep throated growl from Atlas. I rushed to grasp his collar as Pru answered the door. I was amazed at the brazen audacity of the woman; it was the so called Mrs Hope, the clairvoyant. Pru was as charming and welcoming as could be and invited her inside. I waited until she was in the parlour before securely locking and bolting the door, still holding onto Atlas who continued to show an aggressive attitude toward this visitor. This heartless fraud was going nowhere.

Pru, with a quiet charm, invited Mrs Hope to sit, and she drew up a stool to sit opposite. I stayed by the parlour door, still holding Atlas, fervently hoping that the harlot would give me cause to release him. She began,

"I've thought of nothing but Chika since I last saw you, and being here in her home makes me feel very close to her. She seems to be trying to send a message, telling me that she's being well cared for but desperate to come home. I'm also getting the impression that she wants you to give back something you're holding so that the people holding her will release her."

Pru smiled sweetly at her and said,

"Is this what you mean?" and produced the book. Mrs Hope looked quite startled and tongue tied for a moment, but quickly regained her composure and replied,

"I do believe you're right. If I could hold it for a moment I might get something from it." Still smiling sweetly Pru replied,

"Oh no Mrs Hope – if that's your real name – you're not getting your hands on this. We've learned a lot about you and you're going to regret your part in all this."
As though on cue Atlas growled and curled his lip. Mrs Hope's face drained of colour and she spluttered,

"I don't know what you mean. I came here to help you, not be threatened."

"It might surprise you that we've had you followed and we saw who you met..." *which was an exaggeration of the truth "...*when you went to the Raven – the canal barge, and you were observed at the Bunch o' Grapes inn when you left the note with the landlord. Again, you were followed to the gin palace near the Guangzhou where you again met Bill Carter. You are a fraud and you're up to your neck in this no matter how much you deny it."

Sweet Retribution

Pru's manner was still so very quiet and controlled but now it had adopted a very sinister edge to it. Mrs Hope jumped to her feet and turned to flee but I stood in the doorway with a very excited Atlas. His lip was still curled and he was straining against my hold on his collar. She backed away taking refuge behind the sofa. Pru, still sitting and acting in a very placid manner, said,

"Oh, don't worry Mrs Hope; nothing drastic is going to happen to you...**yet**! But please sit down again because you're not leaving here until you've decided to tell the truth and disclosed where Chika is being held." The woman suddenly seemed to lose her ability to speak and her brazen attitude changed to a very nervous and fearful one.

It took some minutes of a silent stand-off before she spoke again. Realisation had finally dawned that her subterfuge was over and she needed to save her own skin. Her voice was now so quiet and subdued that it was almost inaudible saying,

"I'm sorry, I had to do it. They forced me."
I could see she was playing the sympathy card, and asked,

"Who; who forced you?"

"You know who I'm talking about – that wicked money lender from Bread Street and his men. They own me body and soul. My husband owed a fortune in borrowed money before he died – that I knew nothing about, - and now I'm at their mercy and I have to do as I'm told."
There was a resonance with what happened to Dina in what she was saying, but Pru, without being openly hostile, said in quite a matter of fact manner,

"Don't expect any sympathy from us, what you're doing is more than criminal, it's wicked beyond words. The only way you're going to make me feel any better towards you is if you tell us where Chika is."
The woman began to weep and covered her face with both hands and replied in a snivelling way,

"I wish I could, I really do, but I just don't know. They've never told me."

"I don't believe you. You're telling us you don't know where she is yet you've tried to make us believe she's being well treated; you've known all along about her shoes, and the personal message from her, yet you're telling us you don't know where she is."

"Honest, I don't know." She wailed.

"Well, who's been delivering her shoes here? Who's been watching us? Who's been giving you your instructions?" asked Pru.

... "You called him Bill Carter – but I only know him as Billy. He's nasty; uses his fists a lot; a really violent sort. I had to do as I was told or get beaten," she answered.

"But you mentioned the money lender; does this 'Billy' work for him?"

"Yes, he's his main man, does all his nasty work."

Pru hesitated and looked at me as though deciding what to do, but before I could interject she turned again to Mrs Hope and said in a forceful manner,

"I'm going to pay your money lender a visit but you're going to stay here until I get back. Don't think of trying to escape because I can assure you my dog will tear you apart at the first opportunity."

Mrs Hope settled down on the sofa with her head in her hands quietly sobbing as Pru left to visit Finkelstein, leaving me desperately afraid for her safety.

Chapter 30

I spent the afternoon pacing back and forth, doing needless little things such as picking up, then replacing, ornaments on the mantle shelf, straightening cushions; in fact anything to occupy my mind and take my worry away from what was happening to Pru. The situation was made worse by having to detain the clairvoyant. She was still in the front parlour with Atlas on guard at the door. There was no way she could escape and Atlas would attack if she tried.

My heart skipped a beat when there was a knock at the door and with some trepidation I hesitated to unlock until I had asked who was there. My worry caused me to imagine Finkelstein's henchmen, or perhaps Inspector Stone at the door, but my fears subsided as I recognised the voice – it was Tom Blood – and I quickly unlocked. He saw the distress in my face and the nervous fidgeting of my hands and asked,

"What's wrong? Where's Pru?" As he spoke he glanced into the front parlour and saw Mrs Hope, and continued, "What's she doing here?"
I answered,

"She came here with the same clairvoyant rubbish that she spoke before but Pru challenged her – told her she'd been followed and seen to meet up with Bill Carter and she's admitted it was all a scam, so I'm holding her here until Pru gets back."

"Gets back? Where's she gone?"

"Gone to see Finkelstein – face to face."

"My God, is she crazy? Can't we stop her – how long has she been gone?

"Well over an hour. My stomach's been churning with nerves ever since she left."

"Jack, Jack, Jack, why did you let her go?"

"You know Pru. She has a mind of her own and nothing I said would persuade her not to go. She's fetched that book from the bank and she's hoping to use it as a bargaining tool to get Chika back."

Sweet Retribution

"OK, you stay here and watch her..." indicating Mrs Hope, "...and I'll run over to Bread Street. If they're holding Pru or if they've harmed her in any way I'll break some heads," and with that he was gone. He set off at a trot, pacing himself for the mile-and-a-half distance to Bread Street, with a determination to try to intercept Pru on her journey there, or at least prevent any harm befalling her. However, she'd had too much of a start on him and despite his best efforts she'd entered Finkelstein's lair ahead of him.

I spent the next four hours of unbearable anxiety pacing the floor, imagining the unbearable torture the scoundrel was putting her through, but to my relief she returned apparently unscathed. The dreadful worry was now replaced by a desire to take her in my arms, kiss her and show her how much I was relieved to have her back safely, but all I could think to say was,

"What happened? What did he say?" She began,

"Finkelkstein smiled that sickly smile and began wringing his hands together in that avaricious manner that's so much an evil trait of his, and he greeted me as though he was pleased to see me, saying,

...."So, my dear, I take it that at last you've decided to see reason?"

One of his henchmen was quickly between us but Finkelstein waved him away, obviously feeling quite safe. I gave him an icy stare before saying,

"Reason? I'll not lower myself to say what I really think of you. To take a child from her parents and use her as a lever against me – there's no 'reason' in that...you're beyond contempt."

"Ah now, my dear, you have things all wrong. I've not taken your child. I'm sure you know that the venerable boys of Mr Peel took me away and placed me in a cell accusing me of this crime, and then went through this place with a tooth-comb but they didn't find anything – as if they would – and me, a fine upstanding pillar of the community? How absurd. They had to let me go."

175

I asked him,

"Are you telling me that you know nothing about Chika's disappearance?"

"Oh no my dear. That's not what I said; I said I've not taken her. There's a difference – I'm sure you can see?"

"So that means you know who took her and where she is?"

"Er, I might have learned something. It doesn't do to jump to conclusions."

"Do you know who's got her or not?"

"Oh, that depends, doesn't it?"

"Depends? Depends upon what?"

"Well, now we're back to what I said when you arrived. Have you decided to see reason?"

"I take it you're referring to the little brown book you've been so anxious to retrieve?"

"Exactly my dear, my ledger – that little brown book you took from me."

"I didn't come here to fight or have an argument with you; I came to make you an offer. That book is safely locked away in a bank vault and has been ever since I obtained it, but just to put your mind at ease, no-one else has ever seen it or knows about it. I'm now offering you the return of that book or ledger as you called it, in exchange for the safe return of my daughter."

"That would seem a fair exchange but that always supposes that it's in my power to secure her release."

"Don't give me that rubbish, I'm not here to play games, this is an ultimatum. I know that whether or not you're holding her yourself, or if someone else has her, you're behind it all, and unless she's safely released, that book will find itself in the hands of the police."

"Don't be hasty my dear, we may both have regrets if that should happen. Be assured I'll do what I can to have her returned to you. I'll contact you tomorrow." He looked long and hard at me in a whimsical way, as though a fanciful thought had crossed his mind. Then he continued,

"You know my dear, if we'd met much earlier in life and on different terms, we could have made a formidable partnership."
My response was to wrinkle up my nose in a show of disgust and say,

"Huh...I'd have to be desperate to partner a despicable reptile like you." He simply gave a sickly smile but didn't respond.

"I was about to turn on my heels and leave but then I decided to put a little emphasis on the deal. I reached into my pocket and pulled out the derringer. He almost jumped out of his skin, reaching out with his palms turned up towards me, stuttering, "Steady...steady. Please be careful with that thing."
I sneered at him and said,

"You've no need to cringe, I just wanted to show you that I'd come prepared...prepared to kill you...if you'd refused to let my child go. So, now you know what this means to me and if you don't fulfil your part of the bargain I'll be back."

"I half expected his henchman to spring forward but the sight of that derringer made him hesitate. I stepped out into the miserable rain soaked street that seemed almost refreshing after the atmosphere in Finkelstein's lair.

"I'd only gone a few steps when Tom came bounding towards me. He told me you'd informed him where I'd gone and he'd feared for my safety. I didn't say as much to him but I thought that after he'd run all that distance he was in no fit state to have done anything to save me. As we walked home together, I gave him the full account of what happened, just as I'm telling you."

"So, where does it leave us?"

"We wait until tomorrow when he said he'd contact me."

"What do we do with this woman, do we let her go?"

"I think we've got as much out of her as we can. I tend to believe her when she says she was being used. She obviously doesn't know where Chika is. I don't want to compromise anything with Finkelstein so let's let her go."

Lottie arrived to complicate matters. She was always there to lend support, but her view of the situation differed from Pru's. She wasn't at all in favour of releasing the woman until Chika had been recovered. She argued that to release Mrs Hope was to throw away any bargaining power. However, Pru explained,

"I've spent time with her and I believe her when she says she'd been forced into this. When I think back to what happened to Dina, it makes me think that she's expendable, they won't care what happens to her, and she'll probably end up in the Thames too. I don't think she knows where Chika is, and all we'll be doing is making more problems for ourselves with Finkelstein. I'm going to let her go."

Pru's mind was set, and she went into the parlour and said to Mrs Hope,

"We're letting you go, but before you leave let me give you a warning. We're desperate to recover our child and understand this, that if we find you're involved in this any more than you've told us, or if anything happens to Chika, I personally will find you and believe me, I shall take my pound of flesh."

Lottie's face expressed the sheer venom she felt towards this woman and said, "I can assure you, we'll find you and I personally will tear your heart out."

Mrs Hope looked at Pru with such a sorrowful face and tears streaming down her cheeks, and replied, "I'm sorry; this is the last you'll see of me. I never wanted to have any part of this." Her miserable apology washed over Pru who snapped,

"You knew what you were up to and you knew what anguish you were putting us through even though you say you were forced into it. I just hope you suffer for what you've done," and with that I pushed her out through the front door and locked it behind her.

Sweet Retribution

Little did she know that Pru had arranged with Tom to be waiting, hidden nearby, to follow when she left. Concealed in the church porch, he'd waited for the moment she was released, and watched as she hurried away – not towards the ferry as he'd expected, but after looking about her in a furtive manner she made towards a brick built former carpenter's work shed that long had the look of dereliction.

The building was almost opposite our home, a perfect place from which to watch us. Tom let her disappear inside and then approached, careful that he shouldn't be seen. He hesitated at a grime laden window hoping to see inside but the cobwebs and years of filth, plus the low level of light in the building made it impossible. He could hear a raised male voice, obviously displeased, but was unable to catch what was being said. He crept round to the doorway which had been left ajar.

Pressed tight against the crumbling brick-work, he cautiously peered inside to see a rough looking man who had hold of Mrs Hope with one hand on her throat and slapping her face with the other. He was too intent upon hitting her to notice Tom slide in through the doorway.

An arm snaked around the man's throat dragging him backwards which took him completely by surprise. The action was so rapid and forceful that there wasn't time or opportunity to resist. Tom twisted him over as he fell, so that he lay on his stomach and with his knee planted firmly in the man's back, struggle as he might, he was unable to resist or escape.

Tom worked quickly to remove the man's leather trouser belt and dragging his arms behind him, fastened them securely together at the wrist to prevent any resistance. He looked around for Mrs Hope but she'd disappeared. Forcing the man to his knees, for the first time he was able to see his face, and there was the scar. Already fired up with adrenalin coursing his body, Tom was at last face to face with the man who had entered his home and abused his wife. He'd spent long hours thinking of this moment and what he would do to the evil man to exact his revenge. Now, his clenched fists itched to deal out some retribution. The crushing blow that followed jolted Billy Carter's head back and saliva flew from his mouth and blood began to drip from his nose but Billy, unable to protect himself, simply looked Tom in the eye and sneered, as if to say, 'Is that all you can do?' Infuriated, Tom struck him again, this time directly in the eye and for good measure aimed a well directed kick to his groin.

The anger and pent up emotion was boiling over in Tom and he turned away as Billy writhed in agony on the floor. The compulsion was to end this evil villain's existence, or at the very least to surgically remove his genitals. He fingered the knife in his pocket and seriously considered doing just that, but at that moment realised there was the issue of Chika.

Chapter 31

Blood trickling down his face, his torn shirt front, the reddening and swelling around his eye, all spoke volumes as Billy Carter was dragged to our front door. Tom gave a little ironic chuckle and said,

"He's had a little *'accident'* he fell on his face."
Atlas was there in a flash and with what seemed to be an extraordinary perception he sank his teeth into Billy's thigh. Billy screamed and writhed but Tom wasn't letting him go: neither was the dog. I instinctively grabbed Atlas's collar and pulled him away, but upon reflection I ought to have let the dog do his worst. It would have been just desserts for this miscreant who had caused so much misery and pain to so many.

Pru and Lottie quickly followed to the door to find out what the commotion was all about. Lottie was first to react and rushed at Billy, sinking her finger-nails into his face and raking them down his cheeks, leaving considerable scratches. Things were getting out of hand but who could blame Lottie for her vicious attack considering what had happened at the hands of this thug. Pru pulled her back as Lottie said

"Let me get his eyes," but Billy Carter was dragged inside and thrown onto the floor of the parlour where Atlas was set to watch. Pru put her arm around Lottie and led her into the kitchen – it was plain the trauma had returned to her being face to face with her attacker.

The dog's training to sit and guard was a testing time for him. His eyes were fixed exclusively on Billy; saliva dripped from his mouth as he continued to emit that low throaty growl, that made him appear to be looking forward to the next bite.

Tom was first to speak, offering to go to Westminster to alert Inspector Stone that the murderer had been caught, but Pru interjected,

"Wait a minute, let us not rush into anything; let's give it some thought. We've not asked him about Chika yet."
Tom replied,

"I don't think he'll tell us anything, he such a nasty, surly rat, he'll probably take pleasure from keeping us guessing."

"Oh we'll see about that, I think he'll probably be only too pleased to tell us what we want to know – Atlas has a way of persuading people," replied Pru.

In taking hold of Atlas's collar again it was almost as though a switch had been thrown. He strained against my hold and his body reacted like a coiled spring, ready to plunge at Billy who, still seated on the floor, shrank away into the corner, terrified. I spoke calmly to the dog – but actually for the purpose of letting Billy hear – said,

"Steady boy, steady. I'll let you have him in a minute or two if he doesn't co-operate..." and then to increase Billy's terror, I continued, "...He's not been fed today. He only eats raw meat – the fresher the better." Billy's face was beginning to stream with perspiration.

....Pru, careful not to get between Atlas and Billy, bent down so that her face was on the same level as his, and with a steely malevolence in her eye, and venom in her tone of voice, she said,

"I want you to understand that this dog will kill you; tear you apart, at my command. He's trained to go for your scrotum first and when he's done his worst he'll go for your throat. You'll not survive and your pain will be excruciating. I'll stand and watch with a smile on my face. Do you understand what I'm telling you?"

Billy couldn't even speak to reply, his throat just dry and constricted, he gulped and nodded his head. She continued,

"The only chance you've got to live is to tell me where you're holding my daughter."

"I'm not holding her," he whined.

"OK Atlas he's all yours," Pru snapped.

"No, no, don't let him go. Please don't let him go," he pleaded.

"You know where she is. This is your last chance; where is my daughter?"

"Honest, I've not got her. I've only done what I've been told." Carter's whinging showed through, there was no bravado now – the bully boy was showing his true cowardly colours. Tom stepped forward,

"Don't let Atlas have him – give me the pleasure..." he said drawing his knife, "...I'm going to castrate the bastard," and he took hold of Billy's breeches as though to expose his genitals, at which Billy lost control of his bladder, soaking his trousers.

...."Please, please, don't. I can only tell you what the Jew said. He said she was in the hands of a woman somewhere in Limehouse, that's all I know. Let me go please, I'll be no trouble to you again."

Lottie was waiting the chance to turn the screw on Billy and said, "You're going nowhere until I've finished with you, I'm personally going to castrate you," and she turned to Tom and pleaded with him to give her his knife. Whether she was truly intent upon using it or whether it was another attempt to frighten Billy, we shall never know, as Tom refused to let her have it. Never-the-less, the fear in Billy was mounting; his eyes showed abject terror, and once more he grovelled, "Let me go, please let me go. I'll get your daughter free, just let me go."

"How can you get her free if you don't know where she is?" snapped Pru.

"The Jew trusts me. I'll find out who the woman is who's holding her, I promise," he snivelled.
There was a slight lull in conversation and Tom turned to look at us probably thinking that we were truly considering letting Billy Carter go free. He beckoned us aside and whispered to us,

"You seem to be contemplating what to do. Look, we can't keep him here, so we've got two options we either turn him over to the peelers or we let him go. We can surely disregard his promise to find Chika and release her if we let him go because in my opinion he'll flee and that'll be the last we see of him. We've tried so long to catch him and we know he'll get convicted of murder and hang once the police get hold of him. If he knew where Chika was I'm sure he'd have told us. At least with Finkelstein we've got a trade off. He desperately wants the return of that book and it's in his own interests to release Chika to get it, so I don't see any advantage in keeping him any longer. My advice is to turn him over to the police and be done with him."

There were nods of approval from the rest of us – it was obvious to us that it was both impractical and undesirable to keep him any longer, we'd had our revenge and the law would do the rest. Tom set off for Westminster and Inspector Stone.

The huge pair of black carriage horses with the iron barred prison van came to a halt outside our house, drawing onlookers to their garden gates and front doors despite the rain, to see the spectacle. The driver remained sitting on the box seat, reins in hand, keeping the pair at the halt. The horses were showing some white frothy foam on their flanks indicating they had galloped here and they stood impatiently tossing their heads, and scraping the ground with their hooves, making their harness jingle. Billy Carter was marched limping heavily, hands manacled behind him, a police escort either side, and thrown unceremoniously into the van, the door slammed shut after him.

That slamming of the door seemed to be a signal to the horses, still on a tight rein, to begin to dance on the spot ready to race off again. The escorts climbed aboard and with a clatter of hooves the spectacle sped away. Grit and pebbles kicked up by the pair flew in all directions, leaving onlookers to gasp and wonder what had been happening on their doorstep.

Inspector Stone remained with us in the kitchen partaking tea whist we told our tale of how we came to detain the murder suspect. The euphoria of finally ridding ourselves of this dangerous monster was sadly heavily over-shadowed by the fact that Chika was still not found. Now we were faced with the unbearable wait until tomorrow for some form of contact from Finkelstein. Inspector Stone was still kept in ignorance of the arrangement.

Lottie and Tom stayed with us until late, mulling over the happenings of the day and the prospects of what might happen tomorrow. The fake clairvoyant, Mrs Hope, came into the conversation again as we wondered whether we'd been too lenient in releasing her. I couldn't help but feel I'd been gullible in believing that she'd been forced into her part of the abduction and that she knew nothing of where Chika was being held. That feeling was exacerbated by Tom's account that she ran straight back to Billy Carter. I had the feeling it wouldn't be the last we'd hear of her.

Another long sleepless night of worry followed, mixed with anticipation of some form of contact from Finkelstein to bring Chika home to us.

Chapter 32

On any other night the constant patter of the rain against the window panes would probably have been enough to lull us to sleep, but not this night. The howling of the wind and the flashes of lightning were a perfect accompaniment to our mood of dark despair. Still lying awake as daylight broke, the quiet was suddenly disturbed by the savage growling of Atlas as he scratched frantically at the door. I jumped out of bed in an instant, pulling on my britches over my night attire as I scrambled barefoot down the stairs.

Grabbing Atlas by his collar, I fumbled to turn the key and unlock the door, and inching it slightly open to get sight of whoever was outside, my caution suddenly disappeared as I saw Sandra Chung standing there, dripping wet. Even Atlas calmed down, accepting Sandra as no threat.

....Inviting her inside, I apologised for my state of dress. Pru followed me downstairs, more appropriately dressed and somewhat excited, believing that this must be the contact we awaited. However, her excitement waned when she realised that it was Sandra, but was concerned to see the worry lines on her face. She took Sandra's hand and said,

"Sandra, what's the matter? Whatever brings you here at this hour of the morning and in such a state?" Sandra began,

"I didn't know what to think. I was awakened in the night by someone banging on the door. I was afraid to answer it at first but it was so persistent I eventually had to see who it was. It was a woman – I've no idea who she was, it was dark and she was careful to hide her face. She said she'd been sent to deliver a message but she couldn't or wouldn't say who'd sent her. It seemed so strange that she knew me and knew I was a friend of yours. I strained my eyes in the darkness to see her face, but I couldn't. Somehow, whether it was the voice I'm not sure, but something about her seemed vaguely familiar. Why she should pick me I couldn't understand but she said I was to deliver a message to you. I asked her why she couldn't deliver the message herself but she wouldn't explain. I quizzed her to know what was so urgent that she had to wake me in the night to deliver it but she wouldn't enlighten me, just insisted it was urgent. I wouldn't have agreed but with Chika being missing I thought it must be connected so I've hurried here to let you know."

"What was the message?" I asked; I might have sounded rather abrupt but I was so anxious to know. I realised this must be the contact we were desperately waiting for. Sandra replied,

"She simply said, '*Meet me by the 'Raven' – the barge moored at the Regent Dock – two o'clock this afternoon. I'll take you to Chika. Come alone and bring it with you. If anyone else appears with you, the deal's off.'* I was puzzled and asked her about what she meant by 'it' and she said you'd know what she meant. Then she asked me to repeat the message, checking to make sure I'd got it right. As she turned to leave I asked her, "How will they recognise you?" and she replied 'Don't bother your head about that. I'll recognise whoever comes."
I assured Sandra she'd done the right thing and I thanked her. She stayed for breakfast and we mulled over the implications of the message and the identity of the woman, before she set off again in the deluge for the ferry and home.

Pru and I were excited to think we'd be getting Chika home and considered what we'd do to make sure she stayed safe in future. I reflected on the message Sandra brought and there was something about the name of the barge – the 'Raven' – that struck a chord in my memory and realised it was the barge Tom had followed the clairvoyant to on the River Lea. I was convinced that the mysterious woman delivering the message to Sandra, anxious to hide her identity in the darkness, was none other than Mrs Hope.

My mind was full of questions that couldn't be answered; where would she lead us, surely somewhere close by? Would we be face to face with Finkelstein; surely he wouldn't trust anyone else to get their hands on that book? It was time to involve Tom and Lottie, sensible minds who would offer good advice.

Tom listened intently to the story and his eyes lit up as he heard the name 'The Raven' as the barge where we were to meet, and he reminded me that he'd followed the clairvoyant back to that barge. Just like me he was convinced that the mysterious woman, instigating the message, must be Mrs Hope. Her vow before we'd released her, that we'd hear no more of her in relation to Chika's abduction, had actually meant nothing. Tom said,

"We're assuming that it was Finkelstein that sent the message and he's demanded that Pru goes alone – I don't like it." Turning to Pru he continued,
"He's not likely to have Chika there, ready to hand over, until he's got his hands on that book, and so if you do go alone you can't have the book with you otherwise he can just take it from you and you'll have no bargaining power. You've got to insist that he produce Chika first and then you can signal for one of us to bring the book forward. I'm also going to suggest to you that you have both Derringers – and make sure they're both primed and ready to use."

"What if it's all a plan to snatch the book without letting Chika go?" I asked.

"That's exactly why I say the book must remain with you, and you must be within signalling distance to bring it forward if everything goes well with the exchange. The meeting is for two o'clock so I'm going to be there early. Where-ever she takes you Pru, I'm going to follow. I need to be close at hand just in case things turn nasty," Tom said.
We left Tom to prepare himself for the task in hand whilst we returned home with an hour to spare to prime the Derringers and try to settle our nerves before setting

off to find The Raven. The anticipation of being reunited with Chika was thrilling but the nervous fear that things might go awry was overwhelming. I felt tempted to swear to myself that if things did go wrong I'd break someone's head but my more reasonable and rational inner self told me they'd still have Chika and she'd be the one to suffer.

Taking the ferry across to Limehouse Basin, the nervousness increased and Pru was unusually quiet. I tried for the umpteenth time to persuade her to let me be the one to go forward and do the negotiating but she'd have none of it. Finkelstein was expecting her and she was determined to go forward herself. She said, "There's no negotiating to be done. The arrangements are set – it's Chika for the book – nothing more, nothing less."

When we alighted the ferry we went straight to the Regent dock and found the barge, The Raven, tied up to the mooring rings. There was lots of activity on the quay side and aboard the other vessels moored there, but there was no sign of anyone aboard the barge, and no obvious sign of Tom in the vicinity. There was still half an hour to go before the designated time for the meeting so we walked back along the quay to a convenient spot where I could remain unobserved but in visual contact with Pru.

The persistent rain was of no significance as our purpose there filled our minds. I felt inside my shirt, fingering the book, to give myself confidence that the bargaining chip to release Chika was still safe. Time seemed to drag and the stomach churning nervousness increased with every minute.

With ten minutes to spare Pru returned to the barge and stood anxiously waiting. My eyes were peeled and focussed all around Pru but I could see no-one to connect with Finkelstein or his cohorts, what's more there was no sign of Tom either. A church clock somewhere close at hand struck two and it was followed almost immediately by a flash of sheet lightning and a rumble of thunder. It seemed to be an ominous warning of what could be expected. The high state of the Thames water in the basin, and the volume of the cascade from the River Lea, made the usually calm and sheltered mooring, rather turbulent. Even the lock gates of the canal had to be opened to relieve the volume of extra water. The wind was whipping the waves against the wall of the quay and spray was flying through the air. The clippers and other vessels idling there were rocking violently, their masts swaying heavily. The weather couldn't have been much worse.

As I shielded my eyes from the stinging lash of the rain, I saw a female dressed in heavy rain-wear approach Pru from the shelter of a warehouse. She was too distant and too heavily garbed to distinguish who it was, but I suspected it was the clairvoyant woman. The thought went through my mind that her sympathy ploy whilst we held her, had worked – we'd all too readily accepted that she was being forced into this, but now it was obvious she was the one orchestrating it.

There was a brief conversation between them before she led Pru off, towards a two masted schooner tied up at the dock. I watched as they clambered up the gang-plank, holding tightly to the safety rope, as everything moved precariously to the rise and fall of the water and the rocking of the vessel. I could see no activity aboard and Pru and the unknown female disappeared into a cabin aft. Instinctively, I moved closer trying not to become obvious, but my anxiety increased now that I couldn't see Pru.

I must let Pru describe what was happening. She said,
"I thought it had the makings of a hoax. I'd stood there beside the Raven as instructed, in the pouring rain. The church clock had just struck two and still no-one came to meet me. The whole basin was suddenly lit up by a flash of sheet lightning and the thunder roared, making me rather more afraid than I'd felt until this point. Just as my feelings were turning to despair, a woman approached from the warehouse behind me. She was dressed

against the weather but even in those clothes I recognised her; it was the so called clairvoyant, Mrs. Hope.

"My feelings towards her were already bitter, but I held myself in check. I said 'So, your pledge to have nothing more to do with this was actually eyewash. You're up to your neck in this and always have been.' She just sneered and gave me a sour look, then said, "Follow me." I looked over my shoulder hoping that Jack would see the two of us and follow, but I couldn't see him.

"She led me to a schooner, tied up further along the quay, and beckoned me to follow as she climbed the gang plank. Again, I looked about for Jack, worried that he'd lose sight of where I'd gone. The swaying of the ship and the rise and fall of the water made climbing that gangplank precarious and I hung onto the safety rope for dear life. One slip and I'd have fallen into the water and probably been crushed between the ship and the quay.

"On board the ship she led me from mid ship, aft to a cabin. She said, 'You'll wait here and don't forget – I've a score to settle with you.' The anger inside me was rising but again, I held my tongue and said nothing but I thought to myself, 'Have no fear, we'll meet again after this is all done with, and I'll be the one to exact revenge, not you.'

She disappeared and left me alone. Waiting seemed to be part of some torture prepared for me. There was no sign of anyone else aboard – not least Chika – for what seemed a long time. I began to worry that Jack might become concerned about what was happening to me, burst in at any moment and ruin the chance of an exchange.

"After what seemed to me to have been the best part of a half hour I heard footsteps on deck, the door opened and in walked Finkelstein. His garb was soaking wet and his long black hair was stuck to his face. He left a trail of water where-ever he walked. He was a despicable sight but he hadn't lost that sickly manner in addressing me,

Sweet Retribution

"Ah my dear, sweet, lady, I'm so pleased you could make it here in this dreadful weather. Might I ask, have you brought the object with you?" and I replied sharply,

"I can see you've not brought my daughter."

"Oh don't let us take each other to be stupid. We both know it doesn't work like that – I've found your daughter as I promised and she's being taken care of close by. I expect that you have the ledger close at hand too. What we must both do at this point is to show our genuine trust and commitment. To that end I want you to come out on deck with me."

"I followed him to the deck amid-ship and followed the line of his pointing finger. There, in the open doorway of the warehouse, stood Chika held tightly by Mrs Hope. It was at that point I realised the purpose of being there on that schooner – we were elevated, out in the open and obvious to all that were watching. It was his way of ensuring this wasn't a trap; reassurance for both parties. His minions could plainly see us and so could Jack and Tom.

My emotions welled up and I couldn't help the tears that began to run down my face as I meekly waved to Chika. Finkelstein then turned to me and said, "There, I've shown you my good faith, now it's your turn."

I turned and looked along the quay but I could see no sign of Jack, he must have been sheltering from the incessant rain, temporarily out of my view. I panicked and shouted Jack's name but I realised that it was useless against the wind and rain. Finkelstein looked at me with distrust in his face but before he could accuse me of reneging on the arrangement, I said,

"Jack's out there with the book. I just can't see him, just give him a moment or two."

Fortunately, at that moment both Jack and Tom chose to come out into the open, much nearer than I'd anticipated. I waved my signal for him to hold the book aloft so that it could be seen. Finkelstein's eyes lit up and I could sense his excitement that the book would soon be in his hands. The two of us went steadily down the gang-plank and I felt the solid quay once more beneath my feet. We walked towards the warehouse where Chika and Mrs Hope had retreated inside. Finkelstein said, 'Now my dear, signal your man to come forward and we'll do business.'

"My mind was in turmoil, so anxious to be reunited with Chika, but always mindful that we were dealing with this despicable snake of a man. I was still worried there'd come a twist to the exchange but with both Jack and Tom present I believed we had the upper hand if things turned nasty, as we were only dealing with Finkelstein and Mrs Hope.

"However, my reckoning was crushed as we walked through the door of the warehouse to find we were outnumbered. Three other rough looking individuals, obviously Finkelstein's henchmen, stood with Mrs Hope, surrounding a really frightened looking Chika. I couldn't help myself, I made to rush forward and embrace the child but one of the men stepped between us and held me back. In a moment of panic I felt the derringer in my pocket and was tempted to bring it out and use it. Fortunately I managed to keep my nerve. "

At this point I can take up the story again. I produced the book and stepped forward and Finkelstein took Chika by the hand and met me half way. He eagerly grabbed at the book and released Chika who ran into my arms. He laughed hysterically and then, holding his book aloft, he snarled

"All this could have been avoided," and he laughed again as he turned away.

Chapter 33

Chika began to sob uncontrollably and her little body shook as she clung first to me and then to Pru. The flood of tears was tears of relief, and through it all she managed a smile. She stuttered, "I thought they were never going to set me free. I've so missed you Mama and Papa. The woman said she was going to sell me."

She wiped the tears from her eyes and continued, "Can we go home now? I so want to go home." It was at that point that I realised Chika was barefoot and I remembered they'd taken her shoes and used them to make us aware they had our daughter. I picked her up and wrapped my coat around her to shield her from the weather. As I walked from the warehouse I looked back but Finkelstein and his party had all disappeared, obviously through another exit.

My emotions were so mixed up; possibly relief was the strongest. Relief that our daughter was back in our arms and relief that we were finally rid of Finkelstein, but underlying it all was anger and a wish to do something dreadful to him and the woman, Mrs Hope.

Pru's face was a picture of joy; her wet eyes sparkled and the loving smile that had deserted her over these past days, once again radiated from her face, Chika was going to be a spoiled child, covered in a protective blanket of love unlike anything that had gone before. I realised that this overwhelming need to protect her mustn't deny her a childhood with the freedom a child needs, but I also knew it was going to be difficult to let her out of our sight. Tom and Lottie were just as doting as we were.

We didn't rush into probing Chika's memory of the abduction and detention, preferring to let her settle and regain a true feeling of safety within the family. However, little pieces of the overall picture emerged from her without prompting as when she was eating breakfast and she remarked, "The woman only spoke to me when she brought me food and it was mostly bread and milk – she called it 'soaky' – or perhaps bread spread with something sickly. I was so lonely, locked in that room." Another time Chika said, "I thought he was nice to talk to until he grabbed me and carried me off. I started to scream and tried to tell him to let me go but he put his hand over my mouth and I could hardly breathe."

The story was emerging in very small snatches but we thought it best to let her tell it at her own pace. The one thing that weighed heavily on my mind and I couldn't avoid asking was, "Did anyone hurt you or do anything to you?" but Chika's childish mind didn't associate anything with any unseemly behaviour against her, only physical restraint.

The child found it difficult to sleep alone in her own room. The darkness seemed to trigger fear in her and at first a candle night-light was left burning for her. We were conscious of the danger a bare flame posed and we eventually succumbed and allowed her to share our bed. She explained they had moved her about from house to house, house to boat, and then boat to house, never allowed outside the room and always kept in the dark. Her keeper had been a big, fat woman, who coughed a lot. The nightmares and reluctance to sleep alone in a dark room were explained.

When Pru and I had a moment to ourselves I expressed my seething anger at Finkelstein and the clairvoyant woman for the distress they'd caused us as a family, but most of all the trauma they'd put Chika through – all because of a book. Pru was equally condemning of the pair but she was contrite about the part she'd played in taking the book from Finkelstein. I hadn't quite thought of it in the same way.

She was rather remorseful, saying she realised she'd brought it all about in pursuit of Lord Bouverie's loot and making Finkelstein suffer in the process. She mitigated those feelings with the 'excuse' that it was not simply avarice on her part but retribution for the misery they'd put Joe, her first husband, through before he died. It had been a vow to him at his death-bed to achieve revenge – which I totally understood.

It was at that moment of confession that Pru suddenly admitted something she'd kept a secret throughout – she'd had a secret copy made of the contents of the book.

"Why? Don't you realise Finkelstein'll get to know? You'll not keep that a secret and when he finds out, all this will start again."

"Oh no, even the person copying for me knew nothing of Finkelstein, nor did she understand what she was copying as it was all in a personalised mix of Yiddish/Hebrew and code..." she said with a wry smile and continued, "...he thinks he's won, but we'll see."

A feeling of dismay hit me, and the worrying thought that she hadn't given up her quest to take Finkelstein's treasures, and she'd spark the whole dreadful fight all over again. I had to ask, "Is it really worth it?"

"Oh yes, it'll be worth it. He thinks he's outwitted me, the police, the revenue, the excise, everyone. It'll be worth it just to make sure he never gets his hands on any of it – even if it all goes to the bottom of the Thames, it'll be worth it, believe me."

I didn't see it in quite the same way but I couldn't argue. Pru had endured the hardship and misery Bouverie had caused her, losing her husband too; I knew I had no right to voice any critical opinion. I simply asked,

"So, where is this copy and does anyone else know about it?"

"It's in the same bank vault, and no-one other than the lady who copied it knows about it. She believes the book was a valuable artefact from another ancient culture that she was copying for the benefit of academics at the university who would attempt to decipher it."

"What do you really intend to do with it?"

"I've found someone I can trust who understands Hebrew and is familiar with Yiddish. I'm hoping that he'll also be able to interpret the ciphers too. When I have his understanding of what's written I'll be able to see if it allows me to take it any further."

I despaired at the thought of what it all might bring about and said,

"Don't you think that whoever interprets it will realise its significance? What happens if he decides to use it to his own benefit?"

"I've taken that into consideration and if I go ahead with it, I shall have to have some safeguard. I've often told you these things have to have a lot of forethought, this has been in my head for a long time, I've kept everything secret and I'll make sure it stays that way. Finkelstein'll never know until it's too late. If I'm right it's a record of all the smuggled contraband Bouverie brought into the country and a record of his dealings in the slave trade. The excise people and the port authority men were apt to make regular visits to him and therefore he had to hide the contraband until he could dispose of it to private buyers. I believe the book was a record of where and with whom, everything was hidden and that's why he was so desperate to get it back."

"Who's this new found man who's going to decipher Finkelstein's book?"

"I don't want anyone else to know this, but he's an Ashkenazi Jew – an immigrant from some Russian state. I don't know much about his background but listening to the small amount he's told me it's clear he's had a difficult time, discrimination, imprisonment, deprivation and violent attacks by the secret police. He's had to flee from his homeland, it's in turmoil at the moment, on the verge of a violent revolution, and he's desperate for money to bring his wife and children here. They've escaped to Poland and I've promised to help him get them here. That's my safeguard against him using what he learns from the copies."

"How have you come to know him?"

"Sandra Chung introduced me. She pulled a few strings and managed to get him a job as interpreter at the new university."

Sweet Retribution

It was clear, there'd be no changing Pru's mind, and the bitterness of her feelings towards Finkelstein would drive her on. I just hoped it wasn't going to be the downfall of us all.

Sandra came again the following morning, eager to know how the meeting had gone and she was thrilled and filled with tears, to see Chika apparently none the worse for her ordeal. She'd brought Chinese sweat meats as a gift for her pupil and hugged and kissed Chika as though she was her own daughter. Pru explained we hadn't probed Chika's juvenile mind about the abduction, preferring to let her bring out the facts at her own pace. However, she was obviously listening to the conversations that were taking place around her, as she asked,

"What is a raven?" Sandra replied,

"It's a bird. Why do you ask?" and Chika answered,

"I thought it was. I heard Mama talking about it but she called it a 'barge' and I didn't understand."

"A barge is a boat that someone has named after the bird." Chika thought for a moment and then said,

"That fat woman that kept me in that room had a raven in a cage."

"A big black raven in a cage?"

"No, not a black raven. It was all pretty colours with long tail feathers. It was very noisy."

Sandra looked at us with concern on her face and said, "That sounds more like a parrot."
I picked up on her concern and had to ask,

"A parrot; does that mean something to you?"

"I'm not sure but I think I might know who that is; a fat woman with a parrot. There aren't many fat women who keep a parrot in Limehouse. If I'm right she has a house with several rooms that she rents – usually to sailors.

Chapter 34

Sandra led us through the back alleys beyond the rope-makers field off Narrow Street that ran parallel to the river, and into a small back-yard strewn with rubbish. The crumbling brickwork of this end of terrace house still bore the limewash that told of the area's previous history. The old lime kilns had almost disappeared but that's how Limehouse had derived its name. I could hear the squawking of the bird as we approached the door. Surely we were at the right place, the home of Lilly Botham, commonly known in the area as 'Big Lil'? The rough hand painted sign on the wall read 'Rooms to Let'.

I didn't want Sandra to become embroiled in any unseemliness or violence, she'd led us this far and so she left us. Tom strode forward and hammered on the door – no one answered. Again he thumped his fist on the door but still no-one came to answer. We could still hear the squawking parrot but there seemed no other sound and we were about to leave when a window, high above us, was thrown open and a large woman leaned out, shouting,

"What's all the noise about?"
Tom took a step or two back and looked up, saying,
"Come down here, I want to talk to you."
The woman answered in an equally belligerent manner,
"Clear off I'm busy, I don't have rooms vacant and I haven't got time to spend talking to ruffians the likes of you."
Tom put his foot to the door and gave a hefty push and it flew open. He looked up to her again and said,
"Either you come down here or I'm coming up to you, and I'd advise you not to make me climb the stairs to find you, so please yourself."
She replied angrily,
"Stay where you are, I'm coming down," and after a few moments she appeared at the door. Before either Tom or I could speak she said,

Sweet Retribution

"If you're after a room, I ain't got any vacant so you can clear off – I don't want no ruffians here."

Tom stepped forward and stuck his face close to hers and said in a tone as menacing as he could manage,

"Hold your tongue you old witch. We're here to ask you about the child you've been keeping prisoner here."

"What do you mean, keeping prisoner?"

"You know very well what I'm talking about. You've held a child prisoner in a room and I want to know all about it."

"You're obviously talkin' about that little coloured girl. She wasn't bein' held a prisoner. I was asked to keep her safe 'cos she was likely to run away. Her mother took her shoes off her so she couldn't go far."

"You knew you were holding her prisoner and it was you who made sure she couldn't get away by taking her shoes."

"No. I was just told to keep her safe – make sure she didn't run away. They said she'd run away afore and if I didn't look after her proper like, she'd do it agen. I tell yer, her mother was the one who took her shoes when she left her with me. There's a big difference in keepin' the kid safe and holdin' her prisoner."
I asked,

"Who's this 'they' that you keep talking about?"

"It was Billy and his wife, she's their kid. I don't know his other name; he's always in trouble – he said the peelers were after him and he'd got to lie low and that's why he needed somebody to look after his little gel."
I stood back and took a deep breath, her story had a ring of truth, but so had the clairvoyant's and that proved to be a pack of lies. Was I being gullible again? I looked at Tom and seeing the frown on his face, he gave me the impression he was feeling the same.

We'd come here intending to take our revenge on someone for holding Chika prisoner. 'Big Lil' wasn't a very likeable woman but she was convincing in what she was telling us. Her story had a ring of truth about it. It appeared that she'd only had Chika there part of the time of the abduction. Billy Carter had moved the child about during that time, assisted by a woman purporting to be his wife – probably the clairvoyant woman, Mrs Hope, if that really was her name.

'Big Lil' was doing her best to appear indignant but we could see she was sweating and underneath that facade of self righteousness, she was more than a little worried. Tom wasn't for letting her off the hook and we left her with these terse words from him,

"I'm going to check your story and if I find you've been lying to us, I'm coming back to see you and I'll hang you from that window up there by your ankles."
Her face drained of colour as she scurried back inside slamming the door behind her.

When we returned home and told of what 'Big Lil' had to say, neither Lottie nor Pru believed a word of it. They still believed that all who took part were fully aware of what they were doing, and Pru gave the impression of being disappointed in us for letting her hoodwink us. I assured her that Tom had given her a hard time and pressed her for the truth. It didn't seem to satisfy them and I half expected Pru to say she'd herself pay 'Big Lil' a visit, but instead she became rather quiet and withdrawn.

Obviously we all, and particularly Pru, still felt bitter about the abduction and the distress we'd been through, and it was going to take some time for feelings to subside – if they ever would.

Life was coming around to something resembling normal and the only panic was when Atlas heard the night-soil collectors clearing the privy. Fortunately he couldn't get out of the house to attack them but the pandemonium during the night was enough to make us fear for Chika's safety until we realised what it was. I hoped that Finkelstein was sleeping just as uneasily.

Sweet Retribution

Chika surprised me in how quickly she settled and recovered after her return home. She continued to sleep with us in our bed, which wasn't entirely convenient, but we were prepared to indulge her. I'm sure she was beginning to take advantage of our indulgence, as we began to lower our guard. Sandra had taken up her tuition again and she said how pleased with the progress Chika was making. In the quiet of evenings I became a pupil to my daughter as she began to tutor me on the abacus that Sandra gifted her.

The air of normality around us was suddenly and brutally shattered by what at first appeared to be a tragic accident. Sandra Chung, Chika's lovely tutor, had fallen from the ferry and was swept away by the torrent.

Tom heard first and was round to let us know in a flash. Jake, the ferryman, was beside himself with grief when I rushed to the quay to discover what had happened. He explained,

"The weather's atrocious; I was fightin' to row agenst the tide, the blindin' rain and the wind. I'd never known owt like it. Them two ladies were behind me -in the for'ard part o' the boat. I was sat 'mid-ships', wi' me back to 'em, pullin' 'ard on the oars, when suddenly the boat sorta lurched and tilted to one side – I thought for a second we were going to overturn. There was a scream that frightened the livin' daylights out o' me it did. I turned round t' see one o' the ladies frantically clawin' at the other in the water, tryin' to save her, but she went under and disappeared. I swung the boat round and tried to find her but it were hopeless. First time I'd lost a passenger in all them years, I'm still shakin' even now."

"Who was the other woman?"

"I don't know. I've seen her a time or two before but I never asked who she was. I thought they were friends – I seen 'em together before at the ferry."

"Are you sure it was an accident, Jake, or could she have been pushed into the water?"

"Pushed? Whatever makes yer ask that?"

"I don't know I'm just surprised Mrs Chung 'fell' into the water. She's used your ferry many times and she's not the type to over-balance or take risks."

"Yer, I knew the lady, she often paid me to cross an' she was a sensible sort, but I didn't see or hear any argument or anythin' so I thought it were an accident."

I wasn't convinced but it seemed Jake was. Sandra was so used to using the ferry and I couldn't conceive that she'd take any sort of risk, what's more I was under the impression that she could swim. I wanted to know who this other woman was. Jake says he's seen them together before at the ferry. Could it be that she was the woman calling herself Mrs Hope? She'd certainly crossed on the ferry with Sandra before and she'd made threats to Pru when Chika had been released. My common sense was challenging what Jake had told me; what if this other woman had had hit her over the head and knocked her unconscious before pushing her overboard? My suspicions were becoming more feasible the more I thought about it. Pru and Chika would both be distraught.

Chapter 35

The mood amongst us was quite morbid, upset at the loss of Sandra who had become such a close friend and confidant. There were a lot of tears especially from Chika. We'd kept the tragedy from her for a while but it wasn't long before she picked up on the mood that prevailed. We promised her that if Sandra's body was found we'd give her a good funeral and a fitting headstone. It didn't make anyone feel any better about the loss but we needed to express our desire to mark her passing. Chika began to spend quiet moments sat alone, clutching her abacus, the present from Sandra, obviously mourning her friend.

Seeing the child's distress, I made a vow to myself that I was going to do my best to find Mrs Hope, regardless of whether events subsequently found Sandra's tragedy to be accidental or not.

The Port authority, watermen, lightermen, colliers, ferrymen, and sea-going men along the length of the navigable Thames were all alerted by Tom, who was determined to retrieve Sandra, but there was no report of a body being found. It didn't really surprise us as the torrent of flood water and the detritus it carried were enough to conceal anything and carry it far away.

It was two days later that an intriguing report reached us from a bargee, of a suicide attempt when a female had been dragged from the river near St Katharine's Dock, presumably at the Wapping bend of the river. There didn't appear to be any connection with our search for a body but the spark of intrigue was the mention of the ethnicity of the female; she was of Chinese extraction. The report mentioned a head injury and loss of memory; she couldn't remember who she was. We couldn't ignore the report but tracking down the source, the bargee, was proving more difficult than anticipated.

Tom was the ideal person to talk with dockers, ship owners and port authority officials alike and with his background he was well accepted. We discovered that the attempted suicide woman had been pulled from the water by Alf and Annie of the barge 'Cornflower', but where were they now? Apparently their barge plied the canal between St Katharine's Dock, through the Tobacco wharf, into Shadwell basin and out onto the Thames.

We walked until our legs ached but finally caught up with the 'Cornflower' in Shadwell basin. Annie seemed please that someone was actually interested in her rescued charge. She volunteered,

"We noticed her floatin' agenst a tender tied up at Jameson's quay. We thought she was dead – you see these bodies in the water from time to time, so Alf wasn't all that careful with her. He grabbed a boat hook and pulled her round to the steps to lift her out, an' he shouted to me to help him 'cause he thought there might be signs o' life. I wasn't so sure, but we managed to get her out the water and Alf started pumpin' at her chest.

Suddenly there was a noise as the air escaped 'er lungs 'an then the water spewed out as she coughed and began t' breathe. We got some 'elp an' carried her over t' the 'Cornflower'. Once we got 'er aboard I was left to get 'er sodden clothes off 'er and cover 'er wi' blankets. That's when I noticed the wound to 'er 'ead. I thought at first it was somethin' Alf had caused with the boat-hook, but he swears he never touched 'er 'ead. Anyway, she opened 'er eyes an' looked at me bewildered, but I couldn't mek 'eads or tales of 'er; still can't. She doesn't know who she is or why she ended up in the river. I've still got her 'ere in the cabin – where else can she go? She's not well; shiverin' all the time and coughin' like her lungs are goin' to burst."

"Can we see her?" I asked,

"Yer can with pleasure, for what good it'll do yer, but be warned 'cause she's not up to a lot o' questions before she collapses."

Sweet Retribution

"We won't cause her any distress; we just need to see her to find out whether it's the person we're searching for."

Annie led us aboard the Cornflower and I only had to peer in through the hatch to see it was Sandra. I felt overwhelmed and tears welled up in my eyes. I wanted to rush to her and hug her but I realised that her condition was too delicate for exuberance. I thanked Annie profoundly and explained that I would pay her for Sandra's rescue and the care she'd shown her. I would arrange a carriage to collect her and convey her to my home where she'd be treated with the utmost care. Pru, and especially Chika, were going to be ecstatic to learn Sandra was alive and coming home to be with us.

A short walk from Shadwell Basin I found Storey's Yard, where the sign read, 'Hansoms and Carriages for hire. Funerals our speciality'. Bill Storey listened to my requirements and suggested a 'Clarence' that would accommodate Sandra's fragile state, pulled by his old faithful that promised a steady comfortable ride. We could all ride together and I'd be able to look after Sandra on the journey, some three miles or so, to the south bank via the old bridge.

Pru, Lottie and Chika had quite obviously been watching for our return, unaware of events that had unfolded. Seeing the arrival at the garden gate of the Clarence sparked their interest and they gathered to see us dismount the carriage supporting a frail looking female between us. It suddenly dawned on them who we'd brought home. Obviously astounded and astonished to find she was alive, they rushed to meet us, faces alight with joy and full of questions. I had to prevent them crowding the invalid and said,

"Sandra isn't well. Let's get her inside and seated. I'll tell you everything when we've got her at rest."

Once she was seated in a comfortable chair, warm blanket around her shoulders, and another around her legs, I began to repeat Annie's tale of rescue from the river. It was clear Sandra was still bewildered but although she looked at us with vacant eyes, she somehow looked a little calmer amongst us, making me hope there was some recognition. Lottie removed the pad from the crown of Sandra's head which revealed a nasty open wound. She wasn't happy about the state of her hair and so with a bowl of clean boiled water and some cotton-wool she began to wash and clean her head. With a fresh bandage the wound was covered again. Chika sat at Sandra's feet willing her to get well. A bed was prepared for her in Chika's room.

It was useless and unhelpful to Sandra to begin asking questions or discussing things in her presence, but I couldn't help but express my concerns when out of her hearing. Putting the head injury to Jake's story about how Sandra had gone overboard into the river, it convinced me even more-so that she'd been struck over the head and pushed into the water. It was certainly no accident, for such a severe head wound it had to have been deliberate. I needed to find Mrs Hope – it must have been her, and this time I wasn't going to be so easily convinced by her story and ready to let her go.

As the days passed Sandra physically improved to a point that she was eating and drinking more normally. I was not so sure of her mental state. She'd often say "Where am I?" or "Who are you?" and then the next moment she'd be relaxed and easy in our company as though knowing she was amongst friends. That was especially the case when Chika was with her – it seemed almost as though Chika was a calming influence upon her. The head wound was showing signs of healing with the care she was receiving from Pru.

Tom had been over to Sandra's home in Limehouse and made sure nothing was amiss. We'd been concerned that she might have a pet – a cat or a bird – that needed food and water, but it wasn't so. He was content to lock the house and return to us. It was as he was leaving that he was approached by Jean, who wanted to know what he was doing there. She accepted the situation when she learnt that

Sweet Retribution

Sandra had been injured and almost drowned. A few subtle questions from Tom discovered that Jean was one of a number of girls working as *'social workers'* at the Guangzhuo. Sandra was apparently regarded as a saintly mother figure amongst them and they'd become concerned about her absence. He took the opportunity to ask her about Mrs. Hope; whether she was known amongst the girls, but nothing developed. Never-the-less, he made a mental note that Jean was someone he could return to for information in the future.

As he stood waiting for the ferry, his mind wandered over the preceding events around Limehouse basin and he realised what a significance the barge, 'The Raven', had played, and what an obvious starting point that would be to find Mrs Hope. He turned away from the ferry point and made for the Port Authority office and his long time friend Captain Johan Klaus, the Harbour Superintendent. Klaus listened to Tom's quest and with a wink and a nod he produced the log. Unfortunately it didn't prove to be quite the meticulous record of all vessels using the basin as he'd hoped. It obviously concentrated upon sea going vessels but the plethora of local trade barges were another matter.

Tom's next call was the lock-keeper for the Regent's canal which proved a little more fruitful. He learned that 'The Raven' was one of three or four barges owned by someone who liked to keep his identity to the background. It conveyed Barley grain, mostly to Haycock's Brewery on the River Lea.

The last the lock-keeper had seen of the barge was days earlier, on its return to the loading point somewhere up the Hertford Union for another load of grain. It would be back to Haycock's Brewery in about a week. Tom probed deeper, "Who's the bargee?" and the answer was,

"I only knows him as 'Black Johnny'. His surname might be Carson or something similar. His wife's called Queenie. All I'll say about 'em is just be careful if yer have dealin's wi' 'em. Keep yer wits about yer if yer see

what I mean, they're crafty, real crafty, an' he's the sort
to lash out if he's cornered, not really the sort to be
messin' with."

"'Black Johnny'? You say Carson – could it be
Carter?"

"Could be. I'm not sure what 'is name is. I've only
known him as 'Black Johnny' – used to work the collier
barges cartin' coal, that's how he got to be called 'Black
Johnny'."

Tom began to ponder; it just seemed likely the name
could be Carter in view of the connection with Billy
Carter. That Mrs Hope was definitely followed back to
the barge; she was in cahoots with Billy Carter, so is it
possible 'Black Johnny' and Billy Carter could be
brothers?" Things were beginning to add up in Tom's
mind.

Chapter 36

Every day that passed there was an improvement in Sandra's physical well being. The initial biliousness and the fever lasted only days but sadly, the mental recovery was a concern. There had been many times when she'd been reduced to bouts of crying, with pains in her head and the confusion in her mind still persisted. Regularly I'd seen her with fingers entwined in her hair, pulling, almost as though trying to lift her scalp. She'd continued to ask, "Who am I? What's happened to me?" and it took time to get her to accept her own identity, and even then we weren't sure she was convinced. Time and again Pru or I would explain to her who she was and how we'd come to know her, but still she was searching for a memory that constantly eluded her. She was always most settled in the company of Chika, there seemed to be an attachment below the threshold of consciousness; if only we could delve below the surface; stimulate her mind.

I never voiced my fears, even to Pru, but it made me wonder whether the damage was permanent. The wound on the outside was practically healed but the delicate mechanism below the surface was not. The bitterness inside me was intense, to think that someone could inflict such damage to such a sweet woman.

That week, waiting for The Raven to return to Haycocks Brewery with its load of grain, seemed to take forever, but eventually word reached Tom that the barge was approaching the river Lea and the last lock on the Hertford Union canal. We'd agreed to go together to intercept them before they reached the brewery. The lock would be busy and they'd have to wait their turn which would give us the time to reach the tow-path on the Lea before them. Even so, there was an air of urgency between us as we stepped onto the ferry. As Jake rowed us across the Thames I couldn't help but wonder what if anything Sandra felt as she was plunged into the filthy water, no wonder she'd suffered the fever.

Sweet Retribution

As we stepped onto the quay in Limehouse basin the sun broke through the overcast sky, almost as an omen of better things to come. We lengthened our steps as the urgency took hold, until we encountered the mud of the tow-path. With the amount of rain, soaking the ground, the numerous horses pulling the barges had turned the path into mire.

Crossing the junction of the Hertford and Union canal we scanned beyond the lock and ahead of us up the Lea. There was no sign of The Raven. Some half a mile ahead we could see the smoke and the steam rising from Haycock's Brewery.

Had they beaten us, were they already there, unloading their cargo? We hurried on and as we approached we could see two or three barges at the wharf and lots of activity as they were discharging grain. All barges has their own distinctive paint work and Tom could especially remember the colours and lettering on The Raven and he assured me it wasn't one of them. We turned about and walked back towards the canal junction. We hadn't gone far when we saw what we were searching for slowly emerging from the junction into the river, against the flow. A huge bay horse was taking the strain, the tow line taught, as whoever was at the tiller steered the craft. Someone appeared to be leading the horse but at that distance I couldn't see who.

I looked at Tom who appeared perfectly calm and controlled; whereas anticipation and nervous energy inside me was intensifying the nearer the barge came. When about fifty yards away, the person at the horse's head, obviously a woman, let go of the horse and stopped in her tracks; she'd clearly recognised us. She immediately ran back to the barge shouting, "Johnny! Johnny!" in alarm. It was the fictitious 'Mrs Hope', the clairvoyant.

As we ran towards her she looked about her as though seeking to escape but there was nowhere she could flee. I stopped the horse and pulled the pin that connected the towing rope to the swingletree of the horse's harness. With no forward motion of the barge it would have quickly been carried backwards towards the basin by the flow of the river. I looped the rope around one of the posts along the riverside, used as a temporary mooring for vessels. Now secured at the bow, the stern began to swing out away from the bank.

Black Johnny responded to Queenie's call of alarm but the barge had drifted too far away from the bank for him to jump to the towpath. In an instant I saw the resemblance to Billy Carter. It was more than co-incidence could allow, he had to be Billy's brother. Queenie began to back away from us still shouting "Johnny!" but she quickly realised there was no way her husband could reach her to offer assistance; all he could do was shout "Leave her alone."

We were too far away from the brewery behind us, or from the canal junction, for Queenie's shouts to be heard. No assistance was likely and she realised her situation was dire, unable to run because of the clinging mud and feeling panic stricken.

Just as Tom reached her I turned to see Black Johnny run to the bow of the barge and launch himself in a frantic leap to reach the river bank, but it was a leap of despair and it was obvious he was never going to make it. The inevitable splash brought a gasping, spluttering and gurgling as he disappeared beneath the surface. He resurfaced struggling for breath, arms flailing, as he reached for the sparse vegetation of the bank. Queenie pleaded, "Help him. Help him, please help him"

I reached down as best I could but I was in danger of slipping into the water myself. I looked around to find something, anything, to reach him but there was nothing available. Black Johnny's sodden clothing was likely to drag him under again but just at that moment Tom had the inspiration to grab the rope that was mooring the barge. The three of us heaved to bring it closer to the bank and to Black Johnny. A barge laden with tons of grain was too heavy for us to make much headway against the current but the difference we made allowed him to grasp one of the fenders hanging from the craft, and he clung on for dear life.

An unladen barge was returning from the brewery towards us and the bargee could obviously see ahead of him the predicament of The Raven swinging awkwardly across the river, and he stopped and secured his vessel up river. Seeing Black Johnny clinging to the fender and anxious to help, he unloaded a small rowboat onto the water and came to our aid. Black Johnny was pulled from the water and helped shivering, onto the towpath; his strength and aggression had clearly ebbed in his struggle to survive.

The rule of the river had come into play, all those plying a trade on river or canal, would without question assist anyone in difficulties. The newcomer brought the horse back from where it stood nonchalantly grazing, to the stricken Raven, and helped to re-attach the tow line.

With verbal encouragement the heavy legged horse sank on its haunches, leant into its collar and heaved, bringing the barge into motion. Once it was sufficiently near the bank Tom jumped across and took the tiller. I thanked the helpful bargee who returned to his own craft, whilst Black Johnny, Queenie and I trudged the muddy towpath until the Raven entered the slack-water of the brewery quay where she was tied up safely.

Black Johnny was eager to get aboard his barge to dry himself and change his sodden clothing. Queenie, now fully recovered, adopted a belligerent tone and began to berate Tom and me for having caused the trouble. Tom was standing no nonsense and he pushed her backwards forcing her to sit in one of the cabin chairs. I looked forward and saw men clambering aboard and lifting the hatches, ready to begin the unloading. Black Johnny became agitated wanting to go forward to supervise the unloading. It was at that point I saw one of the workmen throw a small wooden chest from the cargo hold onto the deck. Tom was blocking

Black Johnny's access but I could see him nervously eyeing the chest.

Tom pushed himself into the face of Queenie and said,

"You bitch!! You're going to rot in prison for what you did to Sandra Chung on the ferry." She replied,

"What're you talking about? I tried to save her!!"

"You struck her a blow on the head and pushed her into the river."

"Oh no, you've got it all wrong. I tried to stop her jumping into the water and I tried to grab her hair as she went under. I was as upset as anyone. The ferryman turned the boat and we looked around for her, but she didn't come back to the surface."

"We've heard your lies before and they won't wash. We're taking you back to the peelers. You're going to suffer for what you've done."

"You can't prove a thing against me because I've done nothing wrong."

Whilst that conversation was going on, I walked forward and picked up the chest that Black Johnny was so anxious about. I was surprised by the weight. It was about eighteen inches long, ten inches wide and twelve inches in height and it was locked. It was brass bound and had a brass plate on the front. I read the inscription and immediately understood why Black Johnny was so concerned, it read 'Ezekiel Finkelstein'. Underneath the name was the figure of a lion and a number of marks; weird figures that meant nothing to me.

As I carried the chest aft Black Johnny tried to rise to intercept me but Tom pushed him back and threatened to throw him back into the water if he dared to move again. I said nothing but quietly pointed to the inscription. Tom's eyes opened wide in an expression of astonishment. He turned again to Black Johnny, "What are you doing with this?" The reply was a terse and sullen murmur, "Mind yer own business." Tom motioned with a shake of his head for me to distance myself from Black Johnny and Queenie before he whispered,

"What are we going to do with them? We know she struck Sandra over the head and tried to drown her but it's her word against ours. She's admitting nothing and we can't prove a thing. We can't even prove her involvement with Chika's abduction. We're sure of her identity and if we get anything more we know who we're looking for and how to find her so let's just concentrate on this chest, it's bound to hold something important."

Black Johnny snarled,

"I warn yer, don't even think o' tekin' that chest – It'll be at yer peril if yer do. Yer life won't be worth a damn." That confirmed it, it was something important and Finkelstein was going to be the loser.

I wasn't happy about leaving Queenie, and I was sure both Pru and Lottie would have something to say about it, but it seemed the chest was more important. We now knew who 'Mrs Hope' really was and we could surely find her again, or we could leave Inspector Stone to deal with her.

Chapter 37

I fiddled about with the lock but it was too robust and the only way seemed to be to force it – but what damage could it do to the contents. Once again Tom's knowledge came to the rescue and he led me to a workshop down near the East India docks. He tapped the side of his nose with his forefinger, saying, "It's not what you know but who you know. Keep this to yourself – this chap's a friend who works for the Excise people. His job is to access the locks where the owners have conveniently 'lost' the key. It wouldn't do to let anyone else know about our friendship; do you understand?" I nodded my head.

We walked into the workshop where a peg-legged and bearded man of about thirty-five sat at a bench, filing a key. I never did hear Tom speak the man's name but he told me afterwards that the man had lost his leg in a hawser aboard one of the East India Company's ships whilst Tom was ship's mate. Tom saved his life by securing a tourniquet until the ship's surgeon could amputate and tie off the arteries.

The man greeted Tom, as would a long lost brother, before taking the chest and studying it closely for some moments. I watched as he inserted two slender instruments into the key hole. It took but a few minutes before there was a click from the lock and he looked up with a smile, the lid open, and handed it back to Tom. I saw Tom offer him money but it was refused; a favour to repay the debt he owed. There were handshakes and then Tom closed the lid without searching beneath the layer of packing – explaining later that in that way his friend could not be held responsible for anything contained in the chest that might be liable to excise duty. He wrapped it in a cloth to avoid enquiring looks as we left the workshop. I found it hard to suppress my curiosity until we reached home.

Tom uncovered the chest on the kitchen table as Pru, Lottie, Chika and even Sandra gathered round. The suspense was eating up my insides. He threw back the lid and began to carefully remove the linen packing. I could see what appeared to be some sort of elaborate candlestick. Tom lifted it out and placed it on the table and I could see that it was of gold and had seven branches forming a candelabra. It stood about nine inches high and was similar in width. It held no significance for me.

Tom again delved into the box and brought out small golden figures of a lion, an ox and an eagle. Finally, two pieces of golden jewellery attached to cords, obviously to be worn as a necklace. The figures of the lion, ox and eagle were beautiful miniatures, but again, neither those nor the jewellery, meant anything to me.

It was Sandra who took our attention as she placed her hand on the candelabra and stood with a pained look on her face, as if trying to remember something. Whatever it was wouldn't surface in her mind. She turned away and held her head in her hands. She was struggling for a memory but I could see that there was definitely something there in the subliminal; it just needed a key to unlock it. How I wish I could provide a locksmith as Tom had found for the chest.

Tom had been quiet for some moments, just staring at the candelabra, before finally saying,

"There something about this that strikes a chord in my memory. It's a strange design and I'm sure I've seen something similar. I can't remember what it is but something tells me it has a religious connection."

Lottie responded,

"Well, it obviously belongs to Finkelstein; could it be something to do with his religion?"

I couldn't help but quip,

"Seriously? Do you think he has a religious bone in his body? If anything, he's more likely to have a leaning towards some satanic cult."

Lottie replied,

"I agree but I just thought it might be a good place to start..." and then turning to Pru she continued, "...who can we ask who understands Hebrew?"
I forgot myself and blurted out,

"That new Jewish scholar you're helping – the one who's going to translate the copy of Finkelstein's book?"

Pru looked daggers at me and I realised I'd promised not to reveal anything about the copy. It had taken just a moment of distraction to reveal something so secret – thankfully I'd slipped up in the presence of trusted friends. Tom and Lottie looked questioningly at Pru and she said pointedly, looking in my direction,

"That's something that was supposed to be kept a secret to protect everyone. If Finkelstein gets to know, we can expect more trouble."
Tom interjected,

"Oh there'll certainly be more trouble now he knows we've got his chest of trinkets. Come now Pru, who is this new Jewish scholar Jack's mentioned?"

"Keep this to yourselves but he's an exiled Ashkenazi Jew from somewhere in Russia – it seems he got into trouble with the authorities. He's found his way to England but he had to leave his wife and family behind in Poland. Sandra won't remember but she found him a job as an interpreter at the university. I've promised to help him with finances to get his wife and family here from Poland if he'll translate what's written in that copy of Finkelstein's book. His name is Abrasha Yacovc."

Abrasha Yacovc arrived at our home at Pru's invitation and was led into the kitchen where everyone was gathered in anticipation. We were all taken by surprise when Sandra suddenly rose and said,

"Hello Abraham".
She'd spoken without having to think and immediately a huge excited smile lit up her face as she realised at least one small aspect of her memory had returned. It meant very little in the overall return to normality but it gave us all a boost to think that something might be improving.

Of course, Abrasha – or Abraham, which was indeed the literal translation of his name – remembered their meeting at the university. He knew nothing of the turmoil Sandra had suffered in the meantime. All he knew was that he was here to look at some trinkets to see if there was any religious connection with his Hebrew heritage.

As the chest was opened and the items lifted out, his eyes lit up, his jaw dropped, and it seemed for a moment that he was unable to speak. Eventually he said in a breath-taken, accented way,

"Gold!! I never saw a golden Menora before, brass yes, but never gold. This has its origins in the temple of Jerusalem where it provided light from the olive oil that was contained in each of these cups. And look, more gold!!! The Star of David or Seal of Solomon – this controls demons and spirits – it was the magic shield of King David."

Putting it aside he turned his attention to the three golden figures. He caressed the lion and said,

"Tanakh, the lion of Judah – or Aryeh Yehudah in Hebrew. According to the Torah – the scroll of Jacob – the Tanakh is first mentioned in the blessing of his fourth son Judah. It's used to symbolise authority, strength or dominance. It's one of four figures of Merkavah the Divine Chariot. Look, here's more, an ox and an eagle, how wonderful."

Abraham was almost salivating as he next handled the two necklaces that emerged. He explained,

"This is the Chai. It's a combination of two Hebrew letters – chet and yod, which mean living. The other is Hamsa, as you see it's again gold, embellished with enamel, in the shape of a bell with three fingers protruding below. It represents God's hand and brings luck, health and good fortune. They're very common in jewellery of our faith."

We were astounded at his knowledge and listened in rapt attention. He placed the golden ornaments and jewellery on the table and turned his attention to the brass plate on the chest. He studied it for a moment and then picked up the lion again and studied them side by side. Finally, he said,

"Whoever crafted these has made a splendid job but he obviously didn't know about the historical and biblical descriptions contained in the Torah. The lion should be rampant and it's not, it's passant. They're recent castings; there are still rough edges if you look closely, especially on the Menorah."

We were all quite dumfounded by Abraham's knowledge and his perception regarding the castings but in a way it confirmed what I'd thought. I produced the small pouch of stones and said,

"I knew nothing of the significance of any of these items but like you, I thought they were recently cast. These stones make me believe the gold all comes from stolen or smuggled items of jewellery, brooches or trinkets that have been melted down and cast into what we have here..." I pointed to the name on the brass plate of the chest and said, "Ezekiel Finkelstein – he's a wicked criminal who will stop at nothing to accrue wealth at any cost."

"What does a man like that want with religious items like this?" asked Abraham,

"I think the idea is to make any enquiring mind believe they're items necessary to his religion and he can maintain` they've been handed down through eternity. He knows that no-one can prove otherwise or identify the gold after it's been melted and re-cast. On their own, it's impossible for anyone to tie these figures to stolen or smuggled property, but these stones tell the story for me – I think they're from the original jewellery."

Chapter 38

Abraham was paid well for his insight into the golden figures. I'm sure he'd have been delighted to have taken away with him the Menorah – or in fact any of the jewels – but that was out of the question. The contents of the chest were going to be kept intact, for the time being at least, his reward was monetary and he was grateful – it was a sizeable amount and would be put to his meagre savings to bring his family from Poland.

As exciting as it was to lay hands on the chest of treasure, I knew we could expect trouble from Finkelstein and I became paranoid about Chika's safety. Even when Pru and Lottie bravely decided to venture into Westminster with the pouch of stones to see a jeweller, I insisted they take the Derringers as a precaution.

Chika had become attached to Sandra whom she tended to view as a big sister. Sandra however, was anxious to return to her own home, having the idea that amongst familiar surroundings her memory would return. The thought of her home was vague in her mind, only registering what we'd told her, but the huge void desperately needed to be filled. I promised her that we would take her back there soon. Secretly, I was concerned that the ferry across the Thames would spark a fresh trauma, but on the other hand it might possibly be the trigger that would revive her memory.

In the mean time Lottie and Pru were showing the stones to the jeweller. He emptied the pouch onto a black velvet cloth and under his lighting the stones sparkled and shimmered. With his loupe to his eye he separated the stones, placing one to the side with a comment, "Paste". Pru turned to look at Lottie with a look of scepticism on her face, thinking, *"Why a jeweller would set a beautiful golden piece of jewellery with a diamond of paste is beyond me?"* she kept it to herself but Lottie had understood.

Sweet Retribution

The jeweller gauged the other diamonds by size, clarity and weight or carats, the rubies by size, colour and density, as with the emeralds and sapphires. One by one his tweezers picked up the stones, replacing them in the pouch and making a written calculation on his notepad. Handing the pouch back to Pru with a smile, he pensively looked her in the eye and said, "We've known each other for some time and I think we know each other well – so I feel I can say without causing any offence – I know there's something er, 'fishy' about these stones. If you're asking me to buy them, I have to take the risk into consideration. I'm not asking how you came by them but I want you to acknowledge the risk I'm taking."

Pru smiled to herself, knowing this was his pre-amble to a miserly offer, a comment he'd made many times before in his dealings with her. She watched him closely but for the moment didn't reply.

....He hesitated for a moment studying the notepad, then said,

"I could offer a thousand guineas."
Lottie gave a wry little laugh and said,

"You're joking, surely. They're worth ten times that amount."

....Pru kept silent for some moments, then, looking him in the eye and with a placid but serious face, said,

"Jimmy, we've both got to make a profit but please don't take us for idiots. You've kept the stone that you classified as paste, on one side. I'm sure that if I took it elsewhere it would prove to be an exquisite diamond of about two carats, so let's be sensible. We'll be willing to give you a very good margin but a thousand is ridiculous."

With a pained expression he huffed and puffed before saying,

"Prudence, you offend me – as though I'd try to rob you of all people..." he picked up the 'paste' stone and looked intently at it before continuing, "...but alright, I might have made a mistake with this stone, so I'll revise

my offer – say two – two thousand guineas, how does that sound?"
Pru took a moment to consider and then said,
   "Jimmy, as you say, we've known each other a long time and I want our business arrangement to continue in future, so let's say two and a half, and shake hands."
   He shook his head and grimaced and then replied,
   "Two thousand five hundred guineas – alright, it's a deal. You're a hard woman to bargain with."
Pru chuckled and replied, "Jimmy, you know and I know that you've got the better of the bargain but I'm satisfied so I hope you are too, you'll make a small fortune when you've re-cut them and set them in other jewellery."
She offered her hand and he took it.
   Jimmy held onto Pru's hand rather longer than normal in a handshake, and enquired,
   "Prudence, you said you wanted our business arrangements to continue – do I take it that you have something more to sell?"
Pru gave a chuckle and replied, with the gold in mind,
   "Not at the moment Jimmy, but you know how it is – there may well be an opportunity for us both in the near future."

As Pru and Lottie took the way home, Lottie said,
   "I'm surprised at you Pru. I always thought you were a very astute business woman, but you let him get away with murder there. As little as I know about precious stones, I know they were worth far more. Two and a half thousand? Honestly, they were worth at least five, maybe six."
Pru stopped abruptly and faced Lottie, saying,
   "You know that, he knows it, and I know it, but what I have to consider is that he's prepared to take the risk others wouldn't. Then he's got the expense of cutting and re-setting them; but most of all I may need to deal with him in the future. We've no need to be too greedy or he could have simply turned us away or refused to increase his offer and we'd find it difficult to go

elsewhere. Remember, they've cost us nothing. I knew how far I could push him and still keep his good will, so perhaps two and a half isn't too bad."

They continued walking and Lottie began to accept that the deal was probably the best they could achieve but there wasn't much more conversation between them as they wended their way. Suddenly Pru took Lottie by surprise and with obvious delight showing on her face and a lilt to her voice said,

"I think I'll go down to the cemetery tonight, to Joe's grave, to let him know how things have gone."

Whilst Pru and Lottie were gone I watched Sandra and Chika together. There'd been no lessons for Chika whilst Sandra had been recovering, and I wondered just how the injury had affected her ability – just what had it done to her mental capacity? Would her memory fully return and would her ability to teach return with it? She seemed totally relaxed when with Chika and I do believe Atlas played his part. I'm always amazed that an animal appears to know when someone is ill, and does its best to show concern. Small things about Sandra were indicating an improvement – her head wound had practically healed, but the one thing above all that gave us hope was when she remembered Abraham and spoke his name without prompting.

The afternoon was getting late and as Pru and Lottie were passing Lottie's home she decided to go to prepare tea for Tom, leaving Pru to continue alone. I was anxious for her return and stood in the open doorway watching for her approach. I was relieved to see her walking towards me, quite unconcerned. I remonstrated,

"It's not safe for you walking the streets alone – even in daylight." This business with Finkelstein's chest had certainly unnerved me anew. Pru was totally at ease and she replied,

"Why all the worry? Have you forgotten I have the Derringer?"

Sweet Retribution

I suppose I was worrying unnecessarily but my concern was in believing she was carrying a small fortune in gems which would make her an attractive target for footpads apart from Finkelstein's fiends. I asked,

"What did the jeweller say?"

"I struck a bargain with him at two and a half thousand guineas."

"So have you got the money?"

"No, nobody keeps that amount of money lying about. Jimmy's sound, he has to visit the bank and I'll collect in a couple of days. Don't worry, I trust him – two and a half thousand guineas."

I scanned up and down the street as I closed and locked the door, realising there was much to discuss between us but that was difficult with the presence of both Chika and Sandra. I feared the acquisition of the chest and contents was certain to bring intensity to the war between Pru and Finkelstein. He was a loser big time now and he was never likely to sit back and do nothing, on the other hand Pru was cock-a-hoop with the situation. It wasn't just the fortune she'd acquired, it was the humiliating and devastating blow that had been inflicted on her hated adversary; a fitting revenge.

For our part, the only time we could discuss these matters with any privacy was as we lay abed into the night.

"What are we going to do with the gold?" I asked as I stared into the darkness.

"I've not given it much thought..." she answered but after slight hesitation she continued, "...I think it's got to be melted down. It's going to be a huge problem – where are we going to get it melted and who's going to buy it? I've explained the dilemma I faced with the gems in selling them to Jimmy, but it's a dilemma magnified ten times with the value of the gold. Someone like Jimmy wouldn't be in a position to buy it all. I don't think any of us has any idea of how much it's worth but we're looking at a fortune beyond the dreams of us all."

Sweet Retribution

"Tom and Lottie have got as much say in this as we have but I'm beginning to wish I'd thrown it into the cut." I said wearily.

"Forget it for tonight; let's just bask in the thoughts that we're fabulously wealthy – at least for now. We'll see what Tom and Lottie have to say." Pru replied.

We eventually fell asleep only to be rudely awoken by Atlas growling fiercely and scratching at the back door. Daylight was just beginning to break on yet another dismal day. As I cautiously looked out the kitchen window, I could see that the usual river mist was more of a thick fog this morning. My first thoughts were that it would be the night-soil men clearing the privy, but there was none of the usual scraping and clattering. I moved to the parlour and looked out through the front window but there was no cart.

My senses told me that there was something sinister about this situation. Atlas was still frantically scratching and growling. Holding his collar I inched the door open but there was nothing to see. There were still dark areas where the breaking light had not penetrated. I let go of Atlas and he rushed past me into the garden. Everything was quiet and after a few moments Atlas returned to me. I was sure that no-one was there now, but Atlas hadn't been that excited for nothing. I would have questioned myself as to whether I was over reacting had it not been for Atlas – no, there had definitely been someone out there.

After breakfast, when the fog began to clear, I decided to make an examination of the area where Atlas had shown interest, to find marks on the wooden frame of the kitchen window where some sort of lever had been used in an attempt to force it open. It was fortunate that I'd fitted security catches to all the windows after the misfortune that befell Lottie. Whoever the culprit was, he would have been mauled to death by Atlas had he forced an entry. He was probably put off by hearing a frightening beast trying to get to him. Never-the-less, I saw it as another episode of Finkelstein's attempt to fight back, but surely, with all that happened with the clairvoyant and Billy Carter, he would have known all about Atlas. Was I giving Finkelstein more consideration than I should; were there other low-life villains out there trying their luck?

I grimaced, here I was calling others low-life villains, but weren't we just as bad? It just seems wrong when you're the victim, but crime is crime no matter how you parcel it up.

Chapter 39

After much pleading I agreed to accompany Sandra
back to her Limehouse home, hoping that familiar
surroundings might stimulate her memory. It was a long
shot, but her frustration in being unable to remember
even the most personal things, was upsetting for her,
and for us too in seeing her distress.

Wrapped up warm against the fog and cool days that
were now upon us, I accompanied her down to the ferry.
We had to wait for Jake to return from his earlier
crossing and as we stood watching the river, I perceived
a slight change in Sandra. As we'd walked down to the
quay her demeanour had been bright and cheerful with
the hope and expectation that events were going to light
a spark in her memory. Now, as we stood quietly, the
swirling water lapping against the quay, and the mist
sending a chill through our bones, Sandra began to
show signs of nervous agitation.

She was twisting her hands together and shifting her
weight from one foot to the other. At any other time I
would have accepted that she was simply feeling the
chill, but her face was giving her away. I took her hand,
trying to instil some confidence. As Jake rowed towards
us she was becoming increasingly tense, and as he tied
up alongside the steps and invited us into his row-boat,
she turned away and gasped,

"I'm sorry, I can't. I don't know what it is but I can't."
There was obviously some recognition of the trauma that
had befallen her on the ferry, deep in her subliminal.

The answer was to take a hansom cab for the two and
a half mile journey over the bridge and back to the East
End. Following Tom's directions we arrived at the small
terraced cottage on Butchers Row with the white painted
front door and the lace curtains at the window that made
it stand out from the other dowdy cottages in the row, but
something struck me as being odd. The door appeared
to be slightly ajar: I said nothing to Sandra but jumped
down from the hansom to investigate.

Sweet Retribution

I pushed the door open, peered inside and listened for any sound of an intruder but could hear nothing. I was sure I remembered Tom saying he'd locked up before leaving; perhaps I was mistaken. I turned to find Sandra behind me as I stepped over the threshold. I tried to get her to wait at the door whilst I checked, still fearing something untoward, but she followed on my heels as I opened the front parlour door. The scene of devastation was stomach turning. Furniture slashed and broken, picture frames torn from the walls, glass shattered and trampled, books torn, crumpled and thrown across the floor.

Sandra followed me into the room and just stood, features drained of colour, simply aghast. She picked up one of her precious books and attempted to straighten out the pages. Tears began to trickle down he cheeks.

The kitchen was a similar scene. I made a cursory check upstairs where, although there were signs of disturbance, damage was much less an issue. I returned to the parlour to find Sandra had righted a chair and was sat, just staring blankly at the melee. She looked at me and said, "Why?" repeating "Why? Why?" I could do nothing more than place a comforting arm around her shoulders and answer, "I don't know," but of course I did know why.

I'd arranged with the hansom cabbie to return for us after an hour, and I spent that time picking up the furniture and gathering the broken glass, but it was only a token gesture, as much to occupy my time as anything more. It would take us all to completely clean and re-decorate the rented cottage.

Although nothing was said to the cab driver I'm sure he sensed that something was amiss and his usual brusque manner was replaced by a careful, considerate attitude, and the journey home was steady and an almost gentle trot instead of the usual furious gallop. I held Sandra's hand in empathy.

As we travelled along, tears still flooding her eyes and sniffling, I suddenly realised – the trashing of her home had had a devastating effect on her, which meant that there was surely some recognition of the cottage and what it meant to her. Perhaps that's what was needed to stimulate her memory – a shock to her senses?

Pru and Chika were watching for our return as the cabbie delivered us home, and they realised by the look on Sandra's face that things hadn't gone well. I explained as best I could how she'd been affected by the vandalism to her home. Pru was distressed by what had befallen Sandra and fussed around her, offering sympathy. When I had the chance to speak to Pru alone I said,

"It may have been what was needed to shock Sandra's mind into remembering again. She only knew of the house because we told her that was where she lived, but when she got there and saw the damage, her reaction was to cry. She picked up the torn and crumpled books and handled them as though they were precious to her. I'm sure she was remembering. All she could do was ask, 'Why?' I didn't say anything but we know why don't we?"

Pru didn't answer my question but her face was acknowledgement in itself. She grimaced as she said,

"I never dreamt that our feud with Finkelstein would affect anyone else, but it has and I'm truly sorry. Somehow, I'll make it up to her. I'll get Lottie to help me; we'll go to Sandra's cottage, clean up and re-decorate for her."

In the kitchen Sandra sat with Chika drinking hot tea with plenty of sugar, and Pru poured a glass of brandy encouraging her to drink it but Sandra declined. The tears were beginning to dry and she was very quiet and subdued, but then she looked up at us both and said,

"I don't think I could ever go back there to live. I'll have to find somewhere new. My books, my books, and all my things, destroyed, whoever would do such a thing? In all the time I've lived there I never saw such an awful thing before."

I'm sure she didn't appreciate what she'd said, but Pru and I looked at each other and gave a knowing little smile. There was something there in her memory after all. I decided that a gentle little probe would reveal whether anything more of her memory had returned. I asked,

"What happened at the ferry as we waited?" She answered,

"I panicked. I had a vision of falling into the water. It was quite frightening – I didn't know whether I was imagining something or whether I was remembering it, but I felt that I was being held under the water, unable to breathe. The more I think about it I'm convinced she was trying to drown me."

I wasn't quite sure I'd heard correctly and I had to ask her to repeat, "She? Did you actually say 'She' was trying to drown you?"

Sandra hesitated and then said,

"Am I dreaming? I have this recollection that I was with Mrs Hope, the clairvoyant, sitting together at the front. I'm sure the ferryman had his back to us rowing the boat, and he was talking to us over his shoulder. Everything is hazy but I seem to think I challenged her about who she was, and why she was pretending to be a clairvoyant. You see, I'd become quite suspicious of her. I'm sure she was angry with me but I didn't see it coming. Suddenly something hit me on the head and everything from that point on becomes a bit of a fuzz. She pushed me into the water and held me down, I was fighting for breath as I kicked out to swim away from her, but I must have passed out. It's all too much of a haze to be sure that's just what happened..." tears welled up in her eyes and she looked imploringly at us as she pleaded..."am I imagining it? Did it really happen? I think I've been pushing it back, out of my consciousness, unable to believe it could be true. Please tell me I'm not going mad."

Pru sat in front of her and held both her hands assuring her she wasn't imagining it; she wasn't going mad. She said,

"We've purposely said nothing to you about what happened in case we planted some false memory in your head, but what you've just told us is exactly what we believed to have happened. You've just confirmed everything for us."

Sandra wiped the tears from her eyes and after a moment or two's thought, she said,

"Why would she do that? Why would she try to kill me? I wasn't aggressive towards her, I just wanted an explanation, after all she'd been the one to approach me and how did she know that Chika was missing or that I was on my way to visit you when we first met? The more I'd thought about it the more suspicious I'd become of her."

It was unbearable to see her in such a state and I felt she deserved some form of explanation of why she'd become a victim, and I said,

"Sandra, I'm afraid you've unwittingly become entwined in a feud that involves us and a money lender from Cheap Side. His people were the ones holding Chika hostage. It's very complicated and it's become a dangerous situation. It should never have affected you and I'm so sorry, but it has. They were watching us and knew you were visiting, and you became their means of getting at us. We've traced the supposed clairvoyant; her name is Queenie Carter not Mrs Hope as she pretended. She and her husband are bargees and they're both in the pay of the money lender, Finkelstein. She admits that she was with you on the ferry, but she insists that she was attempting to save you when you fell overboard. We didn't accept her story but as you couldn't recall what had happened we couldn't prove she was lying. We shalln't let the matter rest, she'll pay the price for what she did to you."

232

Chapter 40

Morning broke to another depressing day of heavy skies and incessant rain. Lightning lit up the heavens and the thunder that followed made Atlas hide – it was probably the only thing that he feared. I opened the front door to find a card wedged into the frame. It was covered in blood stains. I opened it – a black edged condolence card – and read the scrawled message inside; 'Be warned – you know how to avoid Armageddon.'

Instinctively I realised where it had come from and what it meant. A shudder ran through me causing me to take a step back. I felt something soft under my foot and looked down to see a dead rat. I kicked it from the porch step and realised it had all begun again – it was a message from Finkelstein.

....I was sure, right from the moment I'd taken the chest, that it must end in war between us and I'd asked myself many times since whether it was worth the aggravation, but revenge had driven me, even before I knew what the contents were. Actually seeing and holding the gold had created greed in me like I'd never known before; much as it had in us all. I'd heard about gold-fever in the gold-fields of America and Africa, the madness created in striving to get rich – was this it? I took the card inside but said nothing to anyone and threw it into the fire.

I took down a dictionary, turned the pages to 'Armageddon' and read: '*Hebrew name/ great symbolic battlefield of the Apocalypse or final struggle between the powers of good and evil*' which only confirmed what I'd thought. I looked at both Pru and Chika, worried about what this was leading us to. Pru perceived my glance toward her and came to look over my shoulder at what I was reading. I closed the dictionary, but not before she'd seen what I'd been looking at. She looked at me with a puzzled expression and said,

"Armageddon? What's your interest in Armageddon?" I whispered, "That card I just threw on the fire – Finkelstein!"

"What do you mean, I didn't see a card?" Still whispering I said,

"I wasn't going to tell anyone but there was a card wedged in the frame of the door – you know the type with a black surround that you'd normally send with a message of condolence if someone had died – I burnt it. There was a message inside that said, 'Be warned – you know how to avoid Armageddon', and there was a dead rat on the doorstep. It could only be Finkelstein."
Pru just gave a derisory little laugh and said

"Come on Jack; don't let him get to you? What can he do – he can't go running to the peelers can he?"

"That's not what worries me. He's not going to let us get away with taking a fortune in gold from him is he? You know what's happened to Chika, and Sandra, he won't stop there the next time. He uses the word Armageddon – that means something apocalyptic. Don't tell me that doesn't worry you too?" She didn't reply.

Breakfast continued with the four of us, and on the surface it would have appeared that all was normal, however, my stomach was churning and all I could think about was Armageddon and apocalypse.

After breakfast Tom and Lottie arrived. Tom immediately took me aside and whispered, "It's begun, there was a dead rat nailed to the door and offal and blood spread on the door step, this morning. I have the feeling this is going to end badly for us."

I wasn't at all surprised by what he told me and I explained what I'd discovered at our front door. Clearly, by the tone of his voice and the expression on his face, Tom was as concerned as I was. I asked,

"How has Lottie taken it?"

"She's been rather quiet and I think it's unnerved her."
I could understand her feelings and said,

"The four of us are going to have to sit down together and talk this through."
That was going to prove awkward, having Sandra and Chika in our company, we couldn't involve them, but at the same time they deserved to know if only for their

own safety. Fortunately, Sandra decided to retire early that evening, and with Chika safely tucked up in bed, Tom and Lottie joined us around the kitchen table. I asked,

"What suggestions have we for the disposal of the gold, and what are your feelings about the threat it poses from Finkelstein?" Tom was first to answer,

"I've been making a few enquiries and what I've discovered will give you an idea of the value of what we have. The price varies considerably from country to country but as a rule of thumb, America has set the price at a new twenty-eight dollars per Troy ounce. Our guinea is currently worth two and a half American dollars, so if we weigh the gold we can calculate its approximate value."

Pru was quick to point out,

"Whatever its true value, it's going to be too much for any small jeweller to buy, and any honest and self respecting dealer would realise immediately that there was something dishonest in having that amount to sell. What I'm attempting to say is, even if we could find a buyer they wouldn't pay a market price. We might stand a better chance of finding buyers by selling the smaller pieces one by one over a period of time."

Tom replied,

"I understand that but to sell it over time means that we're going to have it on our hands for years."

Pru answered,

"Well does that matter? It's our security."

"I understand what Tom is saying. We are all good friends and have been for a long time, but we've been reading about 'gold fever' and what it does to people. Tom saw what it did to his friends in India and Africa when those in power imposed draconian penalties in respect of gold; people were executed. Perhaps we're more civilised here but I don't want it to eat its way into our friendship," answered Lottie.

Pru was quick to speak up,

"Why should it come to that? We know we're equal partners and none of us are in desperate need, therefore it could sit in the bank vault until we find the buyers."

I listened to everything that was being said and felt compelled to have my say,

"No-one's addressing what I see as the most important aspect, and that's the danger we're facing from Finkelstein. I begin to wish I'd never seen that chest. Even now, it wouldn't concern me if it went to the bottom of the river..." that caused an intake of breath amongst the others, and they looked questioningly at each other, I continued, "...I know Tom sees the danger we're all in. We've already had someone attempting to break into the house. What will it lead to, someone being killed? What are we to do?"

Pru snapped,

"What do you expect us to do, give it back to him?" which brought an equally terse reply from Lottie,

"That's what I mean – did you hear Pru's tone of voice? I don't want it to lead to arguments. It's going to be another Finkelstein curse; we're going to be at each other's throat," to which Pru responded,

"Well we've always shared alike in whatever we've done, so is the answer to divide the gold by weight now, so that we each can do as we please? That way there can be no argument."

I persisted in my question that no one seemed prepared to answer,

"Whatever we decide to do with it, doesn't answer my concern about the danger we're in. I'm sure we all know Finkelstein's never going to let it rest. He's lost a fortune and he's going to do everything he can to get it back. We've already suffered Chika being kidnapped and the attempt on Sandra's life – not to mention what happened to Lottie – so I'll ask again, what are we going to do, we don't want to live the rest of our lives in fear of what he might do next?"

A moment of silence descended as we looked at each other perplexed, until finally Pru spoke up,

"If he wants war, he can have it. We'll go on the offensive. By all means, let him make the first move, but be prepared, and then hit him hard."
I was watching the faces of Tom and Lottie as Pru spoke and I don't believe they understood any more than I did. I had to ask,

"What do you mean, 'offensive'? What have you got in mind?" Pru answered with a grimace on her face,

"I don't know just at this minute but let me think about it. He's got a soft under-belly just like everyone, and I'll find it."

Chapter 41

Christmas was approaching again and we'd hoped to give Sandra some independence again by restoring her cottage to the condition before it was ransacked. However, the threat of reprisal from Finkelstein's mob had meant that we had to watch our back even more, especially where Chika was concerned – she couldn't be left unprotected. The work at the cottage was progressing slowly in the odd days we were able to devote to it but there was still no enthusiasm from Sandra to return there.

Pru and I were quite content that she remained with us – the old vicarage was big enough to accommodate us all, but we thought it would be better for Sandra to return to her cottage and regain the lifestyle she'd lost. Alas, it was becoming clear that the trauma she'd endured was very deep seated. Her memory had now fully returned and on the surface she was fully recovered, but although she tried to hide it, in truth she was deeply scarred by what had happened.

Atlas suddenly rose from the hearthrug, hackles raised and growling, and made for the front door. I jumped to my feet to grab his collar before someone opened the door. I knew he'd savage anyone he didn't recognise. As Pru opened the door I saw a man dressed in the red breasted attire of the post delivery that had gained the nick-name of Robin Red Breast. He was cautiously stepping backwards up the path as though he was already aware of Atlas, but perhaps he'd heard the growling. A wooden box lay on the doorstep. He didn't stop to give me the chance to ask what it was or who had sent it. Neither Pru nor I had expected any delivery but we accepted that it could be something – books perhaps – that Sandra had ordered. Atlas's attention was riveted on the box, sniffing and whining. I pushed him aside and picked up the box which I found was surprisingly light, and carried it inside. Strangely, there was no address label so I asked myself how did they know where to deliver?

We all gathered around, interested to discover what the box contained and who it was intended for. I couldn't see a means of opening it; it appeared nailed fast. Atlas continued to try to push past me to sniff, whatever it was it had him excited. I took the poker from the hearth and began to prise a board from the box. As the board became detached everyone crowded near to see. Sandra suddenly grabbed my arm and said "Careful, I don't like this." And no sooner had she said it a black head slithered from the box hissing, it's tongue flicking out. Everyone drew back and Pru shrieked in alarm but Atlas, growling pushed forward to attack. The snake slithered from the box and with me holding Atlas back it slid from the table to the floor. For a moment or two I think we were all panicked and at a loss as to what to do, and obviously the snake just wanted to escape. It surprised me how quickly it moved and slid silently under the seats and into the corner of the kitchen into the darkness under a cabinet.

Atlas pulled free and growling began to scratch at the cabinet, trying furiously to get to the snake. Conscious that if we got too close we could get bitten we were all a bit reticent, but something had to be done to dislodge it from it's hiding place. I opened the broom cupboard and grabbed a long handled broom. Whilst Tom did his best to hold back Atlas, I used the broom to poke under the cabinet and with several thrusts the snake was forced out into the open again.

Atlas pulled free again and went to attack the snake again. It raised itself up with it's mouth open showing it's vicious fangs and struck with lightning speed. Atlas winced but still attacked. Pru, with presence of mind, grabbed a coat and threw it over the snake and I took up the poker again and beat it down repeatedly with as much force as I could upon the wriggling outline under the coat until all movement ceased.

Sweet Retribution

Sandra, appreciating the danger, had retreated from the snake, but now perceiving the danger to be passed with its demise, came near again as I cautiously lifted the coat. The snake lay inert and Sandra said,

"I think it's a Black Mamba; if it is it's extremely poisonous and they grow very large but I think this is a juvenile – deadly poisonous just the same."

Everyone had been so afraid and concerned about their own safety that no-one gave a thought to Atlas. I noticed him lying in a corner, very quiet and subdued, and I remembered how he winced whilst attacking the snake. He was unusually quiet and his distressed breathing caused me concern, realising he must have been bitten. I knelt down beside him and could see that his face was quickly becoming swollen and his breathing laboured.

Sandra realised the consequences Atlas faced and took Chika to her room. No-one seemed to know what to do. Pru poured water from the kettle that simmered on the hob, and bathed the swelling. I could only lightly stroke his head in sympathy as he lay, now unable to move. The sad inevitable came some hours later, and an air of sorrow descended upon everyone; Chika was distraught and inconsolable.

Questioning and raw anger welled up inside us; where had the snake come from? Who had sent it? It was all too obvious – Finkelstein! His war of attrition had begun, but where would he get a snake? It didn't take much consideration to realise that the crew of ships arriving at the East India docks or Limehouse Basin from Africa, India and the Far East, would see a profit in smuggling unusual, exotic or dangerous animals into the country and someone like Finkelstein would pay heavily for a 'weapon' the likes of a Black Mamba to use against his adversaries.

The pain and distress of losing Atlas was understandably overwhelming for Chika who cried uncontrollably. Pru, choked with anger, went to sit alone in our bedroom, deep in thought and determined upon retaliation. I shared the grief but I couldn't help but think that we'd brought it upon ourselves – or at least, I'd brought it upon everyone in discovering and hijacking the chest of Finkelstein's gold. It was too late though to dwell on what might have been if I'd not taken the chest – it was done and there'd be no turning back because none of the others would relinquish their share of the spoils.

To my mind we had a fortune in gold sitting there; could do nothing with it; and all it did was bring us grief and misery. I knew my misgivings weren't going to change Pru's mind. The untimely death of her first husband Joe, and the distress and hardship she'd endured in consequence because of Bouverie and Finkelstein, had had such a lasting effect, it generated a hatred so deep seated it festered in her mind. Matters could only get worse in pursuit of Finkelstein's utter destruction. I went out into the garden to be alone with my thoughts and to bury Atlas.

Tom and Lottie were devastated to hear what had happened and Lottie got to work immediately trying to find a replacement for Atlas. The breeder and trainer of Atlas was a personal friend and could offer the choice of a litter. Lottie took Chika to see the pups whilst Pru went out alone, walking by the river. She later confided that she'd been approached by a woman who identified herself as a member of the Salvation Army. Apparently, she'd been watching Pru who she thought was showing signs of depression, possibly contemplating suicide in the river.

Actually, Pru's apparent 'depression' was in fact her deep contemplation of revenge upon Finkelstein. Pru thanked the woman for her concern but assured her she wasn't about to harm herself, and handed the lady a guinea contribution to the cause. In return she was given a Salvation Army leaflet that she promised she would read later.

Sweet Retribution

Back home at the Old Vicarage Pru sat before the fire, with the leaflet. I asked what she was reading and she handed it to me. I read 'Salvation Army' and quickly realised it was an extract from Punch Magazine describing the unjust sentencing of children. I read on;

'Most terrible to imagine the savage satisfaction gleaming in the eyes of a starved, and therefore sullen and revengeful peasantry.'

I quickly realised that it was railing against the transportation of children as young as eight years old, found guilty of setting fire to stacks of hay in retaliation against the greed and avarice of their land-owning employers.

The further I read I realised that the deeper issue was the crusade against Bryant and May, the makers of the 'Lucifer'- the common, cheap, yellow phosphorous matches. It was this yellow phosphorus that was devastating the lives of young girls in the local factory, causing that dreadful 'Fossy Jaw'.

I couldn't understand what interest Pru had in reading this material. Had I only known, it had sparked the embryo of a plan to strike back at Finkelstein in spite of knowing the consequences.

Chapter 42

Secretly Pru began to hoard boxes of 'Lucifers', gun cotton, combustibles and whale oil. She said nothing to anyone of her grave intentions. In daylight hours there was little change in her, spending her time in household activities and devoted attention to Chika who was still grieving for Atlas. It was as darkness fell that it all changed. It was obvious that she was nursing and nurturing that deep hatred that had surfaced again with the death of Atlas. Once again she returned to those occasional unaccompanied forays into the haunts of her past.

This change in her and the return to intrigue, could hardly have gone un-noticed, and I was compelled to say to her,

"Pru, it's obvious that you're planning something and I'm beginning to worry that you're putting yourself in danger again. Whatever it is you're intending, please for my sake and for Chika, forget it."

"There's no need for you to concern yourself, you know I'm more than capable of looking after myself," she answered, still not disclosing what she had in mind. I did notice that the derringer was missing from its box; she was obviously carrying that as a precaution – that was at least some consolation.

That night, I sat as usual, nerves on edge, until the small hours, waiting for her return, always expecting that some disaster had befallen her. Outside, it was raining yet again and the wind was howling in the chimney. I shivered and put another log on the fire. Eventually, I heard the key turn in the lock; unruffled and quite unperturbed she walked in and poured herself a stiff brandy. Her only concern seemed to be for me having sat up waiting for her. I felt compelled to remonstrate that whatever she was up to was going to lead to more trouble. I asked,

"What the devil are you doing? You keep telling me you're more than capable of looking after yourself but I know it's all about striking back at Finkelstein and he's not someone to mess around with. He's going to expect some sort of retaliation and he'll have his thugs on the alert. If you get caught I dread to think of what he'll do."

Pru looked unconcerned as she sat before the fire sipping her brandy. She looked at me for a long moment before answering, but eventually said dismissively,

"Jack, give me some credit, I know what I'm doing. I've told you before it's all about finding his soft underbelly. I've been watching his hovel but he's got too many of his thugs covering his back for me to get anywhere near, so I've got to find some other way of getting to him," and she threw back the remains of the brandy in her glass, stood, put the guard around the remains of the fire, and said, "I'm tired, let's get to bed."

Next morning, after breakfast Lottie arrived to collect Chika and together with Sandra Chung they set off to choose a puppy. Chika had been quite upset at the loss of Atlas and despite the miserable weather she'd been spending time in the garden, prettying the grave where I'd buried him. It was obviously her way of coping with grief and I found it upsetting, but understandable, for her to be affected in this way. I was anxious to replace Atlas; as much to give Chika something to relieve her grief as to find another guard dog.

Whilst they'd gone, inevitably I felt compelled – at the risk of upset – to bring up the issue of Finkelstein, the gold trinkets, the precious stones, and the dangers that came with them. Pru became short tempered with what she saw as my weakness of character and my apparent willingness to hand everything back to him. The atmosphere between us became tense and subdued. Without explaining what she was about, she donned her coat and with a parcel under her arm, she went out. Although I had no idea where she was bound, or what she carried in the parcel, I felt that she wasn't about to tangle with Finkelstein or his thugs in daylight hours, so what was she about?

Sweet Retribution

I admit, I felt that what I had in mind was disloyal to Pru but I was both intrigued and concerned for her. I couldn't just sit at home worrying any longer and so I decided to follow. I had a good idea that she was making for her old haunts around Limehouse which meant that I couldn't take the same ferry without alerting her. By the time Jake had rowed across to the basin and made his return crossing, I was a good hour – probably more – behind her. I asked myself, *'Am I wasting my time – will I ever find her after all this time?'* but my worry drove me on. I paid Jake and climbed the steps onto the quay at Limehouse basin but now, *'where do I go – where would she have gone?'* I felt quite miserable, traipsing around in the mizzle – it wasn't so much rain as a heavy mist that was enough to soak me – which helped deepen the mood I was in.

I wandered around the quay, scouring the vessels tied up there, the crews, the dockers, the merchants, and all the numerous by-standers, for a glimpse of Pru but to no avail. *'Where would she go, surely not to Cheap Side and Bread Street – into Finkelstein's lair?'* Again I dismissed the idea, *'She wouldn't be that crazy; in broad daylight, so where would she go?'* By the time I'd reached the place where the River Lea entered the basin I was beginning to feel it was a wasted effort and the idea of returning home was building. I stood at the entrance to a chandler's shop, finding a little shelter and finally deciding to return to the ferry. Wet and miserable I stood, now with an acrid sting to my nostrils – thin wisps of smoke with an indistinguishable tang, drifting on the light wind, which seemed to be blowing south towards the Thames. I didn't give it much thought to begin with but as I sheltered the smoke grew heavier. I was about to leave, to escape the smell, when my attention was taken by the sound of running feet and shouting.

Suddenly, a figure emerged running full pelt from the tow-path, down the side of the chandler's shop. It was Pru and by the sound of the shouting she was being pursued closely by others. I instinctively reached out and grabbed her arm, swinging her into the shop entrance. Surprised and fearing she was caught she turned to fight, but realised in an instant that it was me, she allowed me to bundle her into the shop just as her pursuers rushed by. I was astounded just how quickly she regained her composure as the counter assistant appeared, alerted by the tinkling door bell. Simply to cover our abrupt appearance I asked for the first thing that came into my head, a chain length of jute rope – which would be a regular requirement of any of the ships crews around the basin. As he disappeared into the rear of the premises to fulfil my purchase, we slipped out again.

Whoever had been chasing Pru had vanished into the throng along the quay. I was desperate to discover what had happened and why she was being chased but we were more concerned at that moment about hiding in the crowd. The whys and wherefores could wait until later. It would have been foolish in the extreme to have returned to the ferry point, as if those pursuing her were Finkelstein's mob, and they must certainly be that mob, they'd realise she'd have to use the ferry to get away and return home. I realised that I was still carrying the key to Sandra Chung's home in my pocket after helping with the renovations there, and it seemed an obvious place to go to lie low for an hour or two.

Despite the renovations the house had a cold, damp atmosphere, possible because of its closeness to the basin and the river, but there'd been no fire to air the place for weeks now. At least we were dry and away from discovery. I could resist it no longer, I had to ask,

"Alright, are you going to explain, what have you done, why they were chasing you?" Pru gave me a wry smile and replied,

"Give it an hour or so and I'll show you. I can get back there across the rope-maker's field without being seen and you'll see what I've done."

"Get back to where?"

Sweet Retribution

"Where the Raven was moored on The Lea. You know and I know that it's owned by Finkelstein. The clairvoyant woman, Queenie, and her husband Black Johnny Carter, are the bargees and are part of his mob. I couldn't get near his den on Bread Street, there were too many of his mobsters around. I told you I was looking for his soft under belly and the only thing that came to me was the Raven. Fortunately there was no-one aboard so I've fired it. I emptied their oil lamps and with what I had with me I spread oil over everything. No-one was ever going to put that fire out, it'll be just a burnt out shell now. Those men that were chasing me saw the fire and saw me jump from the barge as the fire took hold. Fortunately they were too far away to catch me and I'm fairly confident they couldn't identify me – but Finkelstein will know it was me. I just wish it had been a funeral pyre for him and the Carters."

"I knew you were up to something when you left the house, that's why I followed you." She didn't respond but simply smiled. As we waited Pru used the time to wash, and to clean the mud from her clothing and her shoes. After about an hour, it seemed reasonably safe to leave. Pru said, "Follow me," and she led me through back alleys and finally into the rope-maker's field, where, from a safe distance, we could see the black, burnt out hulk that lay smouldering, beside the wooden landing stage. All of the upper structure of the cabin and even the hatches of the cargo hold had all perished, all burnt to a cinder.

The delight showed in her face, obviously satisfied she'd been able to strike back at Finkelstein, but although I said nothing, I didn't see it as much of an achievement. Yes, it was another financial loss for Finkelstein, but that was going to fuel the situation even more, and in the overall scheme of things it wasn't going to harm him in the same way that the snake had harmed us.

Chapter 43

Chika arrived home full of joy, with her new love, a huge energetic bundle, already too heavy for her to carry, that appeared a miniature version of Atlas. Lottie placed him down on the hearth and unwrapped the blanket in which she'd carried him home.

"I've named him Titan," said Chika cuddling the pup close to her cheek.

"Why Titan?" I asked.

"Sandra explained to me that Atlas was a Greek god, one of the Titans and I liked that name. I think Atlas would like him to be called Titan," she replied.

"Then Titan it is," I said.

Lottie explained, "He's a twelve weeks old English Mastiff, just like Atlas, and he's bred by the same lady that bred Atlas. He should have all the same attributes as Atlas; they're loveable dogs but tend to be protective of their home and owners. He'll grow very quickly."

Titan was a small diversion in my troubled mind; he gave me a little more assurance of Chika's safety – even though he was just a pup, but I knew this tit-for-tat feud was going to escalate. I could only try to imagine what Finkelstein might do next and what we could do to prevent it. I still felt responsible for everything that had happened by taking the chest of golden trinkets and wished I'd never set eyes on it. I knew it was useless dwelling on regrets because no-one else felt the same and they were never going to relinquish their share.

Finkelstein was a devious and fiendish adversary and I worried that his next strike against us was going to be far worse than anything he'd done before. For me, the next fortnight was a period of nervous anticipation, always expecting the worst. I realised I couldn't persuade Pru to return to our moorland holding, away from this obsession to destroy him and there seemed nothing I could do to bring the situation to an end. I could understand her loathing of the man and what he represented, because of what had happened to her previous husband, but that bitterness was threatening to destroy us too.

In one of our quiet moments of candour, Pru confessed that she'd seriously considered contaminating the well from which he pumped water for his household needs, perhaps with a dead animal, but she'd eventually rejected the idea because that same supply would probably be used by others. Another plan was to approach contacts amongst the sea-going fraternity to purchase some exotic venomous reptile to release inside Finkelstein's den – as indeed he'd done with the snake that bit and killed Atlas. She wasn't sure what venomous reptiles there might be, but anything with a poisonous bite would do. She'd read about Black widow, Tarantulas or Funnel-web spiders had come to mind, but these extreme ideas carried their own problems for whoever was handling them and thankfully she had eventually rejected them. Although discarded, those ideas showed this fanatical intent that festered inside her.

I feared that when all these extreme ideas fell through, she might be tempted to use her derringer to shoot him and that would surely lead to her arrest for murder. She wasn't going to give up, that was for certain, but how could I dissuade her when she was determined to find some other way to strike back? The situation was beginning to destroy me, I could think of nothing else, and the constant worry for the safety of everyone around us, made me decide that I'd have to take the initiative, but what was I to do?

There was nothing for it but to approach Finkelstein and try to bring this war to an end. I knew I was putting myself in danger to do it and I admit that I was afraid, to the extent that my insides were constantly churning – but it had to be done.

What was I going to say to him to placate him? I lay awake most of the night trying to devise a plan. He was never going to accept anything less than the return of the chest of golden trinkets and that was never going to happen, so what could induce him to bring the feud to an end? The matter filled my tired mind; trying to absorb every facet of the dilemma. No matter how I turned from side to side, buried my head in the pillow or sat on the edge of the bed, trying to resolve the problem, sleep wouldn't come and my fraught mind repeatedly returned to that same issue – the return of the chest and trinkets.

Eventually, unable to sleep, I rose before daylight had broken. I took Titan outside into the frost covered garden to relieve himself. I shivered in the cold air but perhaps that was what was needed to stimulate my brain and it was at that moment that my plan came together. It was going to be so risky and there was no guarantee that it would work – but it was better than sitting around worrying, waiting for Finkelstein's next move. There'd be no point in discussing it with Pru, Tom or Lottie, they'd certainly not agree to what I had in mind and would probably try to stop me. It would need some preparation.

A visit to the foundry was first on the list to obtain scrap pieces of iron, or perhaps lead might be better with a density and weight most akin to gold. Next on the agenda was the blacksmith's forge to have a small balance device made that would fit inside the chest that had held the gold. Finally, I made an advance payment to the canal lock-keeper's son, to row me to a rendezvous on the river Lea when the time came.

I set off for Finkelstein's den on Bread Street, full of nervous dread of the reception I was likely to get. I took my time on the journey, giving myself time to bolster my nerve; constantly fighting against the more sensible messages my brain kept telling me to turn around and forget this dangerous idea. Only the certain knowledge that he'd do something even more diabolical if I didn't attempt to stop him drove me on.

I hesitated for some moments as I turned the corner onto Bread Street; the sight of the pugilistic individual with the broken nose shuffling back and forth outside Finkelstein's domain increasing my nervousness. He'd recognise me for sure but come what may I had to get by him to confront Finkelstein.

Sweet Retribution

Trying to appear as confident as I could, I walked purposefully toward the doorway, calm and determined on outward appearance, but actually feeling turbulence unlike anything I'd experienced before in my bowels. The door-keeper sprang into action, pushing me against the wall with his left forearm across my throat making me struggle to breathe. With his free hand he began a thorough shakedown, frisking me for concealed weapons.

Satisfied that I carried nothing offensive he relaxed the pressure on my wind-pipe. I felt my bladder weaken under the assault but when no further blows came from the gorilla pinioning me, I regained a little of my former confidence, and said, "I'm not here to cause trouble I just need to talk with Mr Finkelstein."

The broken nosed hulk just grunted as though incapable of speaking normally, turned me around, took my collar in his huge fist and pushed me forward through the doorway. With him still holding me as I stood in front of Finkelstein, I felt like some useless glove puppet, unable to utter a word. Finkelstein looked up quite unperturbed and sarcastically asked,

"Well, well, my dear, how nice to see you, whatever brings you to my humble abode?"

I tried my best to speak but all I managed was a croaking noise. I gulped and swallowed and tried again,

"I, er I, I, think you know why I'm here Mr Finkelstein..." I swallowed again trying to ease the compression I felt in my throat, and then continued again, "...We have to come to some understanding. This terrible war that's going on between us is going to end in someone losing their life."

There was a long silence as his gaze became fixated on my face, but showing no emotion. I broke the silence by asking,

"What can be done?" Finkelstein continued to stare at me, in unblinking silence that somehow seemed so malevolent.

Sweet Retribution

Suddenly, that sickly, sweet, rhetoric that was so recognizable in him, changed with a snarl, as he said,

"Have you lost your mind? You have the gall to come here asking me 'What can be done?' You know full well what can be done. You can return to me what's mine – that's what can be done, and unless it is, then I promise..." and he broke off without finishing the sentence, but I knew he was promising to take the feud to another level.

This was no more than I had expected from him, he wanted the chest of golden trinkets returned and he'd stop at nothing to that end. The temptation was there in me to tell him that the gold was never his in the first place, it was all obtained from his criminal dealings in stolen property, but I realised to do so would only antagonise him further, and get me nowhere. My plan was to make him believe I'd do almost anything to appease him and I hoped my truly nervous and frightened image would convince him that I would. I drew a deep breath and bolstered my nerve to say,

"I...I understand sir, I really do, but my partners don't see it that way, so what can I do to bring this to an end?" His eyes drew into a squint and a puzzled expression crossed his face as he searched for understanding, and asked,

"Are you actually telling me you'd be prepared to return the chest, even though the others are opposed?"

"Yes sir, I would, I'd do anything if there was a way," I answered.

Chapter 44

Finkelstein looked at me in amazement and said,

"Do you take me for a fool my dear..." returning to that characteristic sickly smarm, "...and expect me to believe that you'd risk everything to deprive your friends of their bounty?"

"I would, sir, if it would bring this dreadful war between us to an end. I wish I'd never set eyes on the chest." I tried to sound as servile and convincing as possible. Again he stared at me for what seemed an age without speaking which was as unsettling as any assault. Eventually he said,

...."I can't make up my mind whether you're just a fool or an imbecile, trying to take me for an idiot."

"Sir, I'm neither a fool nor an imbecile. I know the risk I'm taking in coming here to offer to return the chest, and I know the risk in depriving the others of the trinkets, but whatever the consequences, they can't be as dreadful as facing this continuous war. I assure you, I am in earnest."

He thought for a moment, with his both hands in front of him, fingertip to fingertip, before he looked up and asked,

"Supposing that for a moment I believed you, how could you possibly obtain the chest – *my chest* – without the others being aware?"

"I've thought about that. It's been away at a foundry somewhere secret, and I'm sorry to tell you the trinkets will all have been reduced to gold ingots by now, but it's being returned and my idea is to intercept it before the others realise." Of course, I knew that the trinkets were safe in a deep vault of the bank, but I thought my story sounded feasible.

"Somewhere secret you say? How will you know how and when it will be returned?"

"It doesn't matter where the foundry is, but how it will be returned. I'm sure I can find that out and then it can be intercepted."

Sweet Retribution

"Mmm, you don't convince me. Perhaps you can come to me again when you have a more plausible story – when you know when the chest will be returned."

"Yes sir, I will, but I believe time is of the essence. As I see it this is the only chance I have to obtain the chest. Once it is back in their hands the contents will be distributed and then all is lost. If it is to work I must act quickly and you must help me."

"Alright, what is to be done? – but I warn you, my patience is thin, and if this is all an attempt to hoodwink me, then you must be fearful of your life."

"Sir, I assure you, this is no attempt to deceive. I shall be in touch with you as quickly as I can. My plan is to intercept the chest, hand it over to you, and then I can make believe that you forced me to hand it over."

"Mmmm, we'll see. You've risked a great deal coming here with this idea, so I'm tempted to give it a try but you've been warned!! I'm still not altogether convinced about you. Come back the moment you know more." That was the signal for the brute holding my collar to pull me around and thrust me out onto Bread Street.

I stumbled out into the fresh, cold air and only then did I realise just how much I was sweating. Finkelstein was a frightening character and it had taken a lot to enter the dragon's den and face up to him. I'd thought I might escape with a few bruises at best if it hadn't gone well but it went better than I'd anticipated.

The consequences had been made clear that if I didn't deliver I'd be made to suffer, so it was up to me to set things in motion – make the plan work. I had the scraps of sheet lead from the foundry and estimated the weight to equal the original weight of gold in the chest. Next I collected the small tilting device ordered from the blacksmith. Finally I fitted a small wooden box I'd made into the chest and filled it with dry sand. Now I was ready. It was two days since I'd visited Finkelstein – now it was time to see him again.

Sweet Retribution

The pugilistic minder recognised me and went through the same procedure again, shaking me down to make sure I wasn't carrying a weapon, and then allowed me, unmolested, to enter the lair. I anticipated Finkelstein would be eager to take the chest from me rather than entrust it to one of his minions, but to allay any suspicions he might have I said,

"Can you send someone to meet me at the landing stage above the junction where the Union canal meets the river Lea? I've arranged for someone to deliver the chest with the ingots to me there at first light of day tomorrow. No-one else knows these arrangements so you can rest assured there'll be only me and who-ever you decide to send, to know what's taking place – no-one to interfere – and I'd like to keep it that way."

"I hope, my dear, that this isn't some sort of trap you're trying to lead me into, because you'll regret it if it is."

"Oh please, sir, don't concern yourself on that account. I just want an end to this fighting..." I was trying to be as convincing as possible but there was a great big knot in my stomach as I spoke, nerves were very difficult to keep in check bit I continued,"...all I ask is that who-ever you instruct to meet me there, on your behalf, is either someone I recognise or who properly identifies himself to me. Above all he must be discrete. I don't want my partners to know what's taking place."

Finkelstein made no commitment but I felt confident he was taking the bait and he'd be there in person to take the chest from me. I was sure he wouldn't chance the recovery of the chest to anyone else with all that had happened previously. Despite the nervous tension I began to feel a sense of elation that my plan was coming together.

Unfortunately, that elation didn't last, and was instead replaced by nagging thoughts that things might go wrong in the execution of the plan, especially as so much depended on a trusted but unworldly youth rowing a boat. I'd spent many sleepless hours devising the plan up to this point and it seemed that another night lying awake and worrying lay ahead. Pru couldn't understand my restlessness, constantly tossing and turning in bed, and my apparent solitary, brooding behaviour, but how could I possibly explain to her what I had in mind?

The church clock struck four in the morning as I left home, carefully locking the door behind me. Again the weather was miserable, wet and cold with a biting wind. It was a long walk to London Bridge and on towards Limehouse. Jake the ferryman, wouldn't be operating at that time in the night, and walking was the only option, but despite the weather the walk freshened my mind and blew away the sleeplessness.

The streets were empty and the only sounds were of the wind whistling in the tree branches and of the swish and swirl of the Thames rushing along. It all seemed so eerie and gave me a feeling of foreboding for what was to come. I shook myself and dismissed those negative feelings from my mind and turned my thoughts to the matters in hand. I hoped I'd convinced my adversary and tempted him to be there in person.

I wondered just what feelings and thoughts were going through his mind, whether he'd lost any sleep – I doubted it – but I fervently hoped he'd have something to disturb his slumbers after this day was over.

The lock-keeper's cottage was in darkness as I waited. My plan depended upon Aaron to row the boat. He was the eldest son of the Jackson family, a normally reliable youth, but had he forgotten the commitment he'd made? A sense of unease began to grip me, but at the moment I was about to begin throwing pebbles at the window, I saw the flicker of a candle.

Aaron had no idea of how vital it was for him to row his boat to the landing stage on the river, or what the chest that I'd left with him the previous day actually contained. He may have wondered why I'd been prepared to pay him so well and in advance too. I now needed to give him specific instructions to make this work.

....I'd chosen the venue on the tow path near the landing stage purposely as it was an open area with no obstructions to view or bushes in which others could hide. The idea was to give Finkelstein a sense of security, sure that he wasn't walking into a trap, and indeed I could assure myself that he hadn't secreted others to entrap me.

The time was approaching; a red hue was beginning to appear in the sky far away on the horizon as dawn began to break, although it was still a dark and dismal rain-swept place. The river was high and running fast, spilling over onto the tow-path in places making the path muddy, murky and precarious, not a place to be walking without the utmost care – ideal!

Two dark figures appeared on the tow-path from near the canal junction, walking towards me. One I could recognise from his silhouette, perhaps it was that exceptionally long dark coat that marked out Finkelstein. The other must have been his minder, probably that pugilistic oaf that I'd encountered outside his den. As they came closer I could see it was indeed the pair. They were puffing visible clouds of breath in the cold air as they progressed carefully along the path, avoiding the puddles. Finkelstein continually looked about him, obviously uneasy, and when close enough he said in a snarl,

"I see no chest – where is it? I hope for your sake I'm not here on a wild goose chase."

"Don't worry, it'll be here, I've every confidence," I answered with a shiver – not from cold but from nervous energy.

As arranged, I could see in the distance Aaron's row-boat slowly approaching. His instructions had been to watch for someone joining me near the landing stage before executing his part of my plan. The three of us watched Aaron's approach and as he got within a few oar strokes of the landing stage the chest could be clearly seen in the boat. I'm sure that Finkelstein grew excited, rubbing his hands together.

....Now it was up to Aaron to follow his instructions precisely. He pulled alongside the landing stage, allowing the flow of the river to press his boat to the structure. Tying a mooring rope to one of the stanchions he stood and lifted the chest from the bottom of the craft. The boat rocked as he stood but he took extraordinary care to follow my instructions and place the chest precariously on the edge of the landing stage, at the same time pulling the piece of cotton that I'd attached, until it broke. He didn't know the purpose of that cotton but it activated the blacksmith's tipping device, allowing the sand to flow from the box inside the chest, altering its point of balance.

Finkelstein, watching with eager anticipation, moved toward the landing stage to recover the chest as Aaron untied and pulled away, allowing the river to carry the boat quickly away. I stepped in front of my adversary and said,

"Be careful, that structure isn't too safe," but he wasn't about to let such considerations prevent him from recovering his chest. During the few brief seconds that I delayed him, the sand flowed from the box to make the chest tip and slide over the edge of the landing stage and with quite a splash it fell into the water.

He uttered a shriek of despair as he lunged to grasp the chest as it fell, slipped on the muddy bank and fell with a huge splash into the river and was immediately out of his depth. Panic gripped me as I reached out to grab him, putting myself in danger of falling into the river too, but to no avail. His minder rushed forward to help, but neither of us could reach him. My stomach lurched as I frantically searched around, for something to help him, a plank of wood, a tree branch, anything, but alas there was nothing.

....The times I'd dreamt of revenge against this evil who I knew was behind my daughter's abduction, were beyond count but now, in this moment of panic, here I was trying to save him.

Despite my revulsion I would never have intended this. It was simply a natural reaction to attempt to save him, but we were helpless. All the two of us could do was watch, totally shocked, as the dirty, foaming torrent, with its stinking debris and detritus, carried him away. That familiar long black greatcoat ballooning up on the surface then gradually sinking as it became soaked, dragging him down.

I can only imagine the fear he must have felt as the deluge swept him along; his fight to survive; his struggle for breath, arms flailing in desperation until his strength ebbed away. Finally, I imagine, he'd experience just dark, choking oblivion as he was pulled beneath the surface. A single image remains imprinted on my mind, that of his ashen face with long strands of black hair plastered to it, that black kippa skull cap washed away, as he finally disappeared beneath the surface.

Now I can't help but wonder, did his past really flash through his mind, and if so what were his final thoughts? Was there the slightest regret of the evil he'd employed against others throughout his life; but then again, do I really care? Is that callous of me? The panic I'd felt as he drowned has now left me and the plain truth is that callous or not, I just feel relief and satisfaction that we're finally rid of him and he's finally got his just desserts."

Chapter 45

I arrived home to be met by a furious Pru, and Chika ran and clung to me.

"Where in heaven's name have you been? Tom is still out searching for you. We've been worried Jack, we thought you'd thrown yourself in the Thames. Why do you put us through this torment?" Pru railed, "Look at the state of you, wet through and covered with mud."
I said nothing but couldn't help thinking of the times I'd spent worrying about her when she'd disappeared into the night on her sojourns into her murky past.

"Let me get out of these wet clothes and I'll tell you where I've been. All I'll say at the moment is you won't be disappointed."

She looked at me with an expression of wonder mixed with anger.

"What do you mean, 'won't be disappointed'?"
I managed a smile and planted a kiss on her cheek then turned my back and went to change my clothes.
Although I'd managed a smile I didn't really feel in the mood to smile – it wasn't every day I'd watched a man drown.

By the time I'd washed, shaved and changed, Tom had returned from his search. I appeared in the kitchen to a graven faced Tom, wanting an explanation for my behaviour. Pru produced a hearty breakfast and a desperately needed cup of tea and I sat down to eat as I talked. I knew it was going to be a story that would take some believing. Who'd believe that I'd venture alone into Finkelstein's den and emerge without some physical scars?

I took my time, and perhaps made it sound braver than it actually was, but I felt I deserved some recognition. When I finally revealed that Finkelstein had drowned they were astounded. Pru threw her arms around me and hugged me close. Then I noticed there were actually tears in her eyes.

Sweet Retribution

Tom was a little less emotional and expressive but I could see he was just as pleased, but ever the practical, he asked,

"How sure are you that he drowned? Did you look down in the basin for a body?"

"Yes, I'm sure he drowned. We followed the river down but there was no sign of him. Give it a day or two and he'll wash up somewhere, but take my word for it – he's dead, we're rid of him." Tom took my hand in a firm hand-shake and said in a very heartfelt manner,

"Jack, I never thought you'd got it in you. Well done my friend."

A huge weight had been lifted from our minds. I'm sure we'll never lose that cautionary look over our shoulder, or the desire to ensure that our doors are locked at night, but unless we believe in ghosts then our nemesis will trouble us no longer.

The days that followed were care-free and quiet, and I found time to return to my books and calligraphy. I now realise that the yellow metal everyone craves no longer has any place in my desires for either adornment or wealth.

Titan growled at the sharp rap, rap, rap at the door. He was certainly showing Atlas's qualities even though only a pup. I answered to find Inspector Stone standing there. The severe look on his face worried me from the moment I saw him. He said in that grave inquisitor's manner,

"We found Finkelstein's body floating in Limehouse basin. We've been making a few enquiries and it seems you were there when he entered the river. What on earth were you doing on the river bank at that time of the morning with a criminal like Finkelstein? The thought crosses my mind, did he fall or did you push him. My guess is you pushed him into the water, do you want to confess?"

I wanted to blurt out a denial but my vocal chords froze. That brief moment seemed to last an age for me and he watched as the colour drained from my features.

He laughed as he saw my discomfort, and he asked, "Is the kettle on?" as he stepped inside without invitation. He sat down at the kitchen table with an air of bonhomie and said,

"We're as glad to see the back of him as you are, but tell me, I'm intrigued, what were you doing on the river bank at that time in the morning with a man who we all suspected was behind the abduction of your daughter?"

I hardly knew what to say and I looked at Pru for help. There was a moment of panic for me but Pru always retained that presence of mind and charm that a good confident trickster always has. She answered with a disarming smile,

"We invited him to meet us there."

His eyebrows seemed to come together in a questioning frown, obviously sceptical of Pru's response, and said in a laughing manner,

"Oh yes, as though I was born yesterday?"

"It's true, it was an attempt to come to terms with him," she retorted.

"What, on the tow-path at that time in the morning?"

"How do you know we met on the tow path or what time it was?" I asked.

"Oh, I know. You see, for some time we've been watching Finklestein, and we know that you Jack, have been visiting him recently. Very little escapes us, but I couldn't understand why you'd choose to visit him – why were you there?"

I tried to summon up as much courage as possible and be as plausible as I could,

"Well, if you had someone watching, you'll know that thug at the door put me through some torment before I managed to get in and see Finkelstein. You'll have noticed that we no longer have the dog, Atlas; he was the reason for me being there. We'd received a package and inside it was a poisonous snake which bit Atlas. It could quite well have been one of us that suffered, but we managed to destroy it. I'm sure it was Finkelstein that sent it although he didn't admit it – that's why I was there. I realised the time had come to try to put an end to all of this warfare and the river bank was my idea of neutral territory."

I couldn't judge whether the inspector believed what I was telling him. He seemed to take time considering my words, weighing up the probabilities, but then he said,

"I accept that you were genuinely trying to put an end to all that, but how did he drown? Did he fall? What happened?"

I couldn't tell him the truth about the chest or the gold, but I stuck to virtually what had happened without mentioning either,

"I'm not quite sure, he seemed to slip. The river bank was muddy and slippery. His feet seemed to go from under him. His minder and I tried to grab him but we weren't quick enough and the river swept him away. We searched down river but we could find no sign of him."

The inspector nodded his head and said,

"That's close to what his minder has said. We interviewed him but he's a well known villain and not very well disposed to talking to the police. He's an ex-fairground bare-knuckle fighter, part brain-dead, so we couldn't entirely believe what he had to say. Now I have your side of the story to corroborate what he said it'll have to go down as 'accidental'."

The relief brought an immediate relaxation to my nervous stomach and I took a grateful drink from my tea that was beginning to lose its warmth. Inspector Stone stroked his chin and said,

"So tell me, what caused all this bad feeling between you in the first place?"

Pru winked at me from behind the inspector and responded before I could say any more,

"It's a long story that goes back years. I operated a shipping business, bringing tea from India. He wanted part of that business with a clear object of smuggling but I wouldn't give way to his demands. He tried to buy me out but when that failed, he tried more 'persuasive' methods like trying to burn down the warehouse and when that didn't work he abducted my daughter. The list of things he'd done against us goes on and on."

"Yes, well I didn't really come here to ask you about that, I wanted your version of how he drowned. We're as pleased to see the back of him as you are, but I actually have another purpose in mind – that book you mentioned. You said that was what was behind your daughter's abduction. What happened to that book?"
I replied,

"I had to return it to him to secure Chika's safe return under threat that we must not involve the police."

Pru immediately interjected,

"He swore he had nothing to do with Chika's abduction but we were sure he was behind it. We desperately wanted her back home with us but he said he'd only help if I returned the book to him and we didn't involve the police. What else could we do? I agreed to return it to him but for what it's worth I took the precaution of having a copy made. You can have that for all the good it'll do you; it's all in a corrupt foreign language."

Inspector Stone drank the remainder of his tea and left with the copy tucked safely in his coat. He'd soon find there were pages missing from the copy; those where Pru found her name mentioned. In a way I hoped he'd manage to decipher Finkelstein's code to establish Bouverie's involvement and although he couldn't be brought to book for his crimes, at least others would learn what an evil man he was too.

Tom and Lottie arrived almost as soon as the inspector left, eager to discover what had been happening.

Sandra brought Chika to the table and the six of us sat together to plan our Christmas celebration which was only a few days hence. It was going to be the best Christmas celebration ever.

I didn't think any of us would ever shake off the caution, that fear of what lay around the corner, that we'd lived with for so long, despite knowing that

Finkelstein was out of our lives forever; or so we thought. It's a strange situation but the evil that had touched our very beings for so long, now began to have another effect.

Christmas was like no other, we were able to open our home to the festivities and invite friends from the wider community, people I'd never met before but who were friends of Pru, Tom's sea-going chums from The Lady Ester and their families. Pru and Lottie had Sandra to help and between the three of them – obviously assisted by Chika – the food was beyond belief. No expense was spared and the local baker and butcher must have made a fortune out of our excess.

It was on Christmas Day that I first noticed a small change in Pru. We'd paid our usual visit together to celebrate Christmas and the nativity at the Church of Saint John which was the highlight for Chika. The scene of the nativity as always held excitement for her but the singing of hymns was sheer joy. Somehow Pru was taking the vicar's sermon and the whole meaning of Christmas more deeply than ever I'd known before. Even after Christmas she'd gone, on her own to the church for the Epiphany and even took Holy Communion. I knew she had Christian beliefs but had never considered her to be devout in those beliefs.

This change became obvious to me when Abraham Yacovc visited us. It was at Pru's invitation but I didn't understand why she'd brought him here, as the copy of Finkelstein's ledger was now in the hands of Inspector Stone and she no longer had need of anyone to decipher it for us.

Pru quickly brought the conversation around to enquiring about Abraham's family. It was clear they were still apart; wife and children still marooned in Poland, and his meagre savings insufficient to bring them over to England. The reason suddenly dawned on me and I understood clearly why she'd invited him; Abraham was reduced to tears as he gratefully accepted Pru's kindness.

This was the effect that release from Finkelstein's evil had brought about on Pru; she vowed that the wealth derived from his evil would be put to good cause. Abraham was the first to benefit but this charity would soon extend to the church, the Sailor's Mission and the Salvation Army to assist their efforts. The stigma and unease was lifted from my mind about everything we'd achieved over evil, and at last Bouverie's and Finkelstein's bounty was going to be put to good use.

———————————————————

About the author - Ernest John Swain.

As a detective in the Criminal Investigation Department and the Special Branch, he worked with such agencies as MI5 and briefly the American Secret Service.

Trained as a firearms specialist he was privileged to provide personal protection for royalty, senior politicians and heads of foreign governments which took him into palaces and stately homes.

He was involved in several dangerous incidents involving firearms that earned him commendations for bravery from a Judge of Assize and from Chief Constables.

Other works by this author:

A Surprising Legacy,
ISBN 978-0-9574852-0-4 Paperback
ISBN 978-0-9574852-1-1 e-book
ISBN 978-0-9574852-3-5 Mobi (Kindle)

The Lightning Tree,
ISBN 978-0-9574852-2-8 Paperback
ISBN 978-0-9574852-4-2 e-book
ISBN 978-0-9574852-5-9 e-book (Mobi Kindle)

The Golden Salamander,
ISBN 9798632662437 Paperback
ASIN B086PPCJJS   Paperback
ASIN B086MC2RRB Kindle e-book

A Burning Issue,
ISBN 9798635337844 Paperback
ASIN B086WPZ7T4   Kindle e-book
ASIN B086PNZLRK   Paperback

The Apprentice,
ISBN 9798637147243 Paperback
ASIN B0874LYDSQ   Paperback
ASIN Bo8739NQF2   Kindle e-book